CW01090953

Mounted Games

Mounted Games, Volume 1

Hannah Conrad

Published by Dimension Seal Studios, 2023.

MOUNTED GAMES

First edition. October 3, 2023.

ISBN: 979-8223866152

Written by Hannah Conrad.

Table of Contents

For the horse girl in us all.

Chapter One

D*ALLAS*
    Dallas could sense the other team bearing down on her with each passing moment.

She tightened her grip on the long pole in her hand, leaning dangerously to one side as her mount hurtled forward at full speed, showing little regard for the rapidly approaching fence. The final carton lie just ahead, half buried in sand from where her teammates had unintentionally jostled it. Luckily, the opening was still facing her, so she didn't have to do any deft acrobatics.

Without even needing to think about her movements, she brought her left foot up, still in the stirrup, and hooked it on the cantle of the saddle. Her body dropped low as she hung expertly from the side of the small chestnut mare, who continued at a gallop in an obediently straight line.

With clenched teeth and an unwavering stare, she lowered the pole until it was near parallel with the ground, her knuckles mere inches from scraping the sand. She punched forward and tilted upwards, spearing the open end of the carton and flipping her arm up in one swift movement. Once sure the item was secure at the tip of the pole, she rocked her body to swing effortlessly back into the saddle.

In the lane beside her, she was more than aware of Amelie doing the same. The other girl made no mistake—it was a race.

Dallas leaned back hard in the saddle and whipped her torso around. The chestnut mare beneath her, reading the sudden change of posture, whirled with ease, nearly prancing on her two hind legs as she turned in a prompt 180.

"Go, Chariot, go!" Dallas yelled, shoving her hand toward the mare's ears and pumping the one elbow that still clutched the reins. Her mare launched forward. She could feel Amelie and Star hot on their heels, breathing down their necks from a mere stride behind.

Star was faster, but Chariot's unrivaled athleticism and deft turn had earned the pair enough of a head start that she and Dallas flew across the finish line first, barely a hoof in front of Amelie and Star.

"Yeah, Dallas!" Brooke yelled, standing in her stirrups and pumping her fists in the air victoriously. "You did it!"

The short palomino below the small strawberry blonde girl snorted, ears twitching at the raised voice on his back, though his expression spelled sheer boredom as he ignored the encroaching chestnut.

Callie merely nodded with feigned disinterest from atop her prancing roan gelding, which she managed to hold in a tight circle with a single hand on her black cotton reins. "Not bad," she muttered, stifling a yawn with the back of her free hand.

Dallas was beaming. She tossed the pole and carton unceremoniously to the ground between the horses and threw her arms around Chariot's neck, dropping the reins completely.

"Good girl, Chariot!" she cooed, scratching at the mare's withers. "You did great!"

"I almost had you," Amelie said, smirking as she struggled to reel in the now very hyped up Star. She was panting from the effort. "One more stride! If Constance hadn't missed the hand-off..." she trailed off, throwing a raised eyebrow at their teammate. Star jigged beneath her, tossing his head up and down and chomping at the bit as he continuously tried to bolt from beneath his unperturbed rider.

Constance shrugged from where she sat on her dappled gray gelding. Janine, who was chewing gum and smiling from her chubby paint gelding, merely nodded in agreement with their anchor.

"Very good, girls," came the approving voice of Miss Nelson. "Janine, I would like to see you vaulting sometime in the near future, as you are spending far too much time trying to find the stirrup to get back on. Team up with Amelie, she's our most proficient vaulter-" Amelie put on her most arrogant grin, "-or Dallas." The grin twitched. "Callie, if you could somehow compel yourself to feel some sense of urgency, that would be nice. And Amelie, for the love of God, please stop sending that pony so much damn energy!"

Amelie dismissed Nelson with a wave of her hand, sitting back in the saddle as Star half-reared and turned on his hindquarters. "Aw, he's fine," she said. "He just wants to do his job."

"Well, he won't be able to do his job if he can't focus," Nelson scolded, shaking her head as she watched the feisty bay gelding giving Amelie a hard time. "Miss West," she placed a hand on Chariot's neck and gave her a pat, "Make sure everyone gets cooled out. And just so all of you know, we're hacking tomorrow. I don't need your ponies," she leveled her stare at Amelie and a pawing Star, "losing their minds."

Dallas nodded. As Captain of the brand new Hoofbeats Mounted Games team, she had very few responsibilities aside from sorting out team line-ups and keeping track of attendance, but Nelson liked to defer leadership to her at any given chance.

As Nelson walked off to start picking up the scattered equipment, Dallas turned in the saddle to grin at her team. "Want to walk down the lane today?" She loved the lane, which was the center cobblestone walkway that wound through the massive grounds that made up the stables around the University. It was lined with trees, different arenas for the variety of sports, the old brick buildings that held their classes, and pastures spotted with horses. In a sense, gorgeous.

The chorus of groans from every other girl but Brooke told her that her idea had not been well received.

"Then we have to go by those snobby hunters," Amelie moaned. "I can't stand them."

Dallas scrunched her eyebrows together, looking between the disapproving faces of her teammates. "They can't be *that* bad, can they?"

"You haven't been here long enough to find out," Amelie mumbled, swiping at a bead of sweat that had trickled down her cheek. Her wild red hair was jutting out from beneath her helmet at crazy angles. "You'll find out how miserable they are soon."

It was true, Dallas *hadn't* been at Hoofbeats University for long, but it had been a lifelong dream of hers to get accepted into the prestigious private university. So, when the school decided to offer scholarships for a brand new Mounted Games program, which happened to be a very under-rated and new discipline that Dallas was *very* good at, she had decided to try out. She practiced night and day for the selection, and, when the day came, Dallas and her little chestnut mare, Swift Chariot, had decimated the competition. So, not only had she gotten a formal invitation to the college of her dreams, she had also been coined Captain. Which added quite a bit of tension, as the assignment was very much to the dismay of Amelie O'Neill and her prized pony, Shooting Star. In the end, though, everything had worked out, because she had been able to finish most of her general education classes at a local university for her freshman year. Going to Hoofbeats for her entire education would have been ideal, but her parents certainly couldn't afford it without the scholarship—besides, in Dallas's mind, better late than never!

Plus, right off the bat, she'd made lifelong friends in her two roommates, Brooke and Callie. Even if Callie wasn't on the same page yet. And, of course, she also got along well with Constance and Janine. Amelie was a different story, though. Dallas still considered them on friend terms, even if the hard-headed girl often disagreed with line-ups—which usually ended up in a screaming match.

As Dallas led the team from the arena and down the cobblestone path, she thought about how amazing it was to have the opportunity to ride for Hoofbeats. The school was old and beautiful, with rolling green fields, massive pastures, miles of beautiful trails and lines of towering trees that loomed in a vast canvas of red, orange, and yellow with the onset of autumn. It was a far cry from Dallas's native country of Japan, and Dallas had to admit that she was a little bit homesick, but it was certainly a gorgeous country.

Possibly the best part of Hoofbeats was the stables. They were state-of-the-art, constructed from imported Irish limestone and rich, polished mahogany. The stalls were massive and cozy, and Dallas had been excited to find that Chariot would even be treated with an automatic water trough (that was heated in the winter, too!) and her own private paddock.

The shoes of the six ponies played a comforting melody as the team meandered down the long stone lane. In a smaller arena to their left, a dressage rider was practicing a piaffe. In another, a girl was lunging a massive gray horse who seemed more than happy to trot in an obedient circle. Ahead, three riders were gathered in the center of a modest jump course.

Dallas watched, vaguely listening to Brooke and Janine's conversation about their upcoming friendly with Appleton.

Her eyes trained on a rather elegant rider who had urged a tall, muscular bay horse into a rocking canter. She found herself staring at the gentle hands of the rider, the muscles of her legs bulging beneath skin-tight tan breeches, the still seat firmly pushing into the glistening leather of what looked like a very expensive saddle. Long, wavy blonde hair spilled from beneath the helmet and a pale, emotionless expression showed the unwavering focus of the rider. She hadn't seen her before, though she had hardly focused on the other disciplines during their very first week, which had involved a lot of confusion from settling into a new home and new routine.

Dallas hadn't even noticed she'd pulled Chariot to a stop next to the four-rail arena fence. She watched the pair sail effortlessly over jumps in a picturesque image of the finest equitation.

"Who is *that*?" Dallas asked in a single, heavy exhale.

Amelie pulled Star up next to Chariot. He had calmed considerably and stood quietly. "You're kidding, right?"

"You know she's been living under a rock since she got here," Callie muttered, bringing Mushroom up alongside the two. "Of course she doesn't know."

"I have not been living under a *rock*," Dallas countered, shooting a glare at her roommate. "I've just been busy adjusting! I've only really met you guys so far."

"That's Alice Thelwell," Brooke said from behind them. Spirit was idly swishing his blonde tail at non-existent flies. "She's the best rider at Hoofbeats. Her family runs the top veterinary clinic in Europe."

Dallas looked on as the pair soared over an oxer as though it was nothing more than a beginner level cross-rail, front legs tucked in close to a broad chest. The rider lifted a passive pair of eyes as she landed and Dallas swore she was looking at *her*, but Alice Thelwell quickly turned her attention back to the regal bay mare beneath her as she pulled her up.

"What are you nerds looking at?" came a voice from one of the riders in the middle of the arena. Two girls, one with a long red braid and one with very straight black hair, strode over on equally expensive looking mounts.

"Oh, hey to you too, Hannah," Amelie snapped back. "How's daddy's money doing?" Star began to paw impatiently at the stone as the temperament of his rider changed with the shift of her seat.

The redhead, the one Amelie was calling Hannah, sneered back. "Oh, it's just fine," she said, tugging on the reins of her powerful looking chestnut. "How's your budget pony?"

"It's so cute that they ride *ponies*," the black-haired girl added, her lip quirking into a grimace. "Never graduated to riding a *real* horse, I guess. Or they could only afford the discount size." She added, shooting a glance to her friend for an approving smile before chuckling.

Dallas could feel Amelie tense at her side. She shot a look over to see the bright red of the other girl's cheeks and quickly made the decision to intervene before her notably fiery temper had the opportunity to shoot off.

"Actually, we're the new Games Team," Dallas said cheerfully, thinking maybe they just didn't understand—after all, it was a very new and small sport in the equestrian world—and needed an explanation. "We ride ponies intentionally for agility purposes. By the way, I'm Dallas West, but you can call me Dallas." She offered a broad, friendly smile and sat a little straighter in the saddle. "And this is Chariot!" she added, patting her mare on the neck.

The two girls just started laughing as though Dallas had said something *very* funny.

"The Games team, huh?" Hannah said, clapping her hand over her mouth and snorting.

"I heard we were getting one of those, but I thought it was a joke," her friend added. "Must be the failed polo players."

"That's so childish."

"I can't believe Hoofbeats even supported this."

"They really are letting anyone in these days."

Dallas could feel blazing heat rising to the tips of her ears as she watched the exchange between the two.

"*Girls,*" came the scolding voice of Alice Thelwell as she walked up behind them. The bay mare's neck was arched prettily and Dallas could see the veins bulging beneath sleek skin. Alice, too, had been pretty going around the ring, but up close she was just plain gorgeous. Dallas felt herself staring and honestly hoped that she wasn't drooling.

"What did I tell you about entertaining Miss O'Neill's jabs? If you two are very much finished, I believe it's time to go untack. I have quite a bit of studying to do tonight," Alice said, leveling Hannah and the other girl through icy blue eyes.

"Yes, Alice," both girls replied in unison.

Dallas felt Alice's eyes turn to her. The blonde studied her for a moment before lowering her chin in a curt nod. "Cute pony," she said in a flat, quiet voice before following the other two to the arena gate.

Had that been sarcasm? Dallas felt her cheeks burning as she glared after the three girls.

"Wow," Amelie snapped after they'd gone. "They are *such* snobs. Barbara's awful, but Hannah..." Amelie growled loudly. "She's the worst! And what did Alice mean when she said to stop entertaining *my* jabs? They started it! That girl is such a bitch."

"Who were they?" Dallas asked, feeling her face beginning to cool as she turned to look back at her team.

"The Hunt Team," four of the girls said together. Constance merely grunted and nodded.

"We told you they were awful," Callie mumbled. "But you don't listen."

Well, Dallas couldn't debate that. They *had* warned her, but she always tried to give people the benefit of the doubt and not judge based on someone else's opinions. Though, she kind of had to admit... her team had been right. As the six turned to walk back up the cobblestone path to the stables, Dallas stayed quiet.

Instead of joining the conversation, she let herself think about the dynamic horse and rider that leapt effortlessly and elegantly over jumps nearly as tall as Chariot. At the passive blue eyes that had met hers for a fleeting moment. She hadn't *seemed* mean, and she was really easy on the eyes—

Dallas sighed and dismounted when they got back to the barn, slipping the bridle from Chariot's head and letting her rub her itchy face on her side as she stood in a wide stance and braced herself. Doing such a thing had always earned a scold from her trainer back home, but Dallas couldn't understand why. Chariot itch. Dallas scratch.

As she stood and let Chariot rub against her, she watched the three girls of the Hunt Team dismount at another barn, the fancier one that cost monthly probably more than a semester's tuition (which Dallas didn't understand why they even had, because the regular stalls were already *really* nice, who needed more?). Alice was pulling the reins over the tall bay's head and, as Dallas watched, ran her fingers in a gentle scratch on the horse's forehead and underneath the throat latch. And then, for one brief moment, Dallas *swore* she saw the other girl look in her direction, but she really wasn't sure, because it was at that precise moment that Chariot decided to throw her head in a particularly aggressive rub and toss her into a bush.

When she climbed out, covered in tiny leaves and brambles to Amelie's howling laughter, she looked back—but the Hunt Team had already disappeared into their own barn.

Dallas was falling asleep.

She felt her eyelids drooping, zoned on the whiteboard ahead. A drop of drool threatened to spill out of the corner of her mouth and she swiped it away with the back of her hand.

Professor Finnelan was droning on... and on... and on.

"Miss West!"

The sharp voice of the professor yelling her name was enough to make her jump in her seat. "Nani?" she heard herself say, blinking in confusion.

Professor Finnelan was staring at the seat that Dallas had decided was her own on the first day—it was next to the windows and she could see the football team practicing sometimes, they had really nice legs—and where she was currently falling asleep. Dallas swallowed.

"Miss West, is there an issue?"

"Er..." Dallas blinked at the teacher with drowsy eyes. "No?"

She could feel everyone in the lecture hall staring at her. Someone coughed delicately behind her and she turned to see Alice Thelwell with a closed fist in front of her mouth. She hadn't known Alice was in her class, though she supposed it made sense if she came from a family of Veterinarians.

"Is there something about Hippotherapy that bores you?" Professor Finnelan asked. Dallas turned back to the front of the lecture hall.

"Uh-" Dallas thought for a moment, looking down at her notes that held nothing more than a squiggled line from where she'd fallen asleep with her pen to the paper. "Is that a rhetorical question?"

Someone sniggered on the other side of her and muttered a, "Damn." Amelie choked back a laugh from where she was sitting in the front of the class. Another cough from behind.

Professor Finnelan looked like steam might start coming from her ears at any moment. "Miss West, you will see me after class today," she said before returning to her very monotone lecture on the psychological benefits of horses for the disabled. Technically, Dallas *should* have been paying attention, because it was very much what she wanted to do in the future, but damn if it wasn't so dreadfully *boring*.

"What an idiot," somebody mumbled from nearby.

Amelie had turned in her chair to throw her a thumbs up and a, "Nice one, West!"

Dallas let her forehead fall to her empty page of notes with a heavy groan. She *knew* she was bound to get herself in trouble—especially with the words that seemed to leave her mouth before she could think—but she had really been hoping it would've been later rather than sooner.

Mucking duty.

Finnelan had given her *mucking* duty.

Dallas could feel the sweat dripping down the side of her temple as she dumped yet another full and very heavy wheelbarrow of manure in the massive pile of disposal behind the stable. Not *only* had Finnelan given her the responsibility of cleaning all the stalls, she had to do it in the morning. Not just the morning. *Five in the morning. On a weekend.* Dallas couldn't think of a more severe form of torture than that.

Plus, she was only halfway through *one* of the barns.

She huffed her disapproval as she wheeled the barrow back into the stable, wincing at the pain of blisters developing on the palms of her hands. Her stomach was growling already and she couldn't wait to finish up so she could get to the cafeteria and at least get *some* decent food before it was all gone.

She was pulling the pitchfork up to enter the next stall when the name on the plate brought her to a pause.

BEATRIX

by BALOU DU ROUET

ALICE THELWELL

Dallas peered through the bars of the stall at the tall mare. A few shavings were clinging to the dappled bay skin, tangled in the long, boxed black tail. She could see the brand on her hindquarters, a curved "H" with what looked like two horse heads on the top. Admittedly, Dallas wasn't very well versed in the different brands of the fancy European warmbloods, but she happened to know this one, because it was the same brand that graced the mount of her idol, Octavia Chariot.

"Hm. Hanoverian," she muttered, glancing again to the shiny golden plaque on the stall door.

"That's correct."

The soft voice behind Dallas made her drop the pitchfork, which clattered to the stone floor and made Beatrix jump to the side in her stall, snorting her disapproval in the direction of her stall door. Dallas whirled to find herself face-to-face with Alice Thelwell—she hadn't even *heard* someone else enter the barn, was she a ninja?-and a hot blush rose to her cheeks. She was dressed like she was going to ride, in tight navy breeches with brown grips, brown paddock boots, a long white shirt, a gray vest. Wavy blonde hair was tied back into a low ponytail. In her hand was a silver tumbler. She looked pristine, like she'd walked out of a Dover catalog.

"Uh, hey," Dallas said, suddenly feeling extremely dirty in her shorts, muck boots, and an old t-shirt that had holes and bleach stains. "Sorry, I haven't done hers yet."

Alice's neutral expression glanced Dallas over—was she judging her? Probably—before turning her attention back to the mare who had thrown her head over the stall door. The blonde girl approached, laying a gloved hand on a clipped muzzle. "No need," she said.

Dallas blinked, taking a step back to pick up the pitchfork that was still lying on the floor. "Huh?"

Alice glanced back at Dallas, one blonde eyebrow raised. "I'll take care of her stall," she said, fiddling with the door latch before opening it and sidling inside with the mare. "It's Dallas, right?"

"Uh—yeah," Dallas said, feeling a blush starting to dust her cheeks. "You can call me Dallas. And it's Alice, right?"

Alice hummed, running her fingers down the white stripe that ran, somewhat crooked, down the mare's face. "Might I make a suggestion?"

Dallas blinked, watching the other girl through the bars, eyebrows knitting together in confusion. "Sure."

"I would highly suggest being a little more respectful in Professor Finnelan's class."

Alice didn't bother to look back at her, which Dallas was grateful for because her whole face was burning a bright red. She stared for a minute, watching as the blonde bent down to pick up one of Beatrix's legs as if she was doing an inspection.

"Oh, uh, okay," Dallas said, lingering an embarrassingly long amount of time before it suddenly hit that Alice wasn't going to say anything else. "Right. Thanks," she added uselessly before hastily grabbing the wheelbarrow and moving to the next stall.

As she cleaned, she could hear a voice in the stall next to her and, at first, she thought Alice was talking to her, but she quickly realized that wasn't the fact at all. No, Alice was talking to her horse. That wasn't weird, Dallas had full conversations with Chariot sometimes. Of course, they were very one-sided, but that didn't matter.

Though, as Dallas listened to the gentle, soothing voice from next door, her movements slowed to a crawl. Maybe she was hoping that Alice would strike up a conversation with her, but no such luck, because a few moments later she heard Beatrix's stall door creak open and the echo of horseshoes disappearing down the aisle. It had been a stupid thought, anyway, because why would Alice want to talk to *her*?

Well, so much for that, Dallas thought, and, with a heavy sigh, got back to work.

Chapter Two

A *LICE*

Alice threw a glance behind her as she led Beatrix from her box, half expecting to see the West girl in the aisle. After all, she'd been in Belle's box for quite some time. She knew that Barbara's mare was quite particular about her cleanliness, so it shouldn't have taken *that* long. The girl seemed nice enough, if not a little bit strange, though Alice couldn't deny she was a little perturbed by the girl's lack of respect for authority. In all honesty, she thought Professor Finnelan's class was extremely dull, too—the woman had a knack for putting people to sleep—but thinking that and voicing it out loud were two very different things.

With a shrug, she turned her attention back to her tall mare, letting her hand fall on the soft skin of her withers as she led her into the cross ties. She set her tumbler of fresh tea down on a wooden stool before walking off to collect her gear from the tack room.

Morning was her favorite time of day, so she made a point to wake up much earlier than her roommates. Hannah and Barbara would be asleep still for a while yet. And not that she didn't enjoy their company, but the solace of being alone with just her mare was too great a temptation not to take advantage of. It felt like she was always surrounded by people, whether her two friends, the riding instructors, the professors, or students eager for tutoring or mentorship. Being a Thelwell meant that solitude was hard to come by.

When she finished lugging her gear back to her mare, who had stood quietly, watching intently, she brushed off her left front leg before lifting it up and running gentle hands down the sides of her cannon bone. The mare had injured her suspensory ligament the year after a particularly high-demand show season, and Alice was constantly monitoring the status of the leg to make sure there was no heat or swelling. Beatrix was the final foal that her mother had bred before she passed, from a rather elite sire and a mare that no longer belonged to the Thelwell Estate, and so, along with being her best friend, the mare was of particular sentimental value to her.

"Looks good," Alice said, to no one in particular, as she straightened her back and began to brush off the rest of the mare's shining coat. Her hand followed the brush with each stroke, carefully feeling for any abnormalities or injuries that could have occurred in her absence. It was a matter of habit, something that she unconsciously did every day. Veterinary studies had instilled a certain level of paranoia, and Alice was constantly scrutinizing bumps or scrapes with the trained eye of a professional.

A low whine down the aisle made her take a step back, out of the cross-ties, to look in the direction of the noise. Dallas had moved on a few stalls but was taking a break, it seemed. She'd slipped in some headphones and was singing along to whatever she was listening to in a series of squeaks and gasps, using the stick end of the pitchfork as a makeshift microphone. Alice turned away to hide a laugh and resumed the care of her horse.

By the time she'd finished tacking Beatrix, Dallas had moved on to another barn and a few other riders had slipped wearily into the stable. A few girls were complaining loudly nearby about being hung over, so Alice quickly tightened her mare's girth and led her by soft, braided leather reins outside. Her shoes—iron in the front, steel in the back—echoed a soothing rhythm against the stone.

The mare stood quietly as Alice brought her next to the mounting block and fussed briefly with her tack, straightening the padded leather of the noseband and checking the girth one last time before mounting the tall mare. Alice's height offered her the ability of mounting from the ground, but she knew it was easier on the mare's back to use the block, and so the slightly slower method was worth the few extra minutes.

"Alright, Bea," Alice cooed, letting a gloved hand fall on a muscled neck in a gentle pat. The mare shook her head, short black mane dancing as she snorted and strode forward.

The morning was crisp but not cold, and dew still settled against the grass from the night before. A few colorful leaves had drifted down onto the cobblestone of the middle lane, un-swept as of yet by the keepers of the grounds, and Alice breathed deep the scent of her favorite time of year. Some of the horses that were on night turn-out were already being led in, following each caretaker with the excited jig that came with the promise of breakfast. Beatrix would eat her meal after her workout. It was too dangerous on a horse's stomach to ride after eating, and Alice didn't have enough time in the afternoon to risk spending too much time at the barn.

Today would be a Dressage day. Though the pair never actually performed in the discipline, Alice only jumped when absolutely necessary—such as when practicing with her team—and otherwise only stuck to flatwork. Dressage was the foundation of training, the very core functionality of the movement of the horse, and so the Thelwell heiress had taken it upon herself to seek private lessons and gain enough knowledge to school at the second level. And as fun as jumping was, a horse only had so many jumps in their lifetime. Beatrix had already shown that too much strenuous activity was unhealthy for her legs, and therefore daily conditioning fell to workouts that were less shock on her weakened ligaments.

And though flatwork could be dull at times, her tall, agile mare was so fluid in her motions, so effortless in her carriage, that Alice was often lulled into the comfort of the ride. The smooth trot, the rocking canter, the easy swap of a lead in the corner or on a straight at the lift of a thigh and a twitch of the wrist. The mare was at her fingertips at all times, and with that came a certain level of pride—Alice had trained the home-bred mare from the ground up from the time she was a preteen.

Beatrix snorted in rhythm as she strode around the arena, ears twitching with each movement of Alice's body to anticipate the next cue. As Alice rode, each tiny correction natural and fluid, she let her eyes wander over the grounds of the stables.

A few riders were trickling out of the stable, mounts in tow. Though Alice was usually the first to the barn and the first to begin her ride on the weekends, others enjoyed the morning just as much and soon she would be joined by a multitude of other riders.

Among them was Dallas. Alice let her eyes fall on the girl each time she went around the arena. She must have finished mucking the stalls, because she was leading her small chestnut pony down the lane. She was still wearing the same ratty t-shirt from earlier, but she'd changed into a pair of breeches and had shoved a black jockey-style helmet onto her head. She could see her long brown hair, tied into a low ponytail, splayed across her back. Alice slowed Beatrix to a smooth working trot, sitting deep in the saddle, as she watched the girl open the gate to the arena she was in and lead the mare inside.

The arena was far from Alice's alone. It was a public, standard arena, which meant that anybody could join—but Alice did find it a bit curious as to why she chose hers in particular, seeing as it was the farthest from the barn. Though, she supposed the other arenas were also occupied, and it only made sense that the other girl join *somebody* else's. Why not hers? She brought Beatrix down to a walk, stilling her hands at the withers and flicking her fingers in a small correction as the mare tossed her head in greeting to the pony.

"Is this alright?" Dallas asked, bringing the pony to a halt—she was a cute little thing, with a tiny white snip on her nose and a kind, but fiery look in her eyes—and peering up at Alice as she grew closer. "I'll stay out of your way."

Alice nodded, but said nothing more as she let her mare walk a little bit more for a break.

The pony had an interesting setup. A regular English bridle, though bitless. The reins simply attached to rings at the side of the noseband. There was a leather strap around the mare's neck, pressing into a wild chestnut mane, that looked much like a stirrup leather. And, the longer Alice looked at it, the more convinced she became that it *was* an old stirrup leather. She wore a small saddle with the stirrups hanging low, nearly reaching to her shoulders.

As Alice observed, Dallas grabbed the leather collar around the mare's neck and deftly leapt onto the pony's back from the ground. The small mare lifted her head a little bit, but otherwise remained calm.

Alice raised an eyebrow. If she tried to do that with Bea, she'd probably just smack against the side of her horse's body and nothing would come of it but a bruised ego and a very agitated horse.

Alice continued her workout, though she couldn't keep her attention from straying to Dallas and her pony. She knew she needed to focus on Beatrix and getting her a little bit more supple to the right, maybe engage her hindquarters a little bit more, but the other girl was proving to be quite the distraction. Before long, the smaller girl and pony were galloping from end to end of the arena—respectfully out of Alice's way, at least—and Dallas was doing some kind of acrobatics where she would leap off mid-gallop, sprint beside the mare and, without skipping a beat or losing speed, grab the strap and launch herself back into the saddle. Only once or twice did she make a mistake, and she seemed to realize it immediately. She would bounce off the ground, let her body drift back down, run again, then correct her jump and hit her mark.

It was... impressive, to say the least. And the girl was clearly fit. She was hardly breathing heavily, and her leg muscles rippled beneath her breeches.

"Hey, Alice!" Hannah greeted with a wave from the arena gate. With a small wave of acknowledgment, Alice eased Beatrix back down to a walk to cool her out and strode over to the gate to meet her friends. Barbara was with her, as usual, and Belle and Cello stood passively with their owners.

"Isn't she bothering you?" Barbara asked, pointing to Dallas, who had brought her pony down to a walk and was hanging all over her neck with loud pats and shouts of praise. The chestnut mare was tossing her head up and down, jigging on her toes as though ready to keep running.

Alice shook her head, letting the reins slide between her fingers to give Bea her head as her two teammates led their mounts into the arena. "She's fine," she said.

"Hey, you!" Hannah hollered out to Dallas, lifting her foot into the stirrup and boosting herself into Cello's saddle. Barbara did the same, gathering the reins as Belle balked a little bit (she was still young and a bit green) and following Hannah's gaze to the other rider.

Dallas seemed to perk up. She sat back in the saddle, legs dangling out of the stirrups, and walked over with a one-handed guide on black cotton reins.

"Scram," Barbara said as she neared, pointing to the open arena gate. "We need this arena."

Alice could see Dallas's expression morph to confusion, her brown eyebrows stitching together as she blinked between the three girls. "There's plenty of room," the girl said, pulling the mare to a halt. "Besides, I was here first."

"No, Alice was here first," Hannah countered, nodding her head in the direction of the blonde. "That means this arena belongs to the Hunt Team. Get out."

Dallas rolled her eyes. Usually, the other riders in the barn listened to anything the Hunt Team had to say. It came with the territory of stealing Championship after Championship, year after year, that the pride of Hoofbeats served as an intimidation factor to others. Dallas, though, seemed to have none of it.

"Public arena," she called out as she whirled the mare with the agility of a reiner and urged the mare into a gallop, which wasn't so much a forward movement as an up-and-down, as she glared over her shoulder. "So find another or get over it."

Alice brought a hand to her mouth, hiding a smile behind her palm as she dismounted Beatrix and excused herself. She hesitated at the gate, taking her time to latch it shut. She didn't bother asking Hannah or Barbara if they wanted to find another arena. Dallas had a good point, they needed to get over it, and it was amusing to finally see somebody sass them back. Alice had been telling the two girls to be more respectful for quite some time or they were going to find themselves up against the wall—and it seemed Dallas was acting as that wall.

And she'd be lying if she didn't enjoy the bewildered expressions on both of their faces as Dallas hopped off her mare, flipped them off while sprinting at the pony's side, then vaulted, one-armed, back into the saddle.

"Hey, Gaywell!"

Alice couldn't stop the audible groan that slipped from her lips as she brought her palm to cover her face. She had long since finished untacking Beatrix, and the mare sat in the cross-ties, enjoying a liniment soak on her legs while Alice polished her saddle nearby, occasionally plucking a peppermint out of a sack and offering it to the content mare.

She had been cozy and relaxed, happy in her own head space. Of course O'Neill had to ruin that.

"Amelie, could you please stop calling me that?" Alice snapped, setting the tack sponge down against the cantle of her saddle and leveling the redheaded American with an icy stare. "It's extremely inappropriate."

Amelie smirked, buckling the helmet—the same kind that Dallas wore—and clutching the reins near the bit of her dancing and snorting pony. That thing was a menace, in Alice's opinion. Poorly trained, disrespectful, and altogether dangerous. Just like the American herself. "Really? Because I think it's super appropriate," Amelie countered, smirking. The pony reached a leg out and pawed at the aisle, anxiously swishing a long black tail.

Amelie had been calling her Gaywell for well over a year—ever since she'd seen Alice kissing her ex-girlfriend goodbye at her car after a short weekend visit—and it was a nick-name that she couldn't seem to escape. She rolled her eyes and sighed deeply, dipping the sponge back into her leather cleaner and rolling gentle circles over the already shining seat of her saddle. "Please leave me alone, Amelie. I'm busy."

"Hm." Amelie glanced down at her. "Looks that way." She reached a hand to Beatrix, who stretched her neck out and smacked her lips against the offered fingers. The redhead tickled her nose, holding the pony back with her other hand as he tried to get closer. "How's her leg doing?"

"If you must know, it's just fine," Alice replied, not bothering to look up. If she ignored Amelie and didn't play her silly games, the girl would go away. It was a proven method of dispelling annoying Americans. But the other girl's attention was quickly drawn away, pulled to the clopping of shoes as another horse strode down the aisle.

"'Ey, Dallas," Amelie called, pulling her hand away from Beatrix, who snorted a disapproval, and directing her gaze away from Alice. Thank God. "I thought you were going to ride with us today?"

"Sorry," she heard Dallas say. Alice glanced up as the other girl stopped in front of Amelie. She wasn't even leading her pony—the bridle had been pulled off and was draped over her shoulder—but the little chestnut mare was following her anyway. Alice let out a breath of approval and went back to scrubbing her saddle. "I was up early anyway," Dallas continued. "Kinda wanted to get it over with so I could go back and take a nap."

You could've avoided that, Alice wanted to say, but it was rude to interrupt a conversation that didn't include her, and so she kept to herself and instead reached into her sack to pull out another peppermint for Beatrix.

Warm air coasted over the side of her face, followed by the tickle of whiskers. Alice felt herself chuckling as she turned to find a chestnut nose with a white snip poking at her cheek.

"Agh, sorry," Dallas muttered, wrapping one arm around the pony's neck to pull her back in. "She loves peppermints."

Alice reached back into her sack and pulled another out. They were the good kind, the ones they gave away at restaurants that melted in your mouth, and she found Beatrix liked them more than anything else. She held one out on a flat hand to the pony, whose ears flicked up and she greedily sucked in the mint.

"Thanks," Dallas said. She slid her hand into the mare's fuzzy forelock and affectionately flopped her ears back and forth. "Kou, Chariot," she muttered to her pony, sliding into her native language with ease. "Mina ni okashi o tanomu hitsuyo wa arimasen."

While Dallas and Amelie continued their conversation, right in front of her and Beatrix, no less, Alice let her eyes skim over the mare. She was a small thing, with a slightly dished face that gave away Arabian heritage. Her copper coat was dappled and healthy, four white legs perfectly alabaster save for a few speckles of sand from the arena. She only wore shoes on her fronts, the backs were barefoot.

The mare rested one hind leg in a way that caught Alice's eye. She scrunched her eyebrows together, letting her gaze follow the cocked pastern all the way up to the angle of the hipbone.

"Alright, see you," Amelie was saying, offering a dismissive wave to the smaller girl. "Later, Thelwell."

Thank *God* Amelie was respectful enough to not call her Gaywell in front of other people. The girl was barbaric, but still had some sensibilities.

"Hey, Dallas—" Alice started. She set her sponge down and lowered her saddle to rest against the wall, rising. "Hold on."

Dallas turned, blinked. She had pulled her helmet off and her brunette hair was damp against her skull, messy with sweat. For the first, time, Alice noticed she had red eyes—how had she not noticed before?—and they were strange, but pretty. "What's up?" she asked.

"Oh, um-" Alice had momentarily lost her train of thought. She coughed into a closed fist, composing herself. "Would you mind pulling her saddle off?"

"Uh, sure?" It was both a question and a statement. Dallas had already undone the girth, which was draped over the saddle itself, so she simply pulled the tack off and into her arms.

"Chariot, is it?" Alice asked, stepping forward and pinching her thumb and two forefingers on either side of the pony's spine. She was short, couldn't possibly be more than 13 hands, and the height was just right for Alice to apply the correct amount of pressure without exertion.

"Ah, yeah." Dallas chuckled, scratching at the back of her neck with her free hand. The pony didn't move, even though she was completely tackless. It seemed like she would follow her rider anywhere. "I kind of named her after Octavia Chariot. She's my idol."

Alice nodded, paying very little attention and instead feeling the change in the spine beneath her fingers.

"You know who that is, right?"

"Of course," Alice mumbled. Octavia Chariot had been a famous Show Jumper who rode for the French Olympic team, everyone in the horse world knew who she was. She reached near the mare's hipbone and felt what she was expecting, but made sure by trailing her fingers down her back once more. Yup. Out at the five. She switched her posture and pressed both her thumbs into the spot, massaging gently at first, but then a bit harder as she expanded her circle. She could feel Chariot's muscles twitching beneath her as the mare leaned away, then a sudden relaxation, a sigh of relief.

"Er..." Dallas was watching curiously, letting the mare lip at her palm.

"She needed an adjustment on her lumbar," Alice said, leveling the shorter girl with a passive stare and giving the mare a scratch on her withers. "Probably from all that jumping around you do. She's fine now. I'd suggest having a chiropractor see her at least once a year, if not twice. Good girl, Chariot," she added with a final pat to the neck.

"Oh." Dallas frowned, scratching at the pony's throatlatch. "Sorry, Chariot," she mumbled apologetically before turning her attention back to Alice. "Thank you, then."

Alice nodded, sitting back down on the wooden stool to pick up her saddle and resume cleaning, signaling an end to the conversation. Dallas seemed confused at first—she lingered for a moment, shifting awkwardly on her heels a though expecting something more to be said—before clicking her tongue at Chariot and leading her away with a quiet, "See you, then."

Alice's hand paused on the flap of her saddle, blue eyes flickering up as she watched the other girl go, the pony following her obediently. She turned back to her own horse, whose eyelids had drifted lazily shut as she slept contentedly in the crossties. "Cute," Alice muttered, though she certainly wasn't talking about the pony, before reaching into her sack to offer Beatrix another peppermint.

"That *stupid* Games team has *got* to go!" Barbara shrilled.

Alice let out a heavy sigh as she dropped her highlighter from the passage of Equine Pharmacology that she needed to become acquainted with for the next week of classes, as per the syllabus. She had gotten all of an *hour* of solitary study time before her two roommates had loudly returned to the rowhouse that the three shared on the edge of campus.

"Alice!"

She slid her reading glasses off and raised a hand to pinch the bridge of her nose. The door of her room hadn't been open, but that didn't stop her roommates from barging in. They were both still in their dirty riding clothes, though they had remembered to take off their paddock boots at the door, a rule that Alice strictly enforced. The barn smelled like barn enough, she didn't need their house to smell like that, too.

"Yes, girls?" she asked with an exasperated sigh, swiveling in her desk chair to meet two very angry stares.

"Amelie O'Neill is absolutely insufferable," Hannah moaned, throwing herself onto Alice's bed—which made Alice cringe visibly, because the girl was filthy— and pounding at the comforter. Barbara folded her arms across her chest, leaning her back against the threshold of the door. "Can't you say something to Headmistress Holbrooke? It's so stupid that they added this team. What kind of sport is Mounted Games, anyway?"

"It's *not* a sport," Barbara insisted. "Absurd that Hoofbeats even allowed it."

Alice begged to disagree, based on the amount of athleticism that she'd seen Dallas display that morning, but she didn't voice her opinion out loud. "What's your grievance?" she asked, raising an eyebrow and rapping a finger against the page of her textbook as she blinked back and forth between the two girls. "I haven't seen them do anything wrong."

"They brought their whole team into the arena while we were trying to ride and started running around like lunatics," Barbara stated, tensing her jaw. "I'm sure that Dallas girl told them to do it."

Dallas hadn't. Alice had heard her exchange with Amelie, the entire thing superficial with no mention of the Hunt Team or, more specifically, acting in spite of her two teammates. She didn't say this, though, and instead pointed out, "The arenas are for public use. Anyone can ride there. If you prefer to be alone, you can ride in the Hunter arena."

"Yeah, but then there's jumps in the way," Hannah moaned. "Why can't the Games team use *their* arena? Instead they dragged half their equipment into ours and started throwing stuff around!"

"Well, it was only a stick," Barbara countered, though the heated glare from Hannah made her stop her argument. "But it was extremely rude and distracting."

"Amelie especially," Hannah said, rolling over on Alice's bed and messing up the covers. It was one thing that her roommates didn't make their bed, but Alice preferred for hers to be neat and tidy.

She finally scolded, "Hannah, would you please remove yourself from my bed?" and the auburn-haired girl quickly withdrew back to where Barbara stood.

"Anyway, Amelie kept running that stupid crazy pony in front of Cello," the girl continued. "He was getting *so* pissed, I wouldn't have blamed him if he kicked the thing right in the face," Hannah moaned. At her side, Barbara nodded her agreement. "I kept trying to tell her to go away but she would just laugh at me."

Alice pursed her lips. She wasn't particularly fond of Amelie O'Neill, not that her feelings were by any means a secret, and she truly did find the behavior despicable—but it had nothing to do with her. "Maybe you should mention her behavior to Miss Nelson. Or if you're more comfortable, Miss Parker." Miss Parker was their personal instructor and coach of the Hunt Team—if anyone could pull leverage, it was her. She was hard-headed and strict, with literal tolerance for possibly dangerous actions.

Her suggestion quickly brought silence to the other girls. They relied on Alice for everything, from helping them study to caring for their own horses to, hell, even being reminded to brush their own damn teeth at night. Quite frankly, Alice had grown tired of it. She was a student at

Hoofbeats, not a babysitter. "Now, if you'll excuse me, I have to study."

Barbara rolled her eyes and stalked off, but Hannah stayed for a moment, a deep frown etched across her face. "Well, I think that stupid team needs to go," she muttered, narrowing her eyes. "They're going to get somebody hurt. I'm sure you'll see soon enough, and then you can come talk to Miss Parker with us."

"Sure thing," Alice replied, waiting for Hannah to get out of her room before shutting the door behind her. She settled back into her desk chair, burying her face into her hands. She had been studying effectively, but now that concentration was broken, and it'd take a little while for her to get back into the mood. Instead, with curiosity ebbing at the back of her mind, she flipped open her MacBook and opened two google search pages:

Mounted Games
and
Dallas West
and started reading.

Chapter Three

D ALLAS
In, one-two.

Out, one-two.

In, one-two.

Out, one-two.

Dallas's sneakers pounded rhythmically over the black top of the track as she ran at a decent clip. She raised her arm and glanced down at her Garmin. Four kilometers—one more to go and she would hit her goal for the day. Resuming the counts of her breath, she lowered her arms a little bit more and quickened her pace.

She had a pretty decent break between Behavioral Psychology and Hippotherapy. Long enough that she could fit in a decent run and still have time to shower so she didn't smell like a ball of sweat in the next class. Besides, the football team started their practice during that break, and she'd be lying if she didn't enjoy watching the athletic girls work out. In a totally non-creepy way. Er—well, she tried not to stare, at least. But, really, who *didn't* appreciate pretty nice leg muscles and perfect—

Besides, just having pretty girls around motivated her to run a little bit faster or a little bit longer than she usually would.

She adjusted her earbuds and focused on completing her run, feeling the sweat trickling from under her sports bra and soaking into the fabric at her lower back. Running was something that she didn't particularly enjoy, though she found the more she did it, the more she didn't mind it. But, regardless, she found it important. If she expected Chariot to be fit, the least she could do was match her pony's athleticism through her own hard work. It was only a fair balance of partnership.

Her Garmin beeped. Five kilometers.

She let herself fall into a walk, breathing deep through her nose to steady her breathing as she walked off the track and shook her ankles to try to loosen her calves.

Normally, she would have jogged back to her dorm building, but she had chosen to run only five kilometers instead of her usual eight (light days were completely acceptable) and so she had plenty of time to get back and shower before her next class. Besides, the campus was pretty, and she loved walking around and looking at everything—the Victorian architecture of the old buildings, the sprawling grass fields, the stables in the distance, the trees that spilled their colorful fall leaves, the variety of monuments of famous alumni that had been erected. There was even one of her idol, Octavia Chariot, just outside the Equestrian Studies building. It was modest, maybe only six feet tall, at most, but it had been clearly been made by an expert's hand. Chariot was curled over the neck of her famous Olympic horse, Swift Wind, as he leapt over an invisible jump. The statue was surrounded by a small fountain, clean and clear save for the few pence that littered the bottom.

She would have stopped and admired the statue, like she usually did, but a few familiar faces were sitting around the outside of it—three in particular, and three that she didn't really feel like interacting with.

Alice seemed okay. She hadn't exactly said or done anything to make Dallas think otherwise, but Hannah and Barbara had already proven themselves just as miserable as the rest of her team had warned. They were constantly making snide comments, throwing insults, and in general just making the life of the entire Games team a living hell any chance they got. She didn't even understand—it wasn't like they had ever done anything to *them*. Well, save for Amelie, she always went out of her way to hassle the Hunt Team.

"Oh, look who it is," a familiar voice piped up just as Dallas was striding by, attempting to go unnoticed. She turned to find Barbara eyeing her from where she sat at Alice's side. The latter had a book spread across her lap, but looked up when her comrade spoke. "It's the Captain of the My Little Pony Club."

"*Barbara*," Alice warned.

Dallas rolled her eyes and slipped her earbuds out to let them fall around the back of her sweaty neck. "Hi to you, too," she mumbled, swiping her damp fringe away from her eyes and glancing to the doors she was headed to on the other side of the class building. Unfortunately, she had to go *by* them to get to the entrance of her dormitory. She started to walk off.

"Hold up, we wanted to talk to you."

Dallas paused and turned again, one eyebrow raised. "What's that?" she asked.

"We just had a question about Mounted Games," Barbara said, throwing a glance at Hannah. "You know, just curious."

"Uh, okay." Dallas blinked. She lowered her arms and stepped toward them. A bead of sweat trickled into her eye and she pulled up the bottom of her shirt to wipe off her face. "What's your question?"

"We were just wondering how we could try out," Hannah stated. The sneer on her face gave her sarcasm away, but Dallas answered her honestly anyway.

"Selection is over," she said. "August only. You'll have to wait until next year, if you're actually interested."

"Well, that's rubbish." Hannah rose, tossing her satchel over her shoulder. "If I had known it was that easy to get into Hoofbeats, I would've tried out for the Games team, too."

Barbara nodded her agreeance. "Wouldn't have had to pay so much for private coaching, either," she added.

"Girls."

Alice slammed her book shut and glared between her two teammates as she stood. "I believe it's time for both of you to move along to your next class instead of picking unnecessary fights."

"Us picking unnecessary fights? She's the one who had her team mess with us all weekend," Hannah grumbled.

"They're a brand new team, one that Hoofbeats's wasting its money on in the first place, and they think they're hot stuff."

Dallas frowned. "I don't know what you're talking about."

"Great Captain." Barbara rolled her eyes. "Doesn't even know what's going on with her own team."

"I said get to class," Alice growled, shoving her book under her arm and starting to walk off to the doors of the Equestrian Studies building.

"Fine," Hannah grumbled, but side-eyed Barbara with a sly grin. "Dallas should probably get busy taking a bath too, don't you think, Barbs? She looks pretty sweaty."

"That's where I was—" Dallas started to say.

But before she could finish, she felt the two girls snagging her arms. She was strong, sure, but not strong enough to fight off two people who had taken her by surprise. In one quick movement, they had pushed her backwards into the fountain and, with flailing arms, she splashed into the water. It was cold and Dallas immediately sucked in a lungful as she fought her way into a sitting position. The two girls were howling with laughter. "What the—" she started.

Nearby, she could hear Alice in snippets.

"Childish—can't believe—out of here—infuriated with—"

But Dallas was hardly paying attention. Her face was burning red with embarrassment as she clambered her way out of the fountain. She had half a mind to beat the snot out of the two right then and there, but that was something she would never do, so instead she squeezed the water out of her tank top and let it dribble onto the cobblestone. The backs of her calves stung and she looked down to find them scraped and bleeding a little bit from where she'd hit them on the edge of the stone bench that surrounded the fountain.

"Dallas, are you alright?"

She felt a hand on her arm and shrugged it off, nose twitching with anger as she glared up at Alice. "Like you care, get off me." She felt tears stinging her eyes but she would *not* give them the satisfaction of crying. Instead, she turned and stormed off toward her dormitory, socks sloshing in her soaked shoes—brand new New Balances, too!—and not even bothering to look back at the trio of assholes, two of which were still laughing at her expense.

"Are you fucking *kidding* me? If they want war, we will give them *war*."

Amelie's eyes widened when Dallas had finished telling the rest of the team what the Hunters had done earlier in the day. She was still furious, and just retelling the story for the second time (she'd already told Callie and Brooke, obviously) made her relive the embarrassment and anger that she'd felt in the moment. She clutched her pint, staring into the amber liquid for a moment before bringing it to her mouth and taking a long gulp.

"*I need a drink*," Dallas had declared when they'd finished Games practice and were finishing untacking the ponies. They'd had to walk past the Hunt Team on the way back to the stables. Hannah and Barbara hadn't laughed—in fact they'd looked away—though Alice had made it a point to look at Dallas and give her a tense nod. Dallas was sure to look away as quickly as she could. She had *not* been in the mood to exchange pleasantries with someone who was, by Dallas's standards, a bitch by association. The girl had already tried to snag her at the end of their Hippotherapy class, but Dallas had simply ignored her and stalked off down the hallway as quickly as she could.

Amelie slammed down her pint and grabbed the pitcher of lager the team had ordered for their table, topping off her own drink before chugging half of it. That girl could put away beer—that was something Dallas had learned *very* quickly on one of the first nights they'd all gone out together.

They were at the place they'd already claimed as their hang-out: a dark, traditional English pub named *LAST WEDNESDAY SOCIETY*. A lot of the pubs in the town around campus had equine-related names, it just came with the territory of being next to one of the most prestigious equestrian universities, though this was one of the few that didn't. The place was cozy and clean, not overly busy, and the proprietor was kind and easygoing.

"I still can't believe they would do that," Brooke said, frowning at her own bottle of Strongbow—"I'm not a beer girl," she had said—and rolling her finger around the top. "They've always been hard to deal with, but they've never done anything like *that*."

"Yes they have," Amelie grumbled. "They shoved me into that manure pile once, remember? Told me, 'you're shite, this is where you belong,'" she said the last in a terrible British accent. "Last year."

"Oh, yeah," Janine said. She threw back the shot of vodka she'd ordered and then took a long swig of her beer. Dallas made a face just watching her. The girl could *drink*. The first night they'd been out, she'd had so much vodka it was a wonder she was still standing, not to mention completely coherent.

"You did kind of ask for that one though." Brooke said. She cringed away from the American's glare.

"Whatever. Anyway, I don't know why Thelwell even associates with them," Amelie grumbled. "I don't like her, don't get me wrong, and she's a total snob, but she's not *that* much of a bitch."

Dallas shrugged. She gulped down the few mouthfuls of beer remaining and poured some more from their pitcher, topping off Constance's while she was at it. The German girl grunted in thanks. "Who cares," she said.

"Speak of the bitches, and the bitches shall appear," Callie mumbled from across the table, where she clutched the beer she was nursing between both her hands.

Dallas swiveled in the booth to find the girls—two of the three that they had just been trash-talking—had walked into the pub. "Are you kidding me?" she grumbled, spinning back around and shrinking down in the seat so she was even shorter than usual, partially shielding herself between Amelie and Brooke.

"Aw, hell, they made a big mistake," Amelie growled. She made a move to stand up but Dallas grabbed her arm and yanked her back down.

"Don't," she said. "Just ignore them."

Dallas had expected the Hunt Team to come over and start giving them hell again. After all, they had *definitely* seem them. It was hard not to, when there were six girls in a booth in a small pub that hardly held anybody. But they didn't. Instead, they grabbed drinks and settled down at the bar where they couldn't even look at the Games team without completely turning around.

"There are so many other places to go," Brooke grumbled, sipping her cider. "Why here?"

"Well, it is one of the better places," Janine said with a shrug. "The rest are the pubs get pretty rambunctious. Plus, this one's closest to the stables." She plucked up a chip from the basket she'd ordered for the table and shoved it into her mouth.

Constance nodded.

"Maybe we should find somewhere else," Brooke suggested.

"No way!" Dallas glared between her friends. "We can't just let them bully us around. They don't own Hoofbeats, or the stables, and certainly not anywhere else. Karera wa o shiridesu."

"English?" Amelie mumbled.

"Assholes."

"Could've just said that." Amelie eyed the beer that was left in their pitcher, gaze flicking between the remaining beer and the girls at the bar. "Hey, I'm going to go get a refill on this."

Dallas still nearly had a full beer. Two was going to be more than enough—she was a lightweight, and she'd hardly eaten much at dinner because she was so irritated—but she knew Janine, Constance, and Amelie liked to drink a lot more, so she just shrugged and took a sip of her lager, turning to Brooke while Amelie slid out of the bar seat.

"How's Frank?" she asked. She hadn't personally met her roommate's boyfriend yet, but Brooke talked about him frequently. Some guy who rode for the Appleton Games team that she had met the year before and started dating recently. From what she'd heard, he seemed nice, and she figured she'd meet him soon enough at the friendly.

Brooke perked up, a content smile sliding across her face as she spun her bottle around. "Oh, he's great! He—"

A loud, ear-piercing shriek interrupted whatever Brooke was about to say and Dallas whirled.

"Oh, I am *so* sorry!" Amelie was yelling.

Dallas's bright red eyes widened as she saw what was taking place. Amelie had dumped the remainder of their pitcher of beer all over Hannah, who had sprung out of her bar stool, liquid dripping off her face and down the white, off-the-shoulder shirt she was wearing. Her hands were raised out to the side in disbelief as she gaped down at her soaked shirt.

"*Amelie!*"

Amelie just grunted and took a step back, but she couldn't hide the wide grin that had found its way across her face. "Damn, I am so clumsy. It looks like you should probably take a *bath*."

"You bloody cunt!" Hannah screeched, stomping into Amelie's face. The proprietor, who was at first both confused and apologetic, had quickly morphed into an expression of anger.

"You two need to get out, right now," the bartender shouted, hastily grabbing towels to start cleaning up all the beer Amelie had thrown everywhere and shoving his finger towards the door. "This is not the place to have petty arguments."

"What?" Hannah's surprised eyes shot to the proprietor, beer still dripping off her chin. "She's the one that did this! I had nothing to do with it!"

"Don't care," he countered. "Both of you, out."

"*Kuso*," Dallas hissed, watching as Barbara jumped to her feet. Barbara was swiping at her grey blazer, which had taken a splash of beer.

"That was so childish," she was saying, scowling and glaring at Amelie, face red with anger.

"That's for my girl Dallas," Amelie growled as she slammed the empty pitcher down on the bar. She then whirled on a heel, storming by the table of the rest of her baffled team. A broad grin tugged at the corner of her mouth as she chucked deuces. "Catch up with you guys later!" she called, tossing ten pounds on the table as she strode by.

Barbara followed a furious Hannah, who was swiping at her face with her sleeves. Her auburn hair was dripping wet on one side. Barbara wrapped her arms around the other girl, muttering something in her ear—probably sweet revenge, Dallas thought—as they left together.

With a loud groan and a slew of Japanese curses that made Callie raise an eyebrow, she let her forehead fall onto the wooden table.

The *last* thing that she had expected to happen, the *last* thing that she had wanted, was to find herself involved in a bunch of drama in her brand new school. And yet, there she was, right in the middle of it.

Chariot was having an absolute blast.

The jumping arena wasn't in use, as it was later in the evening and most teams had finished schooling for the day. Floodlights spilled over the dark lot, leaving the surrounding areas nothing but a black wall.

The Games Team didn't have practice on Wednesdays, but Dallas seriously needed some alone time with her best friend. She'd taken a Behavioral Psychology quiz that she was pretty sure she failed, got assigned a topic for an essay that she had zero interest in for History of Psychology (B.F. Skinner and his idea of radical behaviorism—definitely not something Dallas wanted to research at all), *and* had been dealing with the awkward tension between the Games and Hunt Teams. They'd already gotten a stern talking to from Miss Nelson—apparently the other team had said something to their coach—and Dallas was in the hot seat for "instigating a conflict".

Not that she'd instigated *anything*. Dallas considered herself to be one of the least confrontational people she knew. She tried to be kind to everyone. It wasn't her fault Hannah and Barbara had decided to act like a bunch of children and Amelie had taken it upon herself to get revenge.

Dallas slowed Chariot to a trot, feeling the mare's neck curl with the gentle twitch of the French-link snaffle she hardly ever wore. The mare usually went bitless, because Dallas had taught her how to respond to pressure through a neck rein for gaming, but over fences the pony tended to get rambunctious. She loved to jump.

She glanced around at the arena, at the jumps that she'd lowered a little bit for her pony. Barely even 70 centimeters, because she didn't want to push her mare too hard, but she was certainly looking to take her mind off of her real life issues. Chariot's nostrils were flaring as her hooves skimmed against the surface of the sand, ears flicking back and forth as her chocolate eyes took in the slew of obstacles that surrounded them.

Dallas urged Chariot into a canter, sitting deep in the saddle and squeezing her legs tight against the mare's sides as she guided her to a line of verticals. The mare's ears flew forward and she quickened her stride, head rising with the anticipation of the jump. She flew over the first with ease, three strides, one more, five strides, a small oxer. Dallas felt herself laughing as she stood in the irons like a jockey and brought the pony back down to a trot, and then a walk, with a little pressure from the bit. The mare jigged and danced, ready for more, but Dallas had decided that would be the last of it for the evening. She didn't want to risk getting in trouble—after all, she *really* wasn't supposed to be using the Jumper's arena, though it had been unoccupied—

"Excuse me!"

Kuso.

Dallas looked up from where she'd been slapping the pony's neck in a loud praise to find a woman sliding through the fence and walking towards her. She immediately recognized the woman as the Jump team coach, Miss Willow. Oh, great, now she was in for it. She frowned and halted Chariot in the middle of the arena, feeling her hind legs dance to the side in disagreement with what she was being asked to do.

"Uh, hi," Dallas said, flinching away from the neutral face and the red eyes that flashed from behind frameless glasses. The woman had dark blue hair that she kept in a long braid that draped over the front of her shoulder. "I'm sorry, I just noticed there was no one out here and I kind of wanted to jump, and the only other arena with jumps is the Hunter's—" and lord knew she was not *about* to use *that* arena.

"Oh, it's perfectly alright," Miss Willow replied, a friendly smile spreading across her face. She stopped at Chariot's side, reaching out a hand to stroke down the mare's slightly dished face. "She's a lovely jumper, did you used to compete her?"

"No," Dallas said, maybe a little bit too quickly. "I mean, well, I used to jump a little, but not seriously, and Chariot did pony jumper derbies before I got her, but—well, never together."

Miss Willow nodded, letting Chariot lean into her touch to attempt to scratch herself on the offered hand. "Well, she's quite a lovely jumper. And has a lot of speed. She would be pretty competitive. Wait—" She narrowed her eyes, lowering her glasses a little on her nose. "You're Dallas West, right? From the Mounted Games team?"

Dallas nodded, feeling herself start to blush. "Yeah—I mean, um—" *Be more respectful*, Alice's words echoed in her head. She had meant it for Finnelan, but Dallas figured it should apply to all of her elders. "Yes."

"Cool sport," Miss Willow said with a nod. "I wish that had been around when I was younger, I definitely would have gotten involved. Jumping is a rush, but—" she shrugged, smiling warmly. "Games seems like a whole other level."

Dallas nodded, feeling herself smile. A compliment to her sport felt like a compliment to her. "It definitely is!" she replied. "It's so much fun, and it's great to be part of a team."

"What's your pony's name?" she asked after a moment, running her hands down Chariot's neck. The mare had finally quieted and was simply enjoying the attention.

Dallas kicked her feet out of the stirrups and leaned back coolly, clutching the cotton reins in one hand. She grinned, scratching Chariot's withers with her free hand. "This is Chariot! Swift Chariot. I named her after my idol, Octavia Chariot. And her horse, Swift Wind."

Miss Willow took a sharp intake of breath and looked away for a moment before finally bringing her eyes back to Dallas's. She looked a little... shaken? Dallas found herself confused at the odd reaction, but shoved it off. "I see," she finally said.

"Did you know her?" Dallas asked. Miss Willow seemed young—early thirties, maybe—which would have been about Chariot's age. Had she, well... not disappeared.

Miss Willow grew silent for a moment, her hand slowing its ministrations on the pony's neck, before responding at last. "I... did, yes."

Dallas's crimson eyes lit up and she squirmed in the saddle. Chariot, reading her sudden change in posture, skittered momentarily to the side and huffed through her nostrils. "You knew her? Really? Can you tell me all about her? Did you go to school with her? What was she like? Did you meet Swift Wind?" She was asking too many questions, and she knew it, but she was so excited she couldn't hold them in. She had never met anyone that had personally known her idol.

"She was—" Miss Willow trailed off, lowering her hand from Chariot's neck and taking a large step back. "You know, we should probably save that for another time. It's a bit late, and all the other horses have already been fed. I'm sure Chariot is hungry, and you really shouldn't be riding much longer, it's almost curfew for the stable as it is."

Dallas frowned. "Oh." She slid from Chariot's back, beginning her usual routine of unbuckling the noseband and throatlatch to pull the bridle off before undoing the girth. "You're probably right. Anyway, it was nice to meet you! Thanks for letting me... uh, use your arena." *Thank you for not killing me for using it without permission* is what she probably should have said.

But Miss Willow said nothing. She simply offered a polite nod before striding quickly off the way she'd come, slipping back through the four-panel fence and disappearing into the darkness.

Strange. Maybe she hadn't really liked Chariot that much? But who *couldn't* like her? She had been so cool and such an inspiration for young riders. With a shrug, she turned to her pony and offered a small smile and a scratch to the cheek. "Let's go eat, Chariot," she said to her pony.

Except she'd completely forgotten that Chariot was ready for her post-ride scratch, and instead the pony threw her head against Dallas's side and sent her flying backwards into the sand with a surprised grunt.

Chapter Four

A *LICE*

She had an hour before Hippotherapy—plenty of time to review the many pages of notes that she'd taken during her Equine Nutrition class. Hannah and Barbara had been waiting for her outside the classroom door with a fresh cup of tea that they'd gotten from the café up the street, which she was grateful for even though she had hoped for a little bit of quiet time. Expressing her thanks to the two girls, she stepped outside into the fresh autumn air and breathed deep, feeling the warmth of the tea in her hand and refreshing breeze against the thin fabric of her blue button-up.

Between classes, she liked to sit beside the fountain around the statue of Octavia Chariot. The sound of the steady streams falling into the shallow pool of water brought her comfort, and very few people had the same free period and if they did, the dormitories were right next door. She knew well the temptation to take a nap between classes, although partaking in such was not friendly with her schedule in the least. So, instead, she took her usual seat and pulled out her book to begin reviewing.

Hannah and Barbara were used to this behavior, and so they said nothing. Instead, they sat next to her and gossiped amongst themselves about the pettiest of things: cute boys from Appleton for Barbara, cute girls *and* boys for Hannah, cute horses in the stables for both. It was a never-ending stream of nonsense with the two, and Alice had long since learned to tune them out and focus what was going on in her own mind.

That day, they'd discussed basic nutrition needs for newborn foals from the moment they began to nurse their mothers until they reached the stage of yearlings. Alice was well familiar with this: her family was known for breeding and selling high-end Warmbloods, and so she had often helped her mother, and later the farmhands, care for the foals until the time they were weaned and either sold off or kept as breeding stock.

Beatrix had been the exception. Her mother had always dreamed of having a foal from the handsome and accomplished Balou du Rouet, though she had never seemed to come across a mare with the ideal conformational match until she was in the last stages of her illness. And so Alice had not allowed the filly to be sold or used for breeding—no, Beatrix would be hers to own and compete, a final tribute to her deceased mother. And Beatrix had become all that she expected to be, a picture of conformational elegance and the athleticism of a high-dollar champion. Though, in Alice's mind, she could have been bow-legged and useless and she would have still loved her just the same.

She had become quite involved in her studies, the two girls next to her nothing more than white noise, until she heard light footsteps nearby and Barbara's raised voice.

"Oh, look who it is," she heard Barbara sneer. "It's the Captain of the My Little Pony Club."

Alice glanced up from the book that had held the day's readings, where she was looking for the precise metabolic reaction of a three-month old foal in response to an unusually high iron intake, to see Dallas. She was wearing a sweaty, tight white tank-top that hugged her form in all the right ways, showing off her arm muscles and the smooth skin of her collarbones. And shorts—red running shorts that showed off a *lot* of muscular leg. She yanked her blue eyes back up to Dallas's face in an attempt to not make her staring obvious. Not that Dallas was paying attention, anyway, because she was looking at Barbara with a worried smile.

"*Barbara*," she warned. No good came out of Barbara when she developed the tone she had with Dallas.

The Japanese girl rolled her eyes and tugged some earbuds out, letting them fall around a neck glistening with sweat. Her brunette hair was tugged back into a ponytail, damp at her forehead and around her ears, but soft over muscled shoulders. "Hi to you, too," she said. She swiped at her forehead and turned to walk away.

"Hold up, we wanted to talk to you."

Alice looked to Barbara, shooting her a warning with narrowed blue eyes. *Keep it civil*, they said.

She saw Dallas turn. Alice glanced down at her runners, which looked new and pretty comfortable. She should get some new ones like that. Hers had nearly 500 miles on them. It was about time.

"We just had a question about Mounted Games," Barbara said next to her. "You know, just curious."

"Uh, okay." Dallas stepped forward. She pulled up the bottom of her shirt—sweet and merciful Jesus, those *abs*, good lord was that girl *cut*—and swiped at her face. Alice swallowed hard, feeling her breath hitch in her throat and forcing her mouth to stay closed and her face to stay neutral as she stared. She was *sorely* disappointed when Dallas dropped her shirt and quickly looked away to hide the fire in her cheeks. "What's your question?"

"We were just wondering how we could try out," Hannah said. She was using her petty voice.

Dallas's eyes narrowed, but her answer came genuine and level. "Selection is over. August only. You'll have to wait until next year, if you're actually interested."

"Well, that's rubbish," Hannah muttered. "If I had known it was that easy to get into Hoofbeats, I would've tried out for the Games team, too."

Alice had hardly been paying attention—she was still thinking about Dallas's body, because she had thought the girl was attractive before but, now, my *God*—and she finally snapped back to attention when Barbara said:

"Wouldn't have had to pay for private coaching, either."

"Girls," Alice scolded, shutting her book and directing her attention back to Hannah and Barbara. They were getting out of hand. Dallas had done nothing, and they were just goading a reaction for no reason. "I believe it's time for both of you to move along to your next class instead of picking unnecessary fights."

"Us picking unnecessary fights?" Hannah gave her a look. "She's the one who had her team mess with us all weekend. They're a brand new team, one that Hoofbeats's wasting its money on in the first place, and they think they're hot stuff."

"I don't know what you're talking about," she heard Dallas say.

"Great Captain," Barbara mumbled. "Doesn't even know what's going on with her own team."

Alice let out a heavy sigh. That was enough—they were taking out their frustrations on the wrong person. The Games team had done nothing to them. Despite what Hannah and Barbara were claiming, no one other than Amelie O'Neill had gone out of their way to cause any kind of issue. She didn't know why they were so insecure. It wasn't as though their positions on the Hunt Team were threatened by a sport that had nothing to do with them. "I said get to class," she snapped, shoving her book under her arm and turning to walk towards the Equestrian Studies building, expecting them to follow suit. She would be very early for Hippotherapy, but Professor Finnelan wouldn't mind if she sat quietly and studied while she waited for class to start.

"Fine," she heard Hannah say behind her. And of course, one last slight to poor Dallas. "Dallas should probably get busy taking a bath too, don't you think, Barbs? She looks pretty sweaty."

In all the right ways, Alice had thought, and turned to steal one last glance of the other girl in her athletic gear.

"That's where I was—"

She watched her two teammates grab the girl, whose red eyes widened in surprise, and throw her unceremoniously into the fountain surrounding the Chariot statue. "What the—"Dallas's arms were waving wildly as she tried to catch her balance and stop herself from falling, but to no avail. Her body crashed into the water, which splashed everywhere, all over the side of the statue, the stone bench, and the dry cobblestone.

Alice was outraged.

"That was completely childish. I can't believe you would do that to her. Get out of here, *right* now, I am absolutely *infuriated* with you two!" Alice shouted, anger flaring into the tips of her ears as she stepped forward. It was one thing to argue pointlessly, it was another to assault somebody else—especially a girl who had been minding her own business and was being nothing but friendly. She shot forward, ignoring as Hannah and Barbara backed off in a series of immature giggles, and grabbed Dallas's arm to help her up and make sure she was okay.

"Dallas, are you alright?" she asked. She could see a little bit of blood on some scrapes on the back of her calves. She was completely soaked, water dripping from her clothing, her hair plastered to her cheek and neck. Alice watched as she rang some water out of her shirt, frowning and looking like she might just cry.

Dallas didn't answer. Instead, she shrugged Alice's hand off her arm and shot her an angry look. "Like you care, get off me," she snapped.

Before Alice could say anything else, Dallas had turned to storm off in the direction of the dormitories without looking back. Hannah and Barbara were still laughing and, instead of going after Dallas, which she was tempted to do (though she didn't have a key card for the dormitories, so it probably didn't matter), she whirled on her teammates.

"If you *ever*, and I mean *ever*," Alice struggled to keep her voice level—after all, shouting accomplished nothing—and continued, "touch Dallas or anybody on that team again, I will personally have you removed from the Hunt Team *and* Hoofbeats, unless you want to work your tuition off by mucking stalls until those baby soft hands of yours are covered in blisters." She finished, feeling her eyes flash with the anger that was building inside of her.

Hannah and Barbara had stopped laughing. In fact, they almost looked ashamed of themselves, and if Alice believed for a moment they were actually capable of feeling shame, she might have let her anger die off there. But she knew they would just go back home and laugh about it. That was exactly the kind of people they had become in the last year, ever since they'd let the European Championships go to their heads.

Before Alice could say anything else, the two girls had turned and rushed away.

Alice turned her gaze to the door that led to the dormitories. She could see the trail of wet footprints and dripping water leading there. The door was still in the motion of shutting—if she ran, she might be able to get there. But she knew Dallas wouldn't want to talk to her. No, she probably thought she was just like Hannah and Barbara.

Besides, Dallas had Hippotherapy with her. Maybe she could just catch her there and offer an apology.

So, with a heavy sigh and the twinge of an oncoming headache, Alice wandered off to class in a haze of anger and remorse.

Much to Alice's relief, Hannah and Barbara had decided to go out after a very tense and awkward schooling session with Miss Parker. They seemed frightened of her, like she might go off on them again at any moment for their immature behavior earlier in the day. And, in all honesty, they should have been, because she hadn't nearly been able to scold them in the manner that she had been planning all day.

And so they'd made a point to keep Cello and Belle halted well away from her whenever they'd gathered in the middle of the arena for instructions from their oblivious coach.

She had tried to catch Dallas to apologize after Hippotherapy, but the girl had rushed out of the room as though her seat had been on fire. Alice had lost her in the crowd and had only been able to resign herself to apologizing another time.

With the house to herself, Alice brewed herself a fresh pot of tea and sat contentedly in her favorite leather armchair in the living room. She'd set it up just for herself—the chair was the old one her father used to sit in a long time ago, and somehow still had the imprint of his body even though it had gone unused for years. The floor lamp, too, had been hand selected from the Thelwell Manor. It gave off the perfect amount of soft light for reading, studying, and general comfort. It had been one of Alice's favorite throughout her childhood.

Setting her fresh cup of tea down on the side table, she kicked back in her recliner and opened the book she'd been reading for the last week.

In all honesty, she probably should have been studying or reviewing her notes, but it wasn't often that she found the house to herself and she really just wanted to do something relaxing. And, usually, her reading didn't consist of anything that anyone would consider enjoyable—certainly not fiction—but she had a soft spot for true crime mysteries and allowed herself to fall into something mindless.

She hadn't been reading long and had only covered about a chapter when her mobile vibrated across the table. Great, somebody probably needed some tutoring. Or Hannah and Barbara were sending some half-witted apology. She plucked up her mobile—after taking a sip of tea, because she couldn't let that get cold—and checked her messages.

Hey, Alice. Can we talk?

In an instant, her stomach churned. She tensed her jaw, her fingers freezing over the keyboard of her mobile as she stared down at the text message and the person who had sent it.

Chloe.

Alice took a deep breath and tilted her head back against the soft leather of the chair. In a single moment, her comfort had been completely ruined. She slammed her book shut and tossed it onto the table, instead sinking into a state of anxiety as her mobile lie, the screen still lit, in her lap and she reviewed the text history that she could see on the page.

Tuesday, August 28, 2018
Chloe 23:17
I was just thinking about you, would you want to talk?
Wednesday, August 29, 2018
Alice 07:32
Not really, no.
Chloe 09:57
I miss you. I really just wanted to apologize for everything. I'm not asking for you to take me back or even forgive me for everything I did to you, but I owe you that much.
Alice 10:03
That's great.
Chloe 10:04
Look, can I just... call you? Please?
Alice 10:07
I have nothing to say to you.
Chloe 10:07
Ok.
September 07, 2018
Chloe 01:52
Come on babe can we jut talk a little I realy want to work ths out I miss u
Alice 05:20
First, I am not your "babe" and have not been for months. Second, there is absolutely nothing to work out. Third,

please refrain from sending me drunk texts
at 2 AM.
Chloe 09:52
Sorry.
September 19, 2018
Chloe 19:08
Hey, Alice. Can we talk?

"No, we *can't* talk," Alice grumbled out loud, squeezing her eyes shut. Another text came through.

Chloe 19:11
Please? I'm sorry about that text the other
week.

With a pounding heartbeat, Alice typed out a quick text.

Alice 19:12
I have no interest in talking to you.
Chloe 19:12
And yet you're still texting me back.

Alice slammed the footrest of her armchair down and stood up, lifting one hand to pinch the bridge of her nose. Of course Alice texted her back—Chloe knew that she would, because Alice wasn't the type of person to just ignore things. Her ex was just trying to pull whatever manipulation she had up her sleeve this time.

Chloe 19:14
I'm sorry about everything I've done.

Right. Likely. Chloe had cheated on her—with a guy, no less—and then tried to play it off as though it was a one time thing that had just happened because she was drunk and Alice hadn't been there.

"I was lonely and it just happened. Maybe if you hadn't gone to a school across the country, I wouldn't have been at that party and nothing would have come of it in the first place," Chloe had snapped through tears over the phone.

Like it was Alice's fault that Chloe: a) couldn't regulate her alcohol intake, b) had no self control over her own actions, and c) *cheated on Alice with some random guy at Oxford.*

She should have just deleted Chloe's number and she knew it, but that wouldn't have made any difference because she still knew it by heart. They had been together for nearly two years, it was harder than it seemed from the outside to just block somebody completely out of your life. She remembered telling Barbara that once earlier at the beginning of their first semester at Hoofbeats:

"Just block his number, Barbs. He's a waste of your time and not worth the additional distress."

And she had been dating him for *four years.*

It wasn't until Chloe that she knew her ignorance.

She had told Chloe she loved her. She had come out to her extended family for her. She had used so many weekends skipping time that she could have spent at the stable with Beatrix or with her friends to fly to Oxford to try to keep the relationship alive—something that she wasn't having *any* problems with on her end, because she wouldn't have even fathomed doing the same thing Chloe had done to her.

Alice 19:21
Not interested. Goodbye, Ch loe.
Chloe 19:21
Alice, please...

Whatever. She'd had it. She walked to her bedroom, threw her mobile onto her bed, shut the door, and went right back out into the living room where she threw herself back into her armchair and picked up her MacBook.

Would you like to restore your Google session?

Right. She'd forgotten to put her laptop on the charger and it died. Sure, there was probably something important there. Likely something to do with class and some additional research for certain-

IMGAweb – International Mounted...

Dallas West – Google Search

Oh.

Right.

She'd spent quite some time browsing Mounted Games, watching a few of the videos that she managed to find online and eventually finding the International Association website. The sport seemed interesting, to say the least. Dangerous, fast-paced, and fun, with a clear level of athleticism that rivaled any of the more intense equestrian disciplines.

Dallas—er, Dallas—was a little bit more difficult of a search. Most of what she could find on the other girl was in Japanese and just wouldn't translate properly and she certainly didn't speak that language. Russian, French (including Luxembourgish), German, Italian, Dutch, and Mandarin (it had been an extracurricular when she was a sixth form), maybe. But not Japanese.

What she *did* manage to find, though, was a few pictures on Google images and even a video.

Alice clicked back over to the image search on her page, enlarging the two pictures of Dallas. In one, she was hanging off the side of Chariot, who was galloping at full speed, her tail flagged out behind her and her ears pinned back with the effort of speed. Dallas's hand was dipped into a bucket, either grabbing something out or putting something in, Alice couldn't tell from the picture.

The second was a picture of Dallas and three other teammates grinning with a gold cup clutched between their four hands. They all wore matching shirts—white with a large red circle on the front—and their ponies stood obediently behind them. Chariot's nose was poking over Dallas's shoulder, a scene that made the corner of her mouth twitch into a smile.

Dallas was clearly the most vibrant on the team. Her broad smile gave of a certain vibe of confidence that the other three girls didn't quite have, her brown hair wild from beneath the jockey helmet she still wore, a long brunette ponytail draped over her shoulder.

It had been from Internationals in 2016. Dallas's team, representing Japan, had taken first place in the Junior Master's Division.

She had clicked over to the video she'd found, one that showed Dallas briefly in quite a few races as she and Chariot dominated the other teams handily, when the front door flew open. She slammed the MacBook shut, wincing as the sound continued to play for a moment: "*It's Japan and France fighting for first place, they've both got one more rider-*"

Hannah was soaked. The white shirt that she'd left in was stained over one shoulder and down the side.

"Alice!" Barbara shouted, following the red-faced girl and slamming the door shut behind her (Alice had told her to stop doing that). "That bloody Games team has really hit their limit, look at this!"

Hannah halted in front of Alice, crossing her arms over her chest as she glared at her blonde roommate. Her hair was wet on one side and she reeked of beer.

"Amelie O'Neill dumped a pitcher of beer on me," she said matter-of-factly, leveling brown eyes with blue. "And then said that I needed to take a *bath*. Sound familiar?"

Alice raised one white-blonde eyebrow. Yes, it sounded quite familiar—in fact, it sounded almost exactly like Hannah's words before she *shoved Dallas into the Chariot fountain.*

"It was that Dallas bint," Barbara said, her nostrils flaring angrily. "I bet she told Amelie to do that to get us back. And you say *we're* childish. I don't understand how you can say that those chavs never did anything wrong when they're doing stuff like this." She waved her hands at Hannah for emphasis.

"Alright," Alice said, clenching her teeth and nodding once. "I'll speak to Miss Parker about their behavior."

That seemed to sedate the two girls. Hannah let out a shrill yell of nonsense, throwing her hands in her air before disappearing down the hall to her own room to shower, and Barbara simply went to the fridge and grabbed a bottle of Strongbow ("We didn't even get to finish our drinks," she grumbled) and disappeared into her own bedroom.

Alice shook her head. She was tired of the ridiculous drama between her own team and the Games team, though she *did* agree that something needed to be brought up to Miss Parker. Though, one thing would be left out—Dallas as the instigator. Dallas had shown herself to be nothing more than genuine and she knew how Hannah and Barbara could skew things to meet the expectations of their own reality.

Honestly, she just wished the sudden rivalry would stop. There was no reason for it, other than stubbornness and a false sense of pride, neither of which Alice felt inclined to agree with.

Maybe if she talked to Dallas... after all, Dallas *was* the Captain, she could bring some kind of peace, or at least understanding, to the two vastly different disciplines and stop the headfirst collision that the two seemed to gear towards.

But that would involve talking to Dallas. Who, as it stood, seemed to be entirely uninterested in even acknowledging her existence.

Alice spent the rest of the night thinking about how she would talk to Dallas, how she could get the other girl to understand that she wasn't Hannah or Barbara and there was nothing that the two Teams had to prove. They both competed in equestrian sports, both of which were recognized at international competitions and within the Hoofbeats Equestrian program, and so there was no reason to put each other down.

It wasn't until Alice had settled down for the night to get up early and check up on Beatrix before her morning class that she realized she had forgotten all about Chloe.

She had stayed late at the barn with Beatrix. Her schooling session with Miss Parker had gone rather long, especially when the instructor kept making her re-do a line over and over again ("You look great, I just think we could work on that lower leg a *little* bit more over those fences," she had said) until Hannah and Barbara had long since finished and darkness was settling over Hoofbeats. Alice didn't complain. She was used to it, after all. "One more time" was never one more time when it came to riding instructors.

By the time she had gone back into the barn and begun to brush Beatrix and do her daily post-ride routine of checking for any maladies, the school grounds had grown completely dark. There was only one person still riding in the Jumper arena and the floodlights lit the space between the Hunter arena and the Dressage arena like a stadium.

She led Beatrix from the cross ties, tugging the mare away from the direction of her box and instead out into the open lawn that spread between the barns, the center lane, and the arenas. It was her custom to let Beatrix pick grass following heavy workouts. She enjoyed spending time with her mare that didn't include riding or standing for long periods of time on stone, and one of the better ways to do that was stand guard over her while she grazed contentedly.

As the mare stretched her long neck down and began to rifle through the grass that she wanted, Alice let her gaze wander to the arena and the lone rider.

It was Dallas.

And she was jumping.

That was strange. Dallas wasn't a jumper, nor was her pony, from what she knew. Plus, she was in the jumper arena, which was reserved exclusively for the Show Jumping team. Maybe she had asked for permission?

Either way, Alice found it odd... and fascinating.

She stood at her mare's withers, letting her fingernails gently scratch at her shoulder as she watched Dallas and Chariot take jumps with the ease of a skilled and fluent pair. Dallas's position wasn't the most ideal—her knee crept forward too far and her hips closed a little bit too much over the fence—but all in all it wasn't that bad. Especially for riding a pony, which Alice knew was a bit harder as their center of balance was slightly off kilter from a regular horse.

But Chariot seemed like she knew what she was doing, and she looked like she enjoyed every minute of it. She took each jump at a perfect distance, ears forward as her energetic stride carried her over verticals and oxers with ease.

She could see a shadow moving down the lane. They slipped through the rail of the fence and approached the gleeful rider, who had pulled the small pony up and was hugging her neck. Alice instantly knew who it was. Miss Willow. She was a kind and docile woman, rather young but at the same time incredibly knowledgeable, and she knew that she would treat Dallas kindly. Still, she observed in silence, stepping with the mare as she moved between patches of grass to find what she wanted, snorting into the quiet evening air.

Finally, Miss Willow left Dallas and walked back up the lane. She gave Alice a small wave and a friendly, "Hello, Miss Thelwell!" as she moved past before disappearing into the stable behind her.

Alice looked back down at Beatrix, watching as the mare picked at the grass, almost feeling like she was intruding for watching Dallas and Chariot—but after a moment of reflection, the gentle song of horseshoes approaching made her look back up.

Dallas had already pulled Chariot's bridle off, the girth resting across the saddle. The small chestnut pony was following her owner obediently, showing no signs of looking away or even wandering off. No, she was fully focused on the girl who walked before her with her hands shoved into the pockets of her hoodie, the girl who didn't even look back to see if her pony was behind her. She knew.

"Hey, Dallas," Alice heard herself say before she could even think not to.

Dallas's step faltered and she raised her eyes from where she was staring at the pavement below her to find where Alice stood with a grazing Beatrix. She said nothing, but instead frowned and let out a heavy sigh before continuing forward. Chariot, who had hesitated behind her and glanced over at the other horse with a soft snort, resumed following the small girl.

With some effort, Alice pulled Beatrix's head up—she didn't want to leave the fresh patch of grass she'd found—and met Dallas in the middle of the lane to walk at her side.

"I understand why you wouldn't want to speak with me," Alice said, turning her gaze away from the other girl and instead staring into the light of the stable ahead. "But I wanted to apologize on behalf of the behavior of my teammates."

"Seriously?"

Dallas stopped, and with her, Chariot. She raised red eyes to stare at the taller girl. "It's not as though you really did anything to stop them from acting like that. There's a lot of accountability that comes with just *letting* another person act like that."

Alice frowned, halting Beatrix. The mare stretched her nose out to Chariot and sniffed at her neck. "Well there's quite a bit of accountability for letting a teammate throw a pitcher of beer on somebody," she retorted.

"I didn't *know* she was going to-"

"Well I didn't *know* they were going to do that to you, either," Alice huffed. She rolled her shoulders and straightened her posture, returning her eyes to the stable and resuming her lead of Beatrix just as Dallas stepped forward. "But, if that's what's bothering you, then I apologize for not knowing my friends were going to mistreat you in such a childish manner."

"Fine," Dallas grumbled. "Then I apologize for Amelie being her own person and doing what she wants."

"That's not-" Alice sighed. It was no use arguing the point. She was trying to get on Dallas's good side, not make things worse. "Either way," Alice said, squeezing her eyes shut momentarily, "I will not allow my teammates to treat you—or the rest of your team, for that matter—in any disrespectful manner. And if they do, I would like you to consult me so that I can address the issue accordingly."

Dallas paused once more. The orange light from the barn lit the side of her face, making her red eyes flicker as they turned to Alice. "Prove it."

Alice's eyebrows knit together. "Pardon me?"

"Prove you're not just a bunch of jerks and maybe I'll think about it. Until then, I'm going to let my team defend themselves in any way they see fit."

Alice found herself staring. The girl was looking at her with a resolute frown, crimson eyes burning into her own as she waited for her response. It was intense and unwavering—Alice couldn't help but feel a sudden sense of respect for the smaller rider.

Finally, she cleared her throat. "Fine," she said, pursing her lips. "That seems fair."

Dallas nodded, the corner of her lips tilting upwards in an amused half-smile. "Alright, then. See you, Thelwell."

Last name treatment. Ouch. Alice hated when people called her by her last name—it reminded her of all the expectations she had to meet on a daily basis. Was she taking a page out of Amelie's book? *Redeem yourself, Alice*, she thought.

"You, um-" Alice paused, unsure of how to pay a compliment that didn't sound like sarcasm. She had a tendency to leave her voice a little too flat. "The two of you looked good jumping."

"Oh." Dallas looked down at the ground. She looked unsure, but she responded anyway. "Thank you. She, uh... used to be a jumper, so I like to let her do what she loves sometimes."

Alice nodded. Her hand was sweating against the lead rope as she turned Beatrix away, blue eyes turning to fall on the front shoe of her mare's hoof as she said, "Well, she's a very lucky little pony," before turning and heading off to her own stable without another word.

Chapter Five

D*ALLAS*
"Dude this movie rules, do you mind putting subtitles on?"

Dallas glanced up from where she had been spread out across the couch they shared in the living area of their suite-style dorm, watching as Callie grabbed a bottle of some weird green drink ("It's a kale smoothie," she'd told her one day—weird vegetarian crap) before roughly shoving her legs off the end of the sofa and plopping down. She'd been watching The Grudge—one of her favorite horror movies that she'd fished out of her small collection of DVD's—to gear up for the first Halloween she would ever get to celebrate in style. It had been a slow and lazy day after they'd all had a good two hour long practice in the morning, so Dallas had done nothing but play on her phone and watch movies while Callie had disappeared into her bedroom for a long time, only coming out to get drinks or an occasional snack.

Brooke was out for the weekend with Frank. Apparently they'd had some festival or book release or something they planned to go to downtown that involved cosplay, so Dallas had excused her from the Games practices on Saturday and

Sunday so that she could go. It had taken some convincing on her part to get Miss Nelson on board, but Dallas's charisma had come through and Brooke had hugged her around the neck and told her she was the best Team Captain there was. It was clearly praise as the result of excitement, but it was praise nonetheless, and Dallas certainly took what she could get.

"Uh-huh," Dallas mumbled, picking up the remote off the floor where she'd dropped it and tossing it to her lavender-haired roommate. "You can switch the whole thing to English, I'm not really paying attention anyway."

"Cool," Callie muttered. She did exactly that.

Dallas was very engaged with Google. In fact, she was running a thoroughly extensive search on a certain Alice Thelwell. Curiosity, of course, since she was the star of the Hoofbeats Equestrian Program and, as Dallas had heard it, one of the most highly regarded Hunter/Jumpers in England. Apparently, she had seized the honors of highest point holding rider in the British Show Hunter Association for four years in a row when she was in the Junior ranks, had claimed Champion in the International Hunter Over Fences 3'6"-3'9" division in the Spring of 2018, *and* had won the International Overall Championship Horse and Rider award while representing Hoofbeats the previous year—of which, the entire Hunt Team in itself claimed first place for Highest Point Hunter/Jumper Team.

Along with that, Thelwell Veterinary was one of the most renowned Veterinary services in all of Europe, and, as it was up for debate, the world, only rivaled by Rood and Riddle in the United States. They were also apparently one of the top breeders of different sporthorses—most notably Hanoverians and Holsteiners—although they had been known to produce some of the top money-earning Thoroughbreds in the European racing industry.

All in all, she and her family had a rather notable heritage.

Alice didn't have a Facebook or any other kind of social media, not that Dallas could blame her—she didn't either. Ever since Okaasan had discovered the "wonders" of communicating with their neighbors and spamming meme after meme, she had quickly ditched any semblance of online presence. But there were plenty of pictures on image search. Alice and Beatrix soaring over massive jumps in perfect form, standing next to Miss Parker with garlands and ribbons draped over Beatrix's neck and Alice mounted with a humble half-smile, a few candids of the blonde girl having some silent moments with her large bay mare.

"What are you so busy with?" Callie mumbled, taking a sip of her disgustingly green drink and eyeing the girl at the end of the coach.

"Eh." Dallas closed the Google page and turned her phone off, tossing it onto the coffee table that was littered with dirty dishes and empty water bottles, before turning back to Callie. "Not much."

Callie nodded, raising one eyebrow in a way that told Dallas that she didn't believe that it was 'not much'. She turned her attention back to the movie and seemed quite content in the silence of the moment—after all, it was rare that Dallas was quiet, because she was usually a ball of energy and disrupting both of their roommates no matter what they were doing.

"Hey, Callie?"

Callie grunted, not bothering to look away from the movie as she sank a little bit farther into the couch cushion.

"What do you know about Alice Thelwell?"

"Thelwell?" Callie glanced back at Dallas, narrowing her eyes in suspicion. "Uh, she's a bitch. And she's on the Hunt Team. Those are not mutually exclusive. What is there to know?"

Dallas shrugged, tugging at the waist of her t-shirt and staring at the film with glazed eyes. "Just curious."

"Dunno. Google could tell you more than me," Callie muttered.

Great. Wonderful advice. Dallas rolled her eyes and clambered from the couch, bare feet padding against the hard floor as she slipped into their mini-kitchen and grabbed a fresh bottle of water out of the fridge. Google *did* tell her a lot about Alice—like her accolades, her accomplishments, her family's accolades, her family's accomplishments—but nothing that she *wanted* to know, like what Alice's deal was and why she was so emotionally disconnected from reality and why she associated with people who acted like they were perpetually stuck in a world of immaturity.

Callie's dark eyes followed Dallas as she found her way back to the couch and started chugging her water. "Any reason you want to know anything?" she asked. "Amelie would probably know more, if she's bothering you. They used to be friends or something. Not that I care."

"Amelie? And Alice?" Dallas scrunched her eyebrows together, lowering the bottle of water and staring at the side of her friends face. "That's weird."

"Amelie used to be on the Hunt Team," Callie grumbled. "I don't know the details. I don't care, either. But something to do with a falling out and Amelie threw in the towel and went for Games instead. Again, I don't care. Don't ask me anything else."

Dallas rolled her eyes. "Yeah, yeah. Keep your socks on," she muttered. She took another long swig of water and stared at the television, letting herself zone into her own thoughts.

So Amelie used to be on the Hunt Team. She'd never mentioned that at all—it hadn't come up in any previous conversations, nor had the current three members of the Hunt Team ever brought it up. Dallas made a mental note to ask Amelie about it and then shoved it far from her mind, along with whatever curiosity for Alice Thelwell she couldn't satisfy, before settling back down into the world of mindless horror.

She missed the bucket.

She missed the bucket.

Dallas *never* missed the bucket!

With a yelp of anger and surprise, she sent Chariot spiraling in a 180 and leapt off mid-turn, clutching the reins in one hand as she sprinted to the balled up sock that lie in the sand next to the blue 20 gallon bucket that was sitting slightly off-kilter in the middle of the lane. Hastily tossing it in, she clucked to Chariot, who offered a small rear as she launched off her hindquarters, and let the forward motion of her mare send her spiraling into the air and onto her back. Amelie had already surpassed her and finished up for the other half of the team—her arm had spun triumphantly as she slammed the sock down in the bucket and she was busy trying to pull up Star, who was still bolting along the rail at the end of the arena and disrupting the rest of the ponies. She could vaguely hear Miss Nelson yelling, "Amelie, calm that damn pony down!" as she hooked the cantle and leaned from the side of Chariot.

Dallas used to have to jump off and vault back on to pick up items off the ground, but after learning how to stretch properly and become more flexible, it had become relatively easy to hang off the side of the horse and grab what she needed. Of course, Chariot was a huge part of that—the mare stayed in a straight line without asking and had learned exactly where to turn and even dipped her body pretty drastically to the side with the action. So as her pony whipped around the end of the lane, Dallas's fingers found the remaining, half-buried sock and she threw herself back upright in the saddle just as Chariot launched forward into an all-out gallop.

Normally, she would have pumped her arms or kicked at the mare's side to urge her faster. But the race was over—Amelie's team had already won—and so there was no point. She dunked the last sock in the bucket with the spin of an arm and sat back in the saddle to pull the panting pony up.

"What happened there, Dallas?" Miss Nelson asked just as Chariot slammed on the brakes in front of Mushroom, who was prancing excitedly while Callie inspected the chipped black paint on her nails.

"Too late, I guess," Dallas replied, breathing heavily as she kicked her legs out of the stirrups (the action usually equated with dismounting, and so it calmed Chariot considerably) and brought the mare, nostrils flaring, up to the coach. "I got cocky."

There was a reason she had gotten cocky, and it had a lot to do with the Hunt Team having walked toward their own arena during the race, but she certainly wasn't going to mention that to anybody. Dallas mentally scolded herself for trying to show off. There really wasn't any reason, anyway, it wasn't like the Hunt Team considered them to be a real sport.

Miss Nelson nodded, tossing a tennis ball from a previous race in her hand as she looked over the team. "It happens. Well, I don't think there's much more to improve before we take on Appleton this weekend. We'll work on our hand-offs in our next practice. Until then, I want you all to take it easy on your ponies. They don't need to go into the weekend with," she leveled an accusatory stare at Amelie, "sour minds."

"Yeah, yeah," Amelie grumbled, rolling her eyes and squeezing her thighs to lift Star into a small rear, which earned a scold of, "Stop doing that!" from Nelson. She did it despite their coach's continuous reprimand—after all, rearing was a terrible habit—but getting a reaction was exactly what Amelie was about, and so she'd taught her feisty pony to rear on command.

Dallas wasn't going to lie, she thought it was kind of neat, and she'd taught Chariot to rear a little for receiving hand-offs. It seemed to help for when the taller ponies, like Cookie, came in.

"Cool out," Nelson called with a dismissive wave of the hand, catching sight of Miss Willow and rushing over to the other coach.

Dallas undid the knot of her cotton reins and let them out long so Chariot could stretch her neck as they walked around the arena, mindlessly weaving through poles that were still up from their warm-up. As she walked, her gaze wandered to the Hunt Team's arena. They were warming up at the trot, Miss Parker leaning against a jump standard as she stared down at the phone in her hand. Alice looked perfect, as always—upper body tilted slightly forward, Beatrix's neck and back curved just right, stride long and flowing. Hannah looked good, too, turning her chestnut gelding in a wide circle as she stared down at his shoulder in thought. Barbara seemed to be having a little bit of trouble. Belle was weaving sideways at the fence, a loud, rumbling snort slipping through her nostrils as she eyed something she wasn't particularly confident about.

Suddenly remembering what Callie had said the previous weekend, she found Amelie across the arena, looking bored and letting Star jig his way around some cones, and walked over.

"Hey, want to get a drink tonight?" she asked as she grew near, keeping her voice low so that the rest of the team wouldn't hear. She didn't particularly want to invite everybody else.

Amelie looked up, raising an eyebrow and reaching up to unbuckle her helmet. "Is that a real question?" A slow smirk crept across her lips. "I'm always down for a drink. What's up?"

"We need to sort out the line-ups for the games this weekend," Dallas said, leaning back in the saddle and kicking her legs forward. Chariot turned her head and lipped at the toe of her paddock boot.

"Wow, and you want my opinion this time?" Amelie shrugged, leaning forward to run a hand through Star's roached black mane. "That's a first. Cool, yeah. Last Wednesday?"

Dallas nodded. Amelie had been permitted back into the pub after Dallas had all but shoved her inside to go apologize to the proprietor for her actions. It had been a battle just trying to get the girl to obey, but Dallas was not interested in having to relocate to one of the dirty pubs where people swarmed to play pool and obnoxious drinking games. She tugged at the reins to turn Chariot to the gate of their arena. The mare jigged a little before settling down into her quick-strided walk, neck raised as she looked around at the other ponies and riders in adjacent arenas.

As the team drifted from the arena and back to the barn, Dallas could feel the eyes of the Hunt Team on them. Hannah was staring outright. Dallas couldn't see her facial expression, but if she had to guess, it was one of extreme distaste.

Though, true to her word thus far, Alice hadn't allowed her teammates give the Games Team so much as a menacing glare and her team, too, hadn't gone out of their way to cause any sort of trouble. The air between them was as tense and uncomfortable as ever, and it was far from paradise, but it was progress, at the very least.

"No, I need to anchor for mug shuffle," Amelie was saying as she pointed to one of the races that had been projected as a maybe for the friendly. There would be a total of 20 races and their list held 25 possibilities, meaning that Dallas had no way of knowing which five races would be left off. Though, she *seriously* hoped one would be ball and cone-Brooke, Callie, and Janine all seemed to make a mess of that one. "Star is faster on the straights and I never miss a pole. You should start. Put Brooke and Janine in the middle. Constance's too short for that one and Callie always misses the poles."

Dallas nodded. She had to agree with Amelie's reasoning. "Alright," she said. "You can be anchor for socks, too. No offense, but Star is hard to get hand-offs from. He acts kind of crazy, and this way you don't have to worry about it."

"Sure." Amelie brought her whiskey glass to her lips and took a sip. They'd taken residence at the bar instead of a table since it was just the two of them and it was way easier for both of them to see the paper of line-ups as Dallas scribbled and erased names. The proprietor had side-eyed Amelie when they walked in, but served her without question—an Old Fashioned, because Amelie said girls thought drinking bourbon was hot, though Dallas wasn't sure what girls she was talking about because the pub was empty—while Dallas had just gotten her usual pint of lager. She had never been too keen on liquor and lager was the closest she could get to Sapporo or Kirin.

"Leave Janine out of that one, though," Amelie said, pointing to where Dallas had written Janine into the third position. "She can't vault and Cookie is too tall for her to pick things off the ground. Put Constance there instead. Stan's short enough and she doesn't have to get off."

"Eh, you're right," Dallas agreed again. She still hadn't gotten the firmest grasp on where her teammates strengths and weaknesses lie. Amelie had been around them much longer and knew their abilities better, and Dallas had to wonder why exactly Nelson hadn't made her the Captain. Probably her short fuse. "I'll sit bottles and jousting out," she said. "Sometimes I accidentally knock down more than one target and then I have to reset. You sit out both of the flags."

Amelie nodded and took another sip of her drink before reaching in and plucking out the cherry with her finger. She shoved the whole thing in her mouth. "Sounds good to me, Captain."

"I'll anchor for Windsor," Dallas said, looking at the final race on the page that hadn't been sorted yet. "You start. Constance and Callie second and third." There was no debate from Amelie, so she scribbled in the names and set her pen down before taking another sip of her beer. The question she had really wanted to ask was nagging in the back of her mind, so she figured she would just come out and ask it. It wasn't Dallas's style to beat around the bush. "Is it true you used to be on the Hunt Team?"

The American let out a heavy sigh and stuck her tongue out, plucking a perfectly tied cherry stem off it and tossing it onto her bar napkin. "Fuck, here comes this conversation," Amelie muttered. She brought her drink to her lips and polished it off, letting the ice spread around her mouth as she got every last drop. "Yeah, I did. And I'm assuming you're going to ask me what happened?"

Dallas shrugged. "Well, yeah. I'm curious. If you don't want to talk about it, though, that's alright."

"Nah, it's fine. I'm gonna need more booze for this one." She lifted her hand to the bartender, who was leaning against a pillar watching the Arsenal game. "Two shots of tequila."

"You know I don't take shots—" Dallas started to protest.

Amelie leveled green eyes on Dallas's red, taking the two shots once the bartender had slipped a couple limes over the edges of the glass and shoving one at Dallas. "I don't take shots alone," she countered. "And if you want me to talk about this crap, it's only fair."

Dallas sighed, clenching her teeth as she grabbed the glass and lifted it to cheers Amelie. The other girl threw it back easily and promptly slipped the lime between her teeth. Dallas did the same—although, not with the practiced swallow of the American, she had to take it slow and it burned all the way down—then made a face of absolute disgust and slammed the shot glass down. "Guh." A shudder ran through her body as she pulled the lime out of her mouth and dropped it into the glass. "That was awful."

"I came to Hoofbeats for the Hunt Team," Amelie muttered after ordering another Old Fashioned. She cupped the glass in one hand and stared into the dark liquid. "I never thought it was very fun, but it was what my mom was into and so I had all the good trainers growing up." She shrugged. "Just kind of how it went, I guess. It was me, Thelwell, tweedle dee, and tweedle dum."

Dallas took a long drink of her beer—she was still trying to get the nasty taste of tequila out of her mouth—and stayed silent. She could already feel the edges of her vision getting a little hazy from the shot.

"We got along well enough, I guess. I hung out with Hannah and Barbara mostly. Thelwell kind of does her own thing and I can't say we ever saw eye to eye, but we were cool." Amelie sipped her drink. "We were gearing up for Internationals and had this regional show up in Bristol and it was easy enough to wipe the place clean. Except we kind of went out to celebrate and I got a little drunk—"

Dallas could tell a little drunk meant a *lot* drunk. She relaxed into the bar stool, awkwardly avoiding eye contact as she spun her pint on the lacquered wooden bar.

"Hannah got pretty drunk too," Amelie added.

Dallas's eyebrows stitched together and she glanced over at the red-head, who was blushing furiously and staring at the glowing light above the liquor bottles across the bar. The door to the pub swung open and two girls Dallas recognized from the Dressage team took seats at a table nearby. Amelie glanced over and lowered her voice.

"Anyway, we..." she gazed down at her drink, shrugging. "You know."

Dallas could feel her eyes widening. A hot blush rose to her cheeks and she quickly hid her face behind her beer as she chugged. "Oh," she finally said, lowering her pint and swiping the back of her hand across her mouth. "Got it."

"Yeah." Amelie frowned, fingers drumming against the bar. "I mean, I thought it was fine. It was no big deal, or at least *I* didn't think so, but Hannah started acting really weird and everything got awkward. She started avoiding me and became super bitchy—I don't get it." Amelie licked her lips and picked up the knotted cherry stem, turning it between her fingers. "Anyway, I heard Hoofbeats was starting a Games team and I wanted to have more fun anyway—Hunters is boring—so I sold my horse and got Star and tried out. I didn't really want to be on the Hunt Team anyway, and after Hannah... well, there was no reason to stick around on a team that hated me and I didn't enjoy as it was."

"Oh," Dallas said again, uselessly. She didn't really know what to say. Her hands felt clammy so she wiped them on her dirt-stained breeches (they had just left straight from the barn) and stared down at her nearly finished beer. She *had* intended on asking about what Alice's deal was, but she definitely didn't want to follow Amelie's admission up with lame and unfounded curiosity.

"Could I get two more shots of tequila?" Amelie grunted at the bartender.

Under any other circumstance, Dallas would have absolutely refused to take another shot, but Amelie had just openly shared something she was clearly uncomfortable with, so Dallas resigned herself to another throat burn and made sure to chug the rest of her beer to get rid of the taste.

"Anyway, uh." Dallas stared down at the line-up sheet, desperate to get rid of the awkward silence. She'd dropped a little bit of beer on the corner. "I was re-thinking this. Maybe I should anchor for poles. Chariot's more agile."

Amelie squinted her eyes, her frown twitching back into its signature smirk. "No way, West. Star's way faster. I can't possibly let you do the honors."

Dallas was tipsy.

She shoved her hands into her Mounted Games jacket—the one with the Japanese flag over the heart that she'd been gifted when her team won Internationals—and walked slowly through the dark stone lanes of campus that led to her dormitory. Amelie had gone the other way, toward the flat she shared with Constance and Janine, and so Dallas was left alone in her thoughts as she traipsed below the orange glare of streetlights. Her paddock boots clopped against the uneven pavement and she kicked at some leaves as she went.

As she walked, her fingers traced over the line-up that she'd folded and shoved into her pocket. She wasn't nervous about the friendly with Appleton, but she was a little concerned. Amelie had told her that the all-male university could get a little aggressive with competition. That was the last thing she wanted to go up against: showboating guys who thought they were better riders.

The echoing of nearby footsteps made her glance up. Alice was walking toward her, neutral expression locked ahead, the strap of a thick leather satchel draped across her chest. She looked like she hadn't changed after riding, either. She still wore a pair of tweed breeches and her usual long-sleeve shirt and grey vest, plaid calf-socks rising from her fancy brown paddock boots.

Don't notice me, don't notice me, Dallas thought to herself as she hunched her shoulders over and made a point to stare at the ground as she walked a little faster.

"Dallas?"

Kuso.

Dallas pursed her lips and sighed, glancing up to see the blonde had stopped. Her hair was pulled into a neat French braid and she was wearing frameless glasses—Dallas hadn't even realized she wore glasses—that gave her a different look, one that Dallas briefly appreciated, before continuing on with a dismissive, "Thelwell."

"Hey, wait, I've been meaning to talk to you."

Dallas slowed her stride as the girl whirled and started walking along, adjusting the strap of her bag. "I just wanted to make sure Hannah and Barbara were leaving your team alone. I had a very poignant discussion with them and Miss Parker about respecting other riders and disciplines."

Dallas grunted, twitching her fingers in her pockets. "They've been fine. Haven't heard anything, uh, anything other—otherwise." She mentally cursed herself for tripping on her words. Damn Amelie and her tequila shots.

"Good. Are you headed to your dormitory?"

"Yes."

Alice didn't say anything more, but she didn't bother to turn around and go off in the direction she had been headed, either. Dallas glanced over briefly. The other girl's bright blue eyes were fixed straight ahead, teeth rolling over her bottom lip as though lost in thought.

"Did you have something else?" Dallas asked, correcting a wayward sway of her legs and looking back at the ground to focus on walking in a straight line.

Alice seemed to hesitate. "I just figured I would walk you to your building. It's not very safe to walk alone at night."

"*You* were walking alone at night," Dallas countered. She lifted one hand to swipe at her nose before shoving it back into the warmth of her jacket pocket. "But you're right, the crime rate here is pretty high, I should have considered that."

She felt Alice falter her step at her side and glanced up to see a deep frown settling across the taller girl's features. "There's no need to be cheeky," she said, tightening her grip on the leather strap across her chest. "I'm not sure what you think I've done to you, and if I have done something to offend you, I certainly apologize, but I assure you nothing of the sort was my intention."

Dallas took a deep breath, pressing her lips together as she looked between Alice and the distance she had left to her dormitory—still half the campus—before responding. "Sorry," she mumbled. Alice was right, she *hadn't* done anything wrong. She'd even adjusted Chariot's lumbar of her own free will instead of telling her to just call a chiropractor and spend the money on a farm call and a five minute procedure. *And* she'd stopped Hannah and Barbara from picking on her team.

Alice nodded and continued walking. It had become clear she had no intentions of letting Dallas walk home alone, and so she simply resigned herself to the company and carried on.

"Why are you out here?" Dallas asked finally.

Alice had pulled out her phone and was scrolling through something with her thumb, the light from the screen glaring into the darkness. She frowned and shoved the phone back into the pocket of her vest. "Library," she replied, her tone neutral despite the clear unease of her expression. "There were a few published dissertations I needed for a bit of additional research."

Dallas hummed. She hadn't been in the library herself, yet, but she knew which building it was because it was tall and pretty with wide columns that ran across the top of a shallow and very uneven looking staircase. "Cool," she said.

"And you?"

"Went out," Dallas replied. She pulled the hand holding the line-up out of her pocket and held the folded paper up for Alice to see before shoving it back in. "Got a friendly with Appleton this weekend. Had to plan out the line-ups."

Alice shifted her bag—it looked pretty heavy—and continued looking straight ahead after regarding Dallas's motion with a nod. "What's the line-up for?" she asked after a moment.

Dallas squinted her eyes into the darkness, feeling the cobblestone rolling beneath her boots. She could see the Chariot fountain and the ring of blue lights that lit the water in an ethereal glow. "Four riders per—per race," she replied, tongue darting out of her mouth to wet her lips. "Got to decide who, uh, who goes where. Tactics."

"I see."

Though her voice did not sound like she understood at all, so Dallas felt the urge to elaborate.

"So you have different races, right?" She felt herself growing more confident and hoped she wasn't sounding too drunk—she loved talking about Games and Alice had opened the floodgates. "We have six players, so we—so we need to plan who rides in what race based on their skill—their skill set. Say if Brooke isn't good at a race, we can have her sit out so that someone else who is better can race. It's like, um..." Dallas rolled her hand over the paper in thought. "It's like if Hannah sucked at jumping, she would stick to the flat classes, and since you're good at jumping you would be in the—the jumping classes."

"That makes sense. Hannah is very accomplished over fences, though," Alice said. She was staring thoughtfully at the fountain as they grew near. "So there are multiple races?"

Dallas nodded. "Yep. Two days, ten races a day. They give us a list of possi—possible races the week before, so we have time to plan it out."

Alice hesitated at the Chariot statue, as though she was going to stop there, but instead followed Dallas straight to the door to her dorm building. "And where is this... competition being held?"

"Here for this one," Dallas said. "This weekend. It's just a friendly. Appleton is shipping in. We'll go to their school, uh, next time." She pulled her leather bi-fold out of her jacket pocket and dug through to find her keycard before glancing back at Alice. She was just standing there with her hands shoved into her vest. "Uh, thanks for walking with me. Glad I didn't get mugged," she said with a chuckle, reaching up to scratch the back of her neck with the same hand that held the key card. "Only now you have to walk all the way across campus."

"That's fine, I can handle myself," Alice said with an amused smile. She started to turn, but stopped. "One more thing?"

Dallas glanced up, pausing her card before swiping it. "Yeah?"

Alice started to walk backwards, her smile dissipating as she moved. "It's Alice," she said quietly, before turning on a heel and tossing a hand in the air. "*Not* Thelwell."

Dallas grunted an acknowledgment as the girl strode away and swiped her card, stumbling a little bit into the weight of the door as she pushed herself inside. Her fingers ran over the paper in her hand as she stalked thoughtfully up the stairs.

Maybe Thelwell—er, Alice—wasn't so bad. She had let Dallas talk about Games—a conversation Dallas would have loved to keep going with, because she loved describing her sport to people—without judgment or mocking. That had been nice.

Except she didn't dwell on it too long, because her head was swimming a little bit and she fell up the stairs a moment later. Damn Amelie and her tequila shots.

Chapter Six

A *LICE*

"I don't understand why she continues to message me," Alice blurted as soon as she stepped through the front door, tossing her mobile unceremoniously onto the marble counter in the kitchen as she slumped against it, dropping her satchel to the floor and kicking her paddock boots off. "I have zero interest in talking to her and I feel as though I have made that quite obvious."

Hannah looked up from where she'd been playing with her mobile on the couch. Barbara was laying on the ground, doing some sort of stretch that had both of her legs flat against the wall.

"Chloe?" Barbara asked, turning her head to eye her red-faced roommate.

"Yes, *Chloe,*" Alice hissed. She planted her elbows on the counter and buried her face in her hands. While she had been escorting Dallas to her dormitory, she had received yet *another* message from her nuisance of an ex:

Wednesday, September 26, 2018

Chloe 21:05

Hey, Alice. I know you don't want to talk to me, and I know that you probably hate me, but I could

really use someone to talk to right now and I
would love to hear your voice. Can I call you?
And then a call that she'd silenced in her pocket:
Missed call from Chloe Simoneau
21:08

Hannah grunted, tossing her own mobile onto the couch cushion and sitting upright. She'd changed into a t-shirt with her old stable's emblem on the back and a pair of sweatpants. Alice couldn't wait to do the same. "What's she want this time?"

Alice sighed, plucking her mobile up and walking into the living room to toss it to the waiting redhead. She watched as Hannah turned on the screen and went to Alice's messages—she didn't keep it password locked, mostly because couldn't be bothered with the extra second of time—and read the last few that Chloe had sent.

Wednesday, September 19, 2019
Chloe 19:14
I'm sorry about everything I've done.
Alice 19:21
Not interested. Goodbye, Chloe.
Chloe 19:21
Alice, please...
Chloe 19:22
Can't you just give me the chance?
Chloe 19:24
You're being ridiculous, Alice. I don't
understand why you won't just give me an
opportunity to talk it out with you.
Alice 21:59

Please go away.

And then the most recent. At least she had been with Dallas, who had quickly distracted her with the stumbling speech of an inebriated, yet excited, explanation of Mounted Games. It wasn't until she had left the other girl at her dormitory that she had a chance to reflect on the text message she'd received and the persistent person who wouldn't leave her alone.

"Wow," Hannah mumbled, tossing the mobile to Barbara so she could see, too. The black-haired girl caught it behind her head and held it up over her face to read it.

"Why is she even trying?" Barbara said, rolling over and clambering to her feet to hand the mobile back to Alice. "It's so obvious that you're not interested. Like, at all."

"You should just delete her number," Hannah said, letting herself drop back down into the soft couch. She pulled her legs up a little bit to make room for Alice, who sat delicately on the edge of the cushion. "And you should probably just stop responding. Silence speaks louder than words, you know."

"I suppose," Alice replied. She stared down at the text conversation, at the notification of a missed call, and let her eyes glaze over.

"You don't, uh..." Barbara trailed off in hesitation. "You don't still have feelings for her, do you?"

"*Absolutely not,*" Alice snapped, quickly turning her screen off and leveling an icy glare at her roommate. "How could I possibly have feelings for someone who acted so despicably? If anything, I regret the time I wasted on her when I could have been doing *other* things. Besides, it's been eight months. Any residual feelings I may have had when our break-up was fresh have long since disappeared."

"Eesh, alright," Barbara said, raising her hands in defense. "I wasn't trying to tease the lion. You want me to just block her for you?"

Alice hesitated, glancing down at her mobile before raising an arm and handing it back out to Barbara. She couldn't bring herself to block the girl's number on her own. There were just too many hesitations, like what if something terrible happened and Alice was the only one available? They were ridiculous thoughts. Chloe could find somebody else to crutch on. "Go ahead," she said with a resolute stare.

Barbara took the offered device, tapped the screen for a couple minutes, and then returned it. "Done," she said. "Deleted the conversation, too. Now you don't have to look at it."

Alice clicked open the screen to look. The last message was from Hannah: *When are u heading back from the library?* No more Chloe. She felt herself smiling. "Thank you."

"No problem." Barbara grinned back. "You did the same for me when I broke up with James. Now, if you're completely over her, you can shove her off your mind without being bothered."

"You should honestly just try dating someone new," Hannah suggested. She twirled the end of her long auburn hair around a finger. "It's been a while. You're too pretty to be single."

Alice shrugged. She wasn't opposed to the idea of dating. She'd tried to dip her toes into the water with an app on her mobile recently, but the few girls she'd talked to before deleting it kind of grossed her out. Besides, she'd much rather meet somebody organically. Somebody who didn't live across the country, somebody who was ambitious (Chloe went to Oxford, sure, but that was only because her father was in the French parliament and had connections), preferably somebody who even liked horses, somebody with the body of a Greek goddess. "Maybe," she finally said, finally realizing how exhausted she was. She rose with a stretch. "Goodnight, girls."

With a passive wave, she grabbed her satchel off the floor and went to her own room, where she shut the door behind her and threw herself onto her bed with a huff as she flicked her mobile back on and scrolled once again through the messages.

No Chloe.

Just Hannah, Barbara, Miss Parker, Aunt Marie—who hadn't bothered to message her in over a month—and that was it. She would be lying if she tried to say that she wasn't lonely, that the sudden loss of Chloe and having somebody to talk to hadn't been a difficult adjustment. But she wasn't so lonely that she would seek solace in somebody who had so callously broken her heart, or somebody that she had no emotional attraction to for the sake of filling whatever void was inside her.

Being lonely wasn't ideal, but it was nothing that she didn't have experience coping with. She had been lonely long before Chloe, so finding her way back into the cold arms of solitude had seemed like an almost appropriate fate for a Thelwell.

"One, two, one, two, one, two, jump!" Miss Parker called from the center of the arena.

Beatrix snorted in rhythmic waves as she rocked back onto her hindquarters and sailed effortlessly over the three-tier oxer, dark legs tucked majestically beneath her before snapping out to the front to land into a graceful canter. Alice rolled with her, her hands sliding with the arch of the mare's neck into a perfect crest release, her legs locked around the girth of her wide barrel. She let herself sink slowly back into the seat a stride after her horse landed, her eyes already locked on the outside line that she was headed to.

"Ease her back," Miss Parker was saying. "Eyes up, very good, leg, leg, leg—"

Beatrix took the first vertical easily and landed. Three strides—second jump.

"Leg here, don't let her drop onto her forehand!"

Alice sat back and drove with her seat, feeling the mare's muscles twitching and responding beneath her as she gathered strength for the final obstacle—a 120 centimeter vertical—and launched into the air.

Alice knew her mistake as soon as she made it. She had lingered a little too long before moving into her jumping position, interfered with her horse's natural movement, and forced Beatrix to drop a hoof. One of the rails rocked dangerously in its cups before clattering to the ground just as the mare's front hooves thumped into the soft sand.

With a heavy sigh, Alice drifted back into the saddle, one gloved hand falling to Beatrix's neck in an appreciative pat as she looked behind her at the rail she'd dropped. A dropped rail in a class over fences would be an instant fatality to her marks and would render her completely out of top honors in an instant. "Good girl, Bea," she said, frowning at her own mistake.

"You let yourself get behind," Miss Parker called out as Alice brought the mare back down to a walk and led her back to the center of the arena where her coach and two teammates stood waiting. The young, lilac-haired woman had folded her arms across her chest, peering at Alice through large sunglasses that hid most of her expression. She didn't look upset—Miss Parker remained objective at all times—but Alice could still sense an air of disappointment. "Your seat restricted her movement." She paused before adding, "Again."

They were nearing the end of their schooling session. Beatrix was getting tired, and Alice found herself growing irritated. She could see the Games team off in the main arena, the one Hoofbeats used to host shows, joined by the guys from Appleton, and she was desperately curious to watch a little bit. As it stood, though, she was going to miss most of it before she even dismounted. Turning away from the others, she urged Beatrix back into a trot, did a slow loop around the end of the arena to pick up a canter, and came off the rail to head for the first oxer.

It was a warm day for late September, at least 18 degrees, and both Alice and Beatrix were sweating. Alice had long since stripped out of her vest and pushed up the sleeves of her long-sleeve shirt, but she could still feel hot beads of sweat trickling down her back. Beatrix's neck was dark and wet, streaked with white froth in parallel lines from where the leather of the reins slid back and forth. Neither, though, would subject themselves to the ill effects of being tired. As a pair, they put in the same amount of effort as the beginning of the ride.

Beatrix soared over the first oxer easily, landing on her left lead, just as the pressure of Alice's leg muscles had indicated her to do over the jump. Her hands steadied on the reins, flicking with minor corrections that made the large mare's ears twitch back and forth as they approached the line. She could feel a shoulder bearing out ever so slightly and straightened her seat, added pressure from her inside leg, and—

"Beautiful," Miss Parker called out. "Stay with her—"

Three strides, an effortless leap.

"Now sit back here and ride to the fence—"

Alice was with Beatrix this time, perfectly in tune with the flex of bones and the sway of muscles, hands easing forward without a change in contact as her horse perfectly tucked her legs and cleared the jump with a delicate flick of her hind hooves.

"*Very* nice! Give her a pat, you can be done."

She felt herself smiling. Beatrix's nostrils were puffing and she snorted hard, giving her head a little shake to toss the throat latch around once Alice had brought her back to a walk.

"Remember, first show of the season next weekend. I'll have your classes picked out for you by the end of next week. And don't complain about not knowing what you're signed up for this time. You know very well by now that you should be prepared for whatever I throw at you." With that, she plucked out her mobile and started looking through the many calls she'd received during the lesson—an indication that any retorts would not be heard.

Alice glanced over at where the Games Teams were riding. They were still going at it. Ponies were dashing everywhere, riders were jumping off and back on, loud cheers were erupting every few moments from both teams and the few people who had turned out in the stands to watch. She stared as she cooled Beatrix, transfixed. They were doing some kind of race where they were rearranging cups on a line of poles.

Hannah and Barbara rode up next to her. Cello's head was dipped in exhaustion, but Belle was as perky as ever as she turned her head, tossing her neck over the older chestnut gelding to watch the events taking place with a curious glint in her large brown eyes.

"Bet Andrew's here," Hannah said, tossing a wink at Barbara and raising a gloved hand to point at the Games. "You know he rides for that nonsense now, too."

"Yeah, but he still does the jumpers," Barbara replied, shrugging. "So he's still hot in my book."

"So the degree of attractiveness is now equated with the discipline of the rider?" Alice asked with the quirk of a brow, glancing over at her two friends from below the bill of her riding cap. "I was unaware the two were related."

"That's not what I *meant*, Alice," Barbara groaned, rolling her eyes and scratching the side of Belle's muscular neck. "But it's like... so you prefer guys who play football over rugby because it's a sexier sport, you know?" She shrugged. "I mean, well, not for you with the whole guy thing, but—"

"No need to continue," Alice sighed, watching as Dallas went from a stand-still to a full out gallop. She whipped her pony around the poles, grabbing cups and deftly rearranging them without a break in her stride before bolting back to the end of the arena where the rest of the ponies stood. Her team rose into cheers and she stood in the irons, grinning so wide that Alice could see it from where she sat. "I was just making a joke, anyway. I am thoroughly capable of that, you know."

She guided Beatrix to the center of the arena and dropped her stirrups to dismount in one swift movement. Her feet always felt weird and a little shaky when she hit the ground, especially after a pretty hard work out, and so she leaned up against the mare's bulging shoulder muscle as she readjusted. After loosening the girth and running her stirrups up, she began walking without waiting for her peers, anxious to get to the cheering and laughing that was happening nearby.

"Where are you going?" Hannah asked, jogging a little as she tried to pull Cello—though he wanted nothing to do with it—up to Alice's side. Barbara followed.

Alice nodded in the direction of the competition. "I'm curious," she said, guiding her mare over to the wooden bleachers that lined the lane side of the massive arena.

"You're not going to untack first?" Barbara murmured, holding Belle back and glancing between her own sweaty horse and Alice's.

Alice shrugged, climbing up into a spot at the edge of the stands and clutching the reins between loose, gloved fingers.

At the proximity to her owner's lap, Beatrix stepped closer and nibbled affectionately at her half chaps. Alice reached down and offered the mare a few scratches at the start of her thin white stripe. "She'll be fine for a couple minutes," she said, letting her eyes fall on the arena.

Everything looked different up close. It wasn't as messy a scene as it seemed from the Hunt Team arena, but instead carefully orchestrated with every piece of equipment lined up to perfection. White lines had been drawn into the sand with lime, dividing the lanes between Hoofbeats and Appleton. Miss Nelson and an instructor from Appleton were busy setting up for the next race while the riders mingled at the end of the arena. It was a small event, easy going, showing no signs of stress that Alice was used to during her own schooling shows. In fact, everyone seemed to be having a good time.

Alice watched as Amelie pulled a white band off her helmet and tossed it to Dallas, who slid it on with a smirk and a nod. Across the arena, Nelson and the Appleton coach were throwing some items into the sand. In the middle of each lane was a barrel, a grooming box set carefully on each.

Beside her, Beatrix wiped a little bit of slobber on her breeches.

"He's *so* cute," Barbara was saying. Apparently her friends had decided to stick around and were checking out Andrew Hanbridge, whose feet were kicked out of the stirrups as he leaned back, an arrogant smile spread across his lips as he crossed his arms and watched everything being set up with an unphased look on his face. He, too, had a white band around his helmet. He looked kind of strange, he was tall for the height of his horse, but Alice really didn't give it too much further thought. He was insufferable enough as it was with the imported Hanoverian that he'd had personally trained by Philip Dutton, she didn't want to even know how bad he flexed his testosterone in *this* sport with whatever fancy place he'd bought *this* pony from.

"First rider up!" came a booming voice from across the arena.

Amelie stepped up to the starting box with Star next to an Appleton rider on a taller gelding. The two exchanged a small glance before Amelie rocked back in the saddle, arms moving out to the side as she struggled to keep Star standing straight. He was jumping up and down with his front legs, twirling his hindquarters and chomping at the bit with the anticipation of running.

A flag dropped.

The ponies bolted.

The Appleton rider's horse was larger, but Star was faster. Alice watched as Amelie leapt from her pony's back at the end of the arena, grabbed something from the ground, and started running alongside her pony. She jumped once, twice, missed her mark, corrected and jumped again to awkwardly land on the pony's back at an angle. Even from the modest wooden stands, Alice could see the look of displeasure the American had as she grit her teeth in anger. She missed the barrel and had to whirl Star around, still fidgeting with her legs as she dropped something into the grooming box and took back off to the other ponies.

The Appleton rider had made no mistake. With his height, he had all but stepped onto his pony.

Constance was next, but her pony was dramatically smaller than the others and hardly as fast, plus the Appleton riders had a firm lead. Their second rider had already jumped off. Constance, though, was low enough to the ground that she simply dipped to the side and snagged one of the items right out of the sand, only slowing down momentarily.

Third was Brooke. She seemed more interested in one of the Appleton riders—she kept glancing in his direction—rather than the race itself, and so she was delayed in her start and gave the other team back the length of their lead that the small German had made up. She hopped off her stocky Haflinger and faltered for a moment before jumping back on and heading home.

Andrew and his horse, who looked like a rather regally bred black Arabian—Alice wouldn't have been surprised if she'd gotten him from Godolphin-had already bolted from the starting box to head to the other end of the arena while Dallas's pony still stood behind the line, dancing with excited anticipation as her rider sat calmly, poised and ready.

Brooke flew across the line and Chariot leapt into the air in a remarkable burst of speed. Andrew was already off his pony, but Dallas wasn't too far behind. The small girl had one hand in her mare's chestnut mane, pumping as she yelled something unintelligible.

She was going too fast—she hadn't even bothered to ease Chariot up—and the fence was coming quick. Alice felt herself wincing away, expecting an accident,

but Dallas went hurtling from the back of her pony without breaking stride, sand spraying into a thick cloud as she dipped down almost imperceptibly. Chariot had already turned and Dallas was running with her. The girl grabbed the leather strap she'd tied around the mare's neck, planted her feet, and leapt, muscular legs swinging gracefully into the air as she landed right in the middle of the saddle and kept going without missing a single beat. She sped by the barrel, her arm swinging in a wide arc as she slammed the item home and sped across the line, her legs out of the stirrups and flailing.

Andrew had crossed a couple strides ahead. It was too late, Appleton had won, but Dallas looked thrilled with herself anyway and was smacking Chariot's neck with excitement.

"That's it," the Appleton coach called to the panting riders and jigging ponies that stood in a mass of chatter and laughter behind the start line. "Appleton 16, Hoofbeats 14 at the end of the first day."

Alice glanced back at the Hoofbeats team. Nobody seemed upset. In fact, they seemed rather cheerful as they walked their ponies by the Appleton boys and shook their hands, still mounted. Andrew was sitting on his pony with a haughty smirk as he shook their hands and regarded each one with a look of superiority.

God, she hated Andrew.

Her eyes fell on Dallas. She was leaning back on her pony, legs kicked up with her ankles resting on Chariot's withers as though she was a sofa. The reins lay untouched around the mare's neck as she stood quietly, making no move while her rider squirmed, laughed, and joked with Amelie and Janine.

The brunette turned her head, her gaze settling on where Alice was sitting.

Dallas lifted her hand in a friendly wave and a wide smile and Alice started to raise her hand to return the greeting when somebody to her rear yelled, "Hey!" and she turned to see Avery from the Dressage Team sitting behind her. Alice quickly lowered her hand back to her lap, feeling a hot blush rise to her cheeks as she quickly slid off the bench, gathering the braided reins of her bridle, and led Beatrix back to the barn.

Of course Dallas hadn't been waving to her. Why would she? They weren't friends—far from it, in fact. Alice grimaced, choking on her own embarrassment and knowing that poor Beatrix was going to have to suffer with her very red face buried in her neck for the next half hour.

"*Alice!*"

Not a moment's peace.

Alice let out a heavy sigh, her notes for Hippotherapy sliding out of her hands. "Yes, Hannah?"

Her door was shut, but once again, just as Alice predicted, it didn't matter. Hannah burst inside, flashing a bright grin. She was wearing what she usually wore when she went out and wanted to impress people—tight jeans, a pair of heels that made her dwarf Alice, a white crop top that showed off just how much the girl needed to eat, and one of her many blazers. Tonight it was the beige one.

"Get in, bitches! We're going shopping!"

Barbara skidded into Hannah, wearing an equally devious grin and a light green floral dress that Alice knew wouldn't be appropriate for how cold it was starting to get at night. The auburn-haired girl laughed when she hit the door frame, turning to gently shove the other girl away.

Alice pursed her lips, pinching the bridge of her nose between her fingers as she shook her head. "Absolutely not. I have a lot of studying to do."

"It's *Saturday night*!" Barbara moaned, throwing herself onto Alice's bed and immediately wrinkling the comforter. "Everyone's going to Red Stallion! I got a message from Frank inviting us."

"Define everyone," Alice deadpanned. She let her chin fall back, staring at her bright overhead lamp. She already knew the answer, but she wanted Barbara to say it so she could argue her point.

She wasn't even looking at the girl and she could *hear* the grin. "You know. Frank, Andrewww-"

And there it was.

"I have zero interest in mingling with that knob," Alice muttered, waving her hand dismissively and turning her desk chair back to the notes and books that were spread across her desk. "I'll sit this one out."

"Oh, come on, Alice. Please?" Hannah was begging from the door. "That stupid Games Team will be there and I want you to go so you can see how they treat us. Better yet, maybe if they see you they won't bother talking to us!"

Alice felt her jaw clenching as she stared down hard at her notes. On the one hand, she really did need to study—she didn't want to get any further behind than a month ahead in any of her courses just in case something happened. But at the same time, if the Games Team was going-

"Fine," she mumbled, shoving herself up and ignoring the squeals of excitement from her two roommates. "But keep Andrew out of my sight."

"Oh, look who it is!"

Literally the first person she saw when she walked into the pub was the *exact person she had told Hannah and Barbara to keep out of her sight.*

"If it's not Miss Alice Thelwell herself," Andrew mused, pushing himself away from the bar and stalking over like a dysfunctional lion that had been kicked too many times in the head by a wildebeest. And that was being generous. "I can't believe you're gracing us with your presence. How's Hoofbeats's star rider doing these days? Long time, no see."

"Yes. And it can continue to be a long time. Excuse me," Alice grumbled, ignoring whatever Andrew was retorting with and grabbing the sleeve of Hannah's jacket. She tugged her to the opposite side of the bar where Amelie was standing. She didn't particularly care for Amelie, but she would take the foul-mouthed American over Andrew and his arrogance any day.

"Damn, Thelwell, how'd they manage to get you out?" Amelie said with a sneer.

Alice hadn't exactly dressed up for the occasion. A pair of light jeans that happened to be clean and also happened to fit her particularly well, her favorite navy flats, and a low cut navy v-neck jumper to match. Her hair was pulled back into a ponytail, mostly because she couldn't get it to look the way she wanted down and she'd had enough of it. She didn't want to look like she was *trying*, because, well, it appeared that it didn't matter.

But, either way.

"Gordon's and tonic," Alice said to the bartender with a gentle wave of her hand. Hannah—who seemed extremely distraught at even being near Amelie—had quickly gotten whatever fruity drink was the flavor of the month for her and disappeared to go mingle with Barbara and the Appleton boys. So, once she had her drink in her hand and Andrew was well out of the vicinity (he knew better than to try again), she turned and leaned against the old wooden bar to finally take a look around.

She'd been to the Red Stallion before. It was one of the oldest pubs downtown, one that attracted a lot of tourists to the area because of its age and prosperity, not to mention an egregiously impossible haunting that had been covered by some American ghost hunting team, and the hand-painted portraits of famous racehorses on the walls along with shoes they'd worn in their races. There was Eclipse, of course—minus a shoe, because he was too far back-, Sceptre, Nashwan, Shergar, a few others. Since Alice had been there last, they'd added a very detailed painting of Frankel along with a bib signed by his trainer and jockey. She admired it briefly before turning her attention back to everybody else.

Amelie was facing away from her and chatting with her roommates. Barbara was fawning all over Andrew, who was feigning disinterest in the attention even though Alice knew he was eating it up. Hannah was chatting with Frank and Brooke, who appeared to be a couple based on how he had his arm around the small girl and she was smiling at him as though he hung the moon in the sky. The four other Appleton guys were engaged in a very serious game of pool.

And, at the other side of the bar, clutching a bottle of Harp and in the middle of what looked like a very animated story, was Dallas. Her hair was down and straight, long over her shoulders and the back of the same jacket that Alice had seen her wearing the night she'd walked her to her dormitory. She was half hanging off the barstool as she made wild gestures with her arms at a very disinterested looking Callie.

Dallas caught her eye and, for a second, the glance lingered, though in a moment her expression changed to one of distaste as she turned away and continued her conversation.

Alice frowned. She had been planning to walk over, maybe say hi—but that expression looked anything but friendly. With a long sigh, she brought her drink back to her lips and turned to Amelie, who was trying to catch the bartender's attention.

"The Games looked interesting," she said.

Amelie swiveled an emerald gaze, running a hand through wild red hair as she studied Alice's neutral expression. "Is that sarcasm, Thelwell?"

"No, I-"

"Three shots of Jimmy," Amelie called out when the bartender finally looked her way. Then, she turned her attention back to Alice. "Want one?"

"Absolutely not," Alice huffed, tilting her glass back and rolling her eyes.

"Thought not."

Why had she let Hannah and Barbara sucker her out again? With the meager chance of being able to talk to a girl she thought was cute that wouldn't even acknowledge her existence? She pulled out her mobile and threw it down on the bar as Amelie walked away without so much as another word, idly scrolling through the new articles of Horse & Hound that she'd already read. Though, as much as she tried to look like she was enjoying her solitude, she couldn't help the tug of her eyes as she looked up to find Dallas again.

The girl was talking to the much taller Janine and Amelie. From where she stood, Alice could see the red shorts, the canvas of leg, the bruises that speckled the outsides of her thighs. Likely from all the acrobatics she was doing on a daily basis. Dallas wasn't looking, so she let her eyes mindlessly wander-

Her mobile vibrated.

Amelie 20:32

Whatcha lookin' at, Gaywell?

Alice's eyes shot up from the screen to find Amelie grinning at her, mobile in hand, from where she stood next to Janine. She could feel the flush working its way into her cheeks and desperately hoped the pub was dark enough to hide it. The last thing she wanted to do was give Amelie the satisfaction. And she was *definitely* not going to text her back.

Another vibration, her mobile twitching on the bar. Amelie had turned away and was looking down.

Amelie 20:34

Like something you see?

Alice let her forehead sink into her palm as she squeezed her eyes shut. Amelie was absolutely insufferable. She polished off the rest of her drink and ordered another one—she was going to need it—as she went back to reading the newest article on horse health.

She had just picked up her new drink when a buzz filled her hand.

Amelie 20:38

Waited too long.

Alice turned off the screen and glanced up. Dallas was sitting back in the same bar stool, but Andrew had sidled up next to her, clutching a glass of whiskey and carrying on a conversation as though he'd known her all her life. That was the way he weaseled his way into girls' pants: working the slimy charisma he'd picked up on from having a politician as a father.

Just like Chloe, she thought.

With a heavy roll of her eyes, she puffed out a long breath of air and looked away, down into the clear liquid in her glass and the lime that had submerged, untouched, beneath the ice. If Andrew was Dallas's type, that was perfectly fine. In fact it was *better*, because that would very quickly end whatever sliver of attraction she had for a girl that was simply out of her league. But when she finally pulled her gaze back up to see how the two were getting on, she was surprised to find that neither of them were there any longer.

And the voice behind her startled her so much she jerked her hand and sloshed her drink.

"Quick question, what's your deal?"

Chapter Seven

D*ALLAS*
     Dallas had never even kissed anybody.

That's not to say that she didn't know who she *wanted* to kiss. She knew what she liked when she was five, if that could be believed. There was a girl who lived on the same floor in her apartment building and she remembered doing cartwheels and other acrobatic feats in an attempt to get her attention. It never worked, in fact they had never even become friends nor had Dallas ever learned her name, but it was her first indicator that she was different from the other girls. She wanted to impress them, to enthrall them with her charisma and prowess, to have them look at her in the same way they looked at boys.

Being gay in Japan was drastically different than the western countries—she'd already seen that from the first few weeks she'd been in England—and Dallas was slowly adjusting to the ability to be open with who she was without feeling guilty about it. Not that she was ashamed. She wasn't, she liked who she was and wouldn't change anything about it. It was just different.

She had grown used to hiding her feelings behind jokes and a smile, admiring the girls she liked from afar. Instead, she relied on the yuri manga she hid behind her schoolbooks and pirated poor-quality movies and shows on her laptop to satisfy her growing feelings. And that's not to say she never tried to be outright. When she was 16, she confessed to a close friend in the same way she'd read in her favorite manga, only to be shut down hard. The girl hadn't shamed her, but she made a point to reinforce that she was very, very straight and Dallas was left in a thick cloud of embarrassment at her single attempt at romance.

And so she'd settled into the background and watched as the girls she crushed on fawned over boys from the academy down the street. If there was anyone like her, they were either in the exact same place or someone her eyes fell on with disinterest.

There was the one time Okaasan found her yuri when she was cleaning one day. Dallas was 17 and free-spirited at that point, carried by notions and ideas of western influence, though she channeled all her energy into the Games team and reaching International success. She'd come home from school to find Okaasan crying over tea and they'd had an emotional conversation that fell mainly on the idea of a lack of grandchildren. Dallas was an only child and Okaasan and Otousan had made it quite clear they couldn't wait for her to marry and have a family of her own. It was quite simply cultural normality, the natural flow of life and society. For Dallas, it was the first time she felt like she truly failed her parents and the role she was expected to fulfill, but she was resolved in who she was and continued on as she always had: in the spotlight with her personality and in the shadows with her craving for emotional intimacy.

Her sexuality was not mentioned between them again, though they never inquired about boyfriends, either.

And so England had almost come as a surprise. She'd known the western countries, for the most part, were more accepting of different lifestyles and subcultures. Though Amelie's up-front sexuality had seemed almost over the top at first, Dallas had quickly adjusted—she prided herself on going with the flow—and while she wasn't keen on being as in-your-face as Amelie (and probably never would), she had fallen into a level of comfort that she never felt in Japan.

Even still, her focus remained primarily on Chariot, the Games team, and her position as a student at Hoofbeats. But Dallas had to admit one thing: she thought the girls here were way prettier and she didn't have to feel bad for looking at them.

The Appleton team wasn't as bad as Dallas thought they'd be. Though after the first day they were behind—Appleton had won six, Hoofbeats had won four—the guys never rubbed it in their faces or acted like they were better. Well, except for Andrew. Callie had warned her about him ahead of time and, though Dallas tried to stay open-minded, she quickly found that all she'd said was true. He was arrogant and outspoken, blatant in his perceived superiority when his Arabian ("I had him imported from Dubai," he'd pointed out, even though nobody asked) outran or out-turned the other ponies. Dallas felt a stab of satisfaction every time he made a mistake or was beaten in a head-to-head race.

Quite honestly, he was an asshole.

So when she was leaning against the bar at the Red Stallion to get a fresh beer—only her second, she'd nursed the first one—she had to suppress a groan when he strode over with a cocky smile and a determined look in his eyes.

"Hey," he said, flashing a grin. "It's Dallas, right?"

Dallas frowned, plopping down in the barstool and shoving her empty bottle across the bar to signal she wanted another. "Dallas," she corrected.

He sidled into the seat next to her without even asking if it was alright. "I'm Andrew," he said, never taking his eyes off her even though she kept her gaze locked straight ahead. "Andrew Hanbridge. I don't think I introduced myself to you yet."

His name rolled off his tongue like he thought it was liquid gold, like it held some sort of weight in their community and he was blessing Dallas just by talking to her.

"Uh-huh," she muttered. She wanted nothing to do with him, couldn't he tell? "Another," she said to the bartender when he came over, nodding to her empty bottle of Harp.

"I was going to offer to buy your next drink," Andrew pointed out, bringing his glass of whiskey—straight, on ice, *what a badass,* he and Amelie could be wingmen—and raising an eyebrow.

Dallas shrugged, grabbing the cold beer as it was slid across the lacquered bar. "No, thanks," she said, waving her hand dismissively as she pushed away from the bar to go find one of her friends to talk to instead of the pompous jerk who clearly had intentions.

"Wow," he grumbled, shooting a glare after her. "You're about as polite as Alice."

Alice. Right.

Dallas still didn't know what her issue was. She had walked her back to her dormitory the one night, which was a very nice if not very awkward and unexpected gesture, but then completely ignored her wave earlier in the day. Dallas had been surprised and pleased to see her there watching—the whole Hunt Team, in fact—because she hadn't pegged any of the three as interested in even spectating the Games. But Alice had completely blown her off with a strange stare and immediately walked away.

Hot, cold, hot, cold.

But then she'd walked into the Red Stallion (Dallas had *not* been expecting to see her there) looking like a model straight out of a J. Crew ad and Dallas'd had to wipe her jaw off the floor. She had been trying to fight off a crush since the first time she'd seen the girl her very first week (and had dubbed her Barn Hottie before she knew her name), but every time the girl showed up, it was like she looked ten times better than the last time Dallas had seen her. The *last* thing Dallas needed was another stupid crush on a straight girl.

Though, she couldn't shake the strange air between them. She couldn't decide if Alice hated her or wanted to be on good terms. Earlier, Dallas had looked up from a conversation with Callie to find the girl staring at her, or maybe *through* her, though she didn't even acknowledge her presence and so Dallas had turned away from her in confusion and said to Callie, "I don't get it, what's Alice's problem?"

Callie had just shrugged and said, "Don't know, don't care."

But *Dallas* cared. She wanted to get along with everyone.

So she shrugged off Andrew and strode on over to the end of the bar, where Alice was staring into an untouched drink and looking entirely out of place among the groups of friends that were chatting animatedly and enjoying their time together.

"Quick question," she said, folding her arms across her chest and tapping the bottom of her beer bottle against her waist. "What's your deal?"

Alice jumped—like she hadn't expected someone to be near her, even though she was in a bar full of people—and spilled her drink a little bit. Dallas felt sort of bad, maybe she should have at least said *Hey* or something first, but the question had just slipped out of her mouth.

Alice swiped the back of her hand on her jeans and leveled Dallas with startled blue eyes. "Pardon?"

"You're nice to me one minute, the next minute you act like I don't even exist and give me the cold shoulder. What's up with that?" Arms still crossed, Dallas brought the lip of her bottle to her mouth and took a sip.

"I don't understand what you mean," Alice said. "I wasn't aware that I ever did anything of the sort."

The patron next to Alice slid his empty pint across the bar and stood to leave. Dallas regarded the freshly empty seat with a look of temptation, but made no move to take it. "I waved at you earlier today because I thought it was cool you were there and you totally blew me off."

Alice blinked. Her fingers were tracing the rim of her glass. "I thought you were waving at Avery."

"Who's Avery?"

"Oh."

Alice turned away and finally sipped her drink. This interaction had quickly become way more awkward than Dallas had intended. She brought her beer back to her lips and let her arms fall to her sides while she glanced around the pub. All of her friends were off doing something else. Janine and Callie were playing pool with a few Appleton guys, Brooke was hanging out with Frank and Constance, and Amelie was engaged in a heated debate with Andrew that was steadily escalating in volume.

"You can sit, if you want."

Dallas blinked back to Alice to find uncertain blue eyes watching her. She *did* look rather lonely, and Dallas *had* come to clear the air—

"Alright," she replied, offering a small nod and sliding onto the bar stool. She had no idea what to say now that she'd approached the other girl, because she had been expecting some sort of defensive argument or—well, in all honesty, she hadn't thought that far ahead. "Sorry. About the, uh, confusion. Did you have fun watching? I know it's probably not as cool as jumping or anything—"

"No, it was really great," Alice said quickly. Her eyes flicked over Dallas's face before falling back ahead. "I was only able to see a small amount, but maybe tomorrow I can watch more. You said there were two days, right?"

Dallas nodded. "Yeah."

"Okay."

What a conversationalist. Dallas lifted her beer and chugged.

"Are you ready for the Hippotherapy exam this week?"

And then she spit some of her beer out.

"There's a *test* this week?" Dallas moaned, swiping her mouth with her sleeve and dropping her beer bottle back to the bar. "Are you serious? Since when?"

Alice glanced at her, one eyebrow raised, and frowned. "It's on Tuesday."

Dallas buried her face in her hands. No, she'd had no idea there was a Hippotherapy exam. In fact, she hadn't even looked at the syllabus. *The syllabus that probably held the exact dates of all the exams.* She groaned. "This sucks. Now I'm going to have to spend all night tomorrow studying!"

"I... have a pretty in depth study guide," Alice said after a moment and a long sip of her drink. She seemed to hesitate, spinning her phone on the bar for a moment before adding, "I could uh, text you the link to my Google drive, if you want."

"No, no," Dallas said quickly, shaking her head. "That's okay, I would feel terrible. I'll just study my notes." She didn't know what the hell she was saying, she didn't have any notes, but she definitely knew she didn't want Alice to think she was using her for schoolwork. They were already on some weird kind of thin ice between rivals and acquaintances.

"Oh." Alice turned away and chugged her drink again. She seemed... disappointed? Dallas found herself confused by the reaction—she would have thought the other girl would've wanted her to follow the honor code and do her own work—but she just shrugged and gulped her beer. The first she had drank slowly, because she'd been preoccupied bouncing around and talking to everybody, but the amount of awkward silences between herself and Alice had her drinking way faster than she planned.

"I saw Andrew speaking with you," Alice started, a tentative waver in her voice. "Anything in particular he wanted?"

"Oh, him." Dallas grimaced and polished off her beer. "Seemed like he just wanted to get in my pants. Tried to buy me a drink. I don't know. The guy's a total jerk."

Alice chuckled, ice clinking against the sides of her glass as she twirled it in her hand. "He's a real prat. Rides Jumpers, too. Did he tell you all about his fancy Warmblood?"

"Mmm, no." Dallas felt herself grinning. "Just the Arabian he imported from some Prince in Dubai."

A cackle slipped from Alice's lips and she looked surprised about it, slapping her hand over her mouth. She let herself laugh for a moment before bringing her hand away and saying, "My apologies. I just—I knew it. He tried to brag to me about the fleet of racehorses he's got under Aidan O'Brien. I looked them up. He's got two, they're under his father's name, and neither has broken a maiden."

Dallas laughed, shooting a glance over at Andrew. He was chatting with Barbara again, looking completely bored by whatever she was running off at the mouth. "Hopefully we'll beat them tomorrow. We just made a couple silly mistakes today. Nothing we can't fix." She shrugged, twirling her empty beer bottle in her hand.

"I thought you looked good." Alice glanced at her for a moment before bringing her stare back to her own empty glass. "You were... impressive."

Eesh, the best rider at Hoofbeats was calling *her* impressive. She felt a warm blush creeping into her cheeks and looked at her fidgeting fingers, her pride swelling with the compliment. "Oh. Thanks," she said, finally raising her eyes and offering a small smile.

Alice was regarding the ice in her glass as though it might magically refill itself. Dallas watched her eyes drift to her empty beer bottle and a long pause spread between them before the blonde girl said, "Um—buy you another?"

Dallas took a deep breath, tilting the bottle in her hand and staring at the few drops of liquid left at the bottom. She hadn't been *planning* on having another, two had already been pushing it because she had to ride a whole lot in the morning, but she was sitting at a bar with a super attractive girl and they were actually kind of getting along and having a real conversation—

The patron next to her slammed his pint down with a dramatic flair and an animated gesture, sending a shockwave across the wooden bar.

"You don't have to do that," she said finally.

"No, I insist," Alice replied. Dallas watched her flick her fingers between the drinks as she made eye contact with the bartender, who nodded an acknowledgment. "Think of it as... an apology for unintentionally confusing you." She shrugged, gliding her empty glass across the bar with the arrival of her new drink. "I think I got off on the wrong foot, so let's straighten things out, shall we?"

Alice raised her drink.

With a smile, Dallas grabbed her new beer and let their glasses clink together.

Appleton had won.

It all boiled down to Dallas missing the hand-off in the very first race, the *easiest* race. Pole bending. She should have anticipated that Mushroom would balk a little bit at Chariot's high speed, so when she stretched out her arm with the baton for Callie to grab, she didn't account for the swing of the other horse's hindquarters and the extra distance that grew between them.

She'd had to circle back around to get Callie the baton. They'd lost precious time and, thus, the race.

If the hand-off had been successful, Dallas was positive they would've won. Star was much faster than Andrew's "regally bred" Arabian and there had been no other mistakes. But, as it stood, both of the teams ended up winning five races each. And, since Appleton had won six the day before, they had come out on top with 31 points to Hoofbeats's 29. Had they won pole bending, the two teams would have gone into the tie-breaker, which was set to be the sock race. The team's best race.

The only consolation was that there weren't very many people there the next day. The Hunt Team surely didn't see their folly, because Miss Parker had kept them far longer than their usual schooling lessons. Dallas glanced over occasionally to see the three riders circling in a figure-eight and doing endless gridwork without stirrups. It made her wince—no stirrups had become commonplace for her, but she didn't have to focus on keeping her legs anywhere. They could be parallel with Chariot's spine and it didn't matter as long as she was on top of her horse.

So she was *not* jealous of that.

"Saw you talking with Thelwell last night," Amelie said as they walked the ponies back to the barn. Appleton was already in the process of loading their own ponies into a massive freight van to take them back home. "She wasn't giving you any trouble, was she?"

"No, of course not," Dallas replied. Alice had actually been really pleasant—and Dallas *might* have let her buy her a second beer, which she was still feeling as she brought her water to her lips in a desperate attempt to hydrate. "We were just talking horses." It was warm and the cold bottle was sweating into her hand, so she swiped it across her already dirty breeches. "She seems nice."

Amelie shrugged. "She's never been *not* nice," she replied, guiding Star into one of the wash stalls. Chariot paused a moment to look at him, but turned back to following Dallas, occasionally bumping her thigh with a curious nose in an attempt to find peppermints. "She's just... Alice."

Dallas plucked Chariot's halter off the hook she'd hung it on and held it out. Chariot obediently dipped her head in, letting her owner tug it up and fuss with her ears and forelock for a moment before fastening it. She led the pony into the wash stall next to Amelie and hooked her to the cross-ties—only because Miss Parker would throw a fit if she saw her untied—and started to hose her off.

"Your line up wasn't bad," Amelie called out above the sound of the two hoses spraying off the sweaty ponies.

"Could use a few tweaks, I think, but you wouldn't have known that without seeing how we did today."

Dallas grunted a response, kneeling down to hit Chariot's belly and the insides of her legs. She didn't even hear the clop of horseshoes down the aisle until the three riders were right in front of them.

"Hey, Dallas."

Dallas blinked up from where she was kneeling on a black mat streaked with wet manure and dirt that had been freshly dug from someone else's shod horse (why was it so hard for people to clean up after themselves?) to see Alice standing in front of her. She and Beatrix looked absolutely exhausted. The former's sleeves had been rolled halfway up her biceps and her chest and stomach were patched with sweat. Her helmet was tucked under her arm and wavy strands of loose blonde hair from her French braid were stuck to the sides of her sweaty temples. There was a shadow over her bright blue eyes, but Dallas figured that was probably because of the drinks the night before. Beatrix's head hung low, her nostrils still flaring, sweaty patches of hair stuck to her loosened girth.

The other two members of the Hunt Team kept walking, though Dallas didn't miss the strange look that Hannah shot at Amelie.

"Hey," Dallas replied, switching off the hose with a quick press of her thumb to the nozzle and straightening up. She was suddenly aware of how dirty and sweaty she looked and passed a hand over her loose ponytail.

Chariot turned and glanced back at her, a gentle snort rolling from her nostrils.

"I didn't get a chance to watch," Alice said. She scratched at her nose and left a smear of black across the side from her wet gloves. "How did you do?"

"Lost," Amelie called from the stall next door. "By one damn race."

Alice nodded, looking awkward and out of place as she shifted at her mare's side. Beatrix was gnawing at her bit and giving Chariot a curious look, rear hoof cocking with the sudden gift of relaxation. "Sorry I missed it. But I'm sure you rode great."

She was looking at Dallas when she said it, though Dallas was sure she meant Amelie, too.

"Amelie did." She looked at her wet pony, straightening her hand and swiping down her soaked neck to flick the excess water off. "I missed a hand-off and cost us a race."

"Aw, you don't know that, Dallas!" Amelie yelled. The sound of running water ceased as she turned her own hose off. "Something else would have happened. Murphy's law."

Dallas didn't know what that meant but she said, "Yeah, I guess," and continued to skim the water off her pony's shining copper coat. Chariot stomped a hoof and snorted again, bored but content, her wet tail stinging Dallas's arm as it flicked across her barrel.

"Well, I'll be sure to catch the next one." Alice clucked to Beatrix and the mare perked up. She started to walk off down the aisle but Dallas straightened up and said—

"Next one's in Glasgow."

Alice turned back, one eyebrow raised. "I'll consider trying to make it," she replied, waving a hand dismissively in the air before settling it onto her mare's wet shoulder and walking off.

In an instant, Amelie had slid around the stone wall, green eyes darting between the two riders.

"What?" Dallas asked, squinting at the American.

Amelie grinned, shook her head, and said, "Nothing, Dallas," before disappearing back to her own wash stall.

She failed the Hippotherapy exam.

Okay, she didn't *fail*, but she most certainly got a terrible mark that had resulted in having to see Professor Finnelan after class during her office hours and getting a lecture about how attending Hoofbeats was a privilege and they would not allow mediocrity, even in the case of a full ride. Miss Nelson had been there, too, with the threat of sidelining Dallas if her grades didn't begin to show improvement.

It was in that exact moment that she wished she had accepted Alice's offer to share her study guide. The other girl had gotten a perfect mark. She knew because she had seen it underneath her own paper as Professor Finnelan was handing them out. Her Google drive probably had all kinds of information that would help her with assignments in the class. Dallas would have to ask for those at a later time.

But then she'd have to explain to Alice that she'd done terribly on a test and deal with whatever reaction came along with refusing to accept help in the first place.

She buried her hands deep into the pocket of her jacket as she stalked across the campus. It was dark, and late, but Dallas had found herself unable to sleep and had the unshakable urge to see her pony. Chariot always made her feel better. Her mare was happy to see her no matter what and would always make her laugh with exploring lips and goofy acts—anything to get a peppermint. Plus she was soft and cozy and Dallas could hug her without having to worry about it being an awkward length of time. She had hugged Brooke too long, once, and the other girl had weaseled herself away with an, "Okay, Dallas..."

No, she could hang all over Chariot's neck and the mare would be perfectly content.

It was well after hours and the grounds to the barn was silent save for the horses on night turn-out snorting into the grass as they grazed. Dallas's sneakers echoed across the cobblestone of the middle lane and she kicked at pebbles along the way, staring down with a set jaw and a faraway haze in her eyes. The moon made the buildings and fences cast eerie shadows across the stone, the leaves rustling a harmony above with an on-again off-again breeze.

Dallas hunched down a little bit more into her jacket and slipped into the barn. The lights were off save for a single overhead near the tack room. It was chillier in the stone walls, making her wish she had at least put on a pair of pants instead of staying in her sleep shorts. She strode straight to Chariot's stall and peered in through the bars.

Her pony, who had been reaching up into the hay rack and munching contentedly, sensed her owner and turned around. With a quiet nicker, she walked over and shoved her nose into the offered hand.

Dallas chuckled, unlatching the door and slipping into the stall with her small mare. "Hey, pretty lady," she murmured, ruffling the pony's forelock affectionately and pulling her muzzle up to plant a kiss between her nostrils. "No peppermints right now. Sorry, girl."

Chariot looked anyway, pressing flaring nostrils against the pockets of Dallas's shorts and smacking her lips around the fabric. Dallas stepped forward, wrapping her arms around the mare's soft neck and leaning in. She ran her hand over her back, over her shoulder, scratching at the small white spot on the side of her withers. Her mare didn't move and instead pressed back against her owner, turning her neck to check the back pockets when the front yielded no results.

"You're silly," Dallas mumbled into her mane. She breathed deep the scent of horse, of dirt and hay and the leftover hint of citronella, and let herself relax. When she was with Chariot she could forget about the stress of school and life. She could sink into another world where it was just the two of them and no one else.

But it never lasted forever. It couldn't.

After a while, Dallas pulled away, stroking the mare's soft neck and picking at a spot of dirt before backing off. "See you tomorrow, Chariot," she said, affectionately pinching a hairy muzzle that was still looking for treats before slipping from the stall and returning the latch. It was late, way past any semblance of an acceptable time to be out and about, and Dallas had an 8 a.m. She sighed at the idea of the lack of sleep she was going to get and strode through the barn, peering through the bars at the other horses as she went.

She found herself pausing at Beatrix's.

Burying her hands into her pockets, she stood on her toes and peered into the stall. The large bay mare was laying down, stretched out on her cushion of cedar and straw, her lips flapping as though dreaming. Cute. Dallas smiled at the sight and started to walk away until she heard a groan.

It was coming from Beatrix's stall.

She back-peddled, eyebrows stitching together as she squinted into the stall. Beatrix was sitting up a little, but there was something not quite right. Her brown eyes looked distant, her nostrils a little too wide to be relaxed or sleeping. As Dallas watched, she craned her neck and nibbled at her side, huffing dramatically and letting another quiet groan echo into the silence of the night.

Kuso.

Dallas stepped across the aisle and flicked the overhead on. With the additional light she could see the sweat that coated the mare's soft neck, the heavy up and down of her barrel. No, something wasn't right at all. Dallas had seen it plenty of times before and knew exactly what was wrong.

She whipped out her phone and immediately called Miss Nelson.

No answer.

Well, she didn't have the number of any other coaches. But every stall had emergency information—it was required under the Hoofbeats safety rules in case anything happened—and so she found the number she needed and dialed.

A sleepy, confused voice answered after a couple rings. "Hello?"

Dallas took a deep breath, rolling her tongue and teeth across her bottom lip as she looked at the distressed mare, and said, "Alice, you need to get to the barn. Now."

Chapter Eight

ALICE

Alice grunted awake at the sudden shrill of her mobile going off beneath her pillow. She slapped her hand around until her fingers wrapped around the vibrating device and lifted it, squinting her eyes at the overly bright screen to see who would possibly be calling her in the middle of the night.

INCOMING CALL

071392287856

01:17

Not a number she recognized. She hit accept and held the phone to her ear, letting her eyes drift back shut as she mumbled, "Hello?"

"Alice, you need to get to the barn, now."

She let out a heavy sigh and rolled over onto her back, forcing her eyelids open as she pulled the mobile away from her face and regarded the lit screen for a moment before saying, "Huh?"

"It's Dallas—I mean, it's Beatrix, she's colicking, just—ugh, just get here!"

Alice didn't even wait to hear the dial tone signaling the call was ended. She was slinging her covers away and leaping up in a flash of anxiety, nearly knocking over her side table to turn her lamp on as she yanked on the first pair of jeans she could find and threw a jumper over the t-shirt she'd been sleeping in. In a matter of moments, she was yanking paddock boots over a pair of mismatched socks and banging her way through the dark house, slamming doors and cabinets as she dug for the tube of banamine that she knew was lying around somewhere, not really caring if she woke Hannah or Barbara. Which, she probably did, but she didn't stay to find out—she grabbed her keys, her wallet, and her phone, and was out the door before even five minutes had passed.

Beatrix had been absolutely fine earlier that day. They'd had their usual workout, nothing strenuous, just Dressage and a little bit of conditioning, and she'd eaten her oats with the same veracity that she always showed. When Alice had finally left the stable, long after most of the other riders, Beatrix had been happily snacking on a fresh pad of hay that she'd placed into her feeder.

Besides, Beatrix *never* colicked.

Why was she colicking *now*?

Alice hardly ever drove. She couldn't remember the last time she'd even gotten behind the wheel of her Mazda—likely weeks ago-but it would take two minutes to get to the stable versus the ten or fifteen it would take on foot. She held her breath as she turned the key and thank God, she still had petrol, before stalling out putting it into first and letting out of slew of curses before taking off. The roads were completely empty, void of any other cars and life aside from a couple of people standing outside a pub that was still open, and so she may have made a couple illegal turns. But in the dead of the night, it was mostly just her and her panic, so she justified it that way.

She racked her brain for any sort of symptom she may have missed during her time with her mare. She had completed her routine inspection as usual, carefully feeling each tendon and ligament for heat and running her hands over every inch of her tall horse's body for any sign of distress. Beatrix had acted completely normal. She had begged for treats, was willingly moving forward, drank a few gulps of water after their workout, passed manure in the cross-ties—

Alice pounded a palm on the steering wheel. "You bloody idiot," she grumbled to herself. She still hadn't pinpointed a moment in time that the mare hinted at being ill, but as her caretaker, Alice let the responsibility fall solely on her shoulders. Beatrix relied on her. She had failed her.

She could already see the dark outline of her mare before she even pulled her car into the modest parking lot next to the main barn. The floodlights over the Games arena glared down, bright and obnoxious against the black sky of near midnight. Even from a distance, she could see Dallas's gaze locked on the ground as she trudged along, one hand shoved into the pocket of her jacket, the other clutching the lead rope as she dutifully led Beatrix around the outside of the arena in monotonous circles.

Alice all but ran up to the two, hissing as sharp wood scraped against the soft skin of her palm as she clambered through the rails of the fence. Dallas glanced up in acknowledgment but didn't stop walking.

"When did you find her?" she asked. There was another question—*what are you doing out here at one in the morning?*—but Alice didn't raise that topic because if Dallas *hadn't* been there, the situation could have been much worse than it appeared to be.

"Um... about fifteen minutes ago," Dallas said. "Found her lying in her stall. I got her up as soon as I noticed something was wrong."

"Thank you." Alice pulled the tube of banamine from her pocket.

Dallas regarded the medicine with a cool ease before nodding at the white smears around the mare's lips. "Already gave her some. I had a tube in my first aid kit."

Alice blinked at the other girl as she walked by her side, taking in the sight of her mare: the sweat-coated neck, the flaring nostrils, the gut noises that rumbled against her hand when she placed a palm on her barrel. Her tail was raised and flagged a little bit to the side and occasionally she would try to stop, pawing at the sand in preparation to roll. Dallas would just tug the rope, cluck, offer a word of reassurance, and keep her moving.

"Chariot colicked once," Dallas clarified, giving her a tense smile. "Got too excited on her first day home and fed her four times and rode her twice in between. Dumb move, don't do that, that's a recipe for disaster. I'm kind of an idiot, though." She scratched the back of her neck and looked away.

Alice would have laughed but she was a little bit stressed out, to say the least. She reached for the lead rope. "You're not an idiot. Thank you, Dallas. I've got her. You can go back to your dormitory."

Dallas shook her head. "It's alright. I don't mind staying and keeping you two company. We can just hand her off every once in a while. Besides," the other girl's eyes skimmed over Alice's messy appearance and the blonde suddenly felt extremely self-conscious, "you look like you just woke up."

"Of course I just woke up, Dallas, it's one in the morning! What did you think I was doing?"

Dallas hummed, turning to face Beatrix as the mare stopped to paw once more. She urged her forward with a gentle, "It's alright, girl, you can do it," and scratched her gently on the shoulder. The large mare huffed and lurched back into a walk, head hanging low, large eyes drooped with discomfort.

Alice shoved her hands into the front pockets of her jeans. It was cold, and Dallas was wearing shorts—why in the world was that girl always wearing shorts?—and Alice had to wonder how she wasn't freezing. She let her eyes run over the smooth skin, the bruises dotting the pale canvas of her thighs, until she realized the other girl was looking at her and she turned away and blushed.

Dallas let out a long yawn and Alice moved in, weaseling the lead out of her hand—which was very cold—and taking the mare away before the other girl could oppose. "You can go lay down in my car, if you want," Alice offered, unclipping her keys from a belt loop and holding them out to reinforce her invitation. "Or, you know, just go back to your dormitory. I won't be bothered by it."

"Nah, I'm fine." Her eyes, a dull maroon in the darkness, fell on where Alice's car was parked and she said, "Would've pegged you for fine German engineering."

"I prefer Japanese models," Alice murmured—and then promptly felt a red hot blush stinging her ears at the realization of her own comment. She cleared her throat into a closed fist and added, "Better gas mileage and less expensive repairs."

Luckily, though, Dallas didn't seem to notice. She paused her stride momentarily as Alice had to force Beatrix to keep walking once more. Alice was fully aware of the shorter girl's jacket sleeve rubbing against her arm and felt herself swallowing hard at the realization of the proximity.

"Don't you have a show this weekend?" Dallas asked after a moment's silence and another hard tug on the rope by Alice.

"Not anymore," Alice mumbled. Miss Parker would probably try to get her to ride one of the horses the school owned, but that would honestly be a waste of time. Points were given based on a horse and rider combination—riding another horse would be money unnecessarily spent. No, better to just sit the upcoming show out and enter a few more classes in the next.

Alice glanced down and realized the other girl was wearing her runners, which were barely even tied, and didn't even have socks on. She frowned. The sand in her shoes had to be uncomfortable.

"I don't understand how you're not cold," she mumbled. "I'm freezing."

Alice shook her head and laughed, switching the rope to her left hand to rest a palm against Beatrix's shoulder, which was moving mechanically as she plodded along, the muscles rippling beneath her sleek flesh. "Maybe you shouldn't wear the shortest shorts on the planet at night in the middle of October, then. My offer stands for the car."

"Nope." Dallas grinned and skipped ahead a little bit, making Beatrix raise her head and flick her ears forward. The mare snorted an acknowledgment and kept on trudging. "Can't get rid of me that easy!"

She was cute. Her long hair swayed around her shoulders and pale jawbones as she let a broad grin slide across her face. Alice couldn't help but smile back.

It should have been a truly dreadful situation. After all, she was walking in a circle in the middle of a cold October night with her sick mare when she really would have rather been sleeping in her warm bed. But Dallas was there—bright, cheerful, and very adorable Dallas—and so Alice found that she really couldn't complain about the circumstances, at all.

By the time Beatrix was feeling better—and Alice knew because she left a heap of manure in the middle of the arena and was no longer trying to roll away her discomfort—the sun was starting to peek over the horizon and through the line of trees that spread in a barrier around the Hoofbeats stables. She was exhausted and could feel the heavy bags beneath her half-lidded eyes, the palm of her hand stifling a yawn every other second. Between all the stirrup-less riding Parker was making them do and walking her horse for nearly four hours, she was almost grateful that she wouldn't be able to ride her mare for a few days. Her legs needed rest.

She looked to where Dallas had curled up against the fence by the gate, her legs stretched out of hoof-pocked ground. The other girl had dragged Chariot's dirty winter blanket from the tack room and had it wrapped around her body, her head tilted back against the wooden post and her mouth wide open as she slept. Dallas had champed her way through most of the night and had only settled down about an hour ago, refusing to sleep in the car or just go back to the dormitories, "Just in case Alice needed her to take over."

Company had been very much appreciated. The exact source of the company had been even more appreciated.

"Hey, Dallas."

Alice knelt down and placed a hand gently on the sleeping girl's shoulder. Her eyes fluttered open, a weary, dull red staring back in momentary confusion before Dallas yawned, raised her arms in a deep stretch, and said, "Morning, sunshine."

Alice rose and stepped back, patting the mare's neck. She was much more alert than she had been over the night, but it was easy to tell that she, too, was exhausted. A back pastern bent with every pause in stride as she tried to rest her weary body.

"Do you need a break?" Dallas asked, yawning again as she clambered to her feet. "I'll walk her." The collar of her jacket was sticking up and Alice suppressed the urge to reach out and fix it.

Instead, she shook her head and offered a tired smile. "No, she's feeling better. I'm going to put her in her paddock so she can keep moving around. Come on, let's go."

She waited while Dallas gathered the blanket into her arms and opened the gate for her and her horse, yawning all the way across the cobblestone lane and into the stable. The birds that lived in the trees and rafters had woken in a harmony of early morning chirps and Alice felt her stomach gnawing with discomfort from being up all night. She wanted so badly to climb back into bed, but she had a class in a few short hours and so that need would have to wait to be fulfilled.

Dallas disappeared to go put the blanket back into her tack stall while Alice led Beatrix through her box and into the small paddock that connected to it. The mare stepped away with a snort, lowering her nose to begin sifting through a pile of hay. Good, she was interested in food. Alice let out a sigh of relief and unclipped the rope, leaving her halter on, just in case.

She found Dallas all but laying on Alice's monogrammed mahogany tack trunk in front of Beatrix's box. The girl was struggling to stay awake, unfocused eyes staring off into the distance. "Good?" she mumbled, sleepy gaze turning to Alice.

"Good," Alice confirmed. "Come on, let me give you a ride back to your dormitory. If you walk I'll likely find you passed out somewhere in the middle of campus."

Dallas chuckled and didn't even bother to retort. She obediently followed Alice to her car and slid into the passenger seat, slumping against the faux leather and barely even managing to buckle her seatbelt. "Nice car," she barely managed to mumble before letting her head drift sideways.

She fell asleep somewhere between the stable and the three minutes it took to get to her dorm building, but the sound the car pulling to a stop woke her back up. Alice slid the car into neutral and held her foot on the brake, glancing over at the Japanese girl as she fumbled with the door handle.

"Hey, Dallas?"

"Hmm?"

Dallas turned to face her, suppressing another yawn.

"Thank you. Again."

Dallas nodded, a slow smile spreading across her lips as she lingered, one leg dangling from the open door of the car. "Sure." She hesitated and took a deep breath, then said, "Can I ask you something?"

Alice felt her eyebrows knit together as she studied the other girl—the messy brown hair, the tired eyes, the bare legs prickled with goosebumps-and nodded. "What's that?"

"Do you suppose we're friends now?"

She didn't know whether or not to be hurt that Dallas didn't think that they were friends *before* or to be excited that Dallas was considering them friends *now*. Play it cool, Alice. Stay neutral. She licked her lips and tightened her grip on the steering wheel. "If you like."

"Cool." Dallas nodded again and pulled herself out of the car, pausing for a moment for a final glance before adding, "I like."

The door slammed shut. A bit hard—Alice certainly would have scolded Hannah and Barbara for that—but she didn't necessarily care. She was tired and smiling, watching the brunette as she dug her key card out of her wallet and disappeared into the sliding doors of the dormitory.

Friends. That was okay. Alice could certainly settle for being friends.

"Bloody hell, Alice, you've got *me* wet," Hannah said from her doorway.

Alice froze mid air-grind with her hands out to the side. Her gaze snapped to the door of her room, where Hannah stood with a shit-eating grin and her mobile held sideways in front of her face. She could feel the blood rushing to her neck and face and lunged forward.

"Delete that! Now!"

"No *way*," Hannah howled, jerking her phone away from the desperate blonde and breaking into shrill laughter. "That's quality content right there. I'm adding this to my wank bank."

Alice dropped her bright red face into her palm, gritting her teeth together.

At least I've got you in my head

"Hayley, too," Hannah said through laughs, propping herself up against the door frame and folding her arms over her chest—mobile snug and hidden against her abdomen—as she nodded at Alice's MacBook. "Who's got *you* feeling saucy?"

In long, embarrassment-fueled strides, Alice stormed over to her MacBook and muted Spotify with the press of a button. She *had* been studying for an upcoming exam in Equine Nutrition, but her favorite Hayley Kiyoko song came on and Alice had been feeling it because thoughts of Dallas were plaguing the back of her mind, and so she had started dancing. In a tank top. And her underwear. *Because it was her room and private personal space and she could do what she wanted in it.*

And, of course, now Hannah had a bloody video.

"Why do you feel the need to enter my room without announcing yourself?" Alice moaned, running a hand through her wavy blonde hair and crossing her arms tight over her chest in some sense of self-preservation as she leveled an icy blue stare at her roommate.

"What's going on?" Barbara mumbled from down the hall. Alice could hear the creak of her bedroom door and her bare feet plodding against the hardwood floor.

Hannah was smirking. "Knock? Then how would I catch you doing things like this? I mean, *shit*, girl," she hissed, holding her phone up. "Hey, Barbs, look at this-"

"*Delete that!*"

"Absolutely not! Don't worry, I'll only send it to everyone you ever crush on."

"Wow, Alice, I don't think I'm so straight anymore."

"I've got an idea. You're single, I'm single, this is hot as hell, let's-"

Alice groaned and buried her face in her hands again. "Hannah, I told you not to flirt with me! That's so weird and inappropriate. And both of you, get out of here! This is an invasion of privacy!"

"Eh." Hannah waved a hand dismissively, turning to walk off. "You're not my type, anyway. Too sexy. I prefer boyish charm."

Barbara blinked at Alice for a moment from where she stood in her sleep clothes, somewhat confused but also entertained, with one black eyebrow quirked. "I mean, damn, though," she muttered, inhaling deeply and letting her eyes trail over Alice's body before following her roommate.

Alice lunged for the door and pressed it shut, turning the lock this time for good measure. She had asked time and time again for her roommates to either knock or announce themselves before entering her room, and *time and time again* they barged in without any kind of warning. One of these days she was going to be

doing

something

inappropriate.

She let out a heavy sigh and slammed her MacBook shut. It was late anyway and she was still trying to get her sleep pattern back in order from being up all night earlier in the week with Beatrix. The mare had settled out just fine and seemed completely back to normal, but Alice wasn't about to take her to the show. Hannah and Barbara were going without her, which would be pretty nice, because she'd have the flat to herself and wouldn't have to worry about them *barging into her room.*

She paused for a moment before flicking out her lamp, staring through her window to gaze across the street and the university beyond. It was always a sight she could appreciate: the ornate architecture reaching into the night sky, the bright stars that glimmered overhead. In the distance, she could see some of the rolling fields of the stables and the very edge of the barn that held her mare. She liked to look every night, just to remind herself of where she was and what she was doing.

Just as she was settling beneath the covers, her mobile vibrated on the other side of her pillow. Nobody texted her—unless it was Hannah sending that stupid video, in which case she would kick her all the way across campus—and so a message so late in the night was a little strange.

Thursday, October 4, 2018
Dallas 22:08
Heeeeeeeeyyyy what are you doing :3
Dallas?

She blinked down at the message, kicking her bare feet against the cold sheets as she pushed herself up to sit against her headboard. She'd saved the number, obviously, in case she ever needed to call or message the other girl, and she'd be lying if she tried to say she hadn't hovered over an empty screen for a while trying to think of something to say without coming across as weird, but Dallas texting her out of the blue was... a pleasant surprise.

She'd started to type out a response, deleting it once (because she was going to say "About to go to sleep", and if she said that Dallas would likely stop talking to her) and typing out something new when-

Dallas 22:09
Wrong person sorry

Alice's thumb froze over the keyboard and she frowned down at the dim screen until a couple more messages popped up in rapid succession.

Dallas 22:09

just kidding
Hey Alice

Her disappointment quickly turned to amusement as she chuckled and let herself drift down against her pillow, rolling over onto her side.

Alice 22:10
You sure about that?
Dallas 22:10
Yep

Well, now she didn't really know what to say. Chloe had always told her she was terrible at texting—she was usually delayed in her responses and "too formal", whatever that meant— and so she didn't want to say something stupid.

Which seemed fine, because dots lit up on her screen indicating Dallas typing, anyway.

Dallas 22:11
how's B?

Her muscles were shaking a little and she tried to relax. Why was she nervous? It was just Dallas and it was just texting. No big deal, right?

Alice 22:12
She's great, thanks again.
Dallas 22:12
(*^ω^)

Whatever that meant.

Dallas 22:12
still not going t his wknd?
Alice 22:12
Unfortunately not.

She needed to go to bed—she had a quiz in Microbiology and a presentation in Pharmacology—but now her adrenaline was on high and she didn't want to close her eyes at all.

Dallas 22:13

we are going to LWS tmrw night if u wanna come!

She was about to ask what LWS before she realized it probably meant Last Wednesday Society and mentally scolded herself for almost asking a ridiculous question.

But... we. That meant the rest of the Games team, probably. Girls that really didn't seem to welcome her company in the least. Especially Amelie O'Neill.

Alice let out a long sigh and tensed one calf muscle, rolling her jaw as she stared off into the darkness of her room. Light from somewhere else in the flat was still flooding in through the bottom of her door: either one of her roommates was still awake (unlikely, they had to wake up early to prepare for the show) or they left on a light unknowingly (more likely, they always did that). She flicked her eyes back to the screen and realized she'd let time go by just thinking about a response.

Alice 22:17

Maybe.

A few minutes passed and Alice was starting to think that her message was a little too terse and was considering what else she could say when-

Dallas 22:21

Pleeeeease? :3

I owe u drinks

2 to be exact

maybe 1 more as interest
Dallas 22:22
so 3 drinks
I guess 4 if u want 4
thats a lot tho
how about just 3
(/ω/)

Alice laughed and turned her face into her pillow, twitching her toes into the sheets. She nibbled at her bottom lip and tried to stop the blush from working into her cheeks as she typed back.

Alice 22:23
How terribly convincing.
Dallas 22:24
sounds like a yes

She *did* want to go and hang out with Dallas, but-

Alice 22:25
We'll see.
Dallas 22:25

-_-
Alice 22:25
What are you still doing up?
Dallas 22:26
texting you duh :3
its not late
wait
is it too late
ughh

Good lord, she messaged at the speed of light. Every time she moved to start typing something back, Dallas had already sent three more before her thumbs could even hit the keyboard.

Dallas 22:27
i'm so sorry
(/ω/)
Alice 22:28
lol. It's fine, Dallas.
Dallas 22:28
ok
good
:3
Dallas 22:30
tmrw?
Alice 22:31
Fine.
Dallas 22:31
ok see you there! :3 night!

Well, okay, *that* happened. With a sigh, she typed out one final message and hit send before shoving her mobile back under her pillow.

Alice 22:32
Goodnight.

So she was going out with Dallas. Well, and the rest of the Games team, but that was besides the point, because, well—Dallas would be there. She pulled her covers up to her chin and flexed her fingers into them, squeezing her eyes shut and trying hard, while also failing miserably, to suppress a grin that she was pretty sure she fell asleep with.

Chapter Nine

D*ALLAS*

She lost again. Why was Constance *so* much better than she was?

With a disgruntled groan, she threw the controller down on the ground beside her and slumped against the couch. Brooke, curled up at the edge of the sofa above her, patted her head gently and said, "Aw, it's okay, Dallas, you almost got her that time!"

Constance, with a victorious grin, dropped the controller down on Janine's lap and fell onto her back from where she sat cross-legged on the floor in front of the television. On their massive television, flashes of Princess Peach speeding by Dallas's Yoshi rotated across the screen. They'd been playing for the better part of three hours and Constance had won *every single race.*

Janine had invited Dallas and her two roommates over to the flat she shared with Amelie and Constance following their Games practice, which went well but it had been colder outside than usual and therefore entirely uncomfortable and not very fun. But, now, they were warm in the small, dark den where Amelie had been diligently stoking a fire for most of the evening. Dinner had consisted of crisps and marshmallows, which was acceptable in Dallas's book.

"Don't feel bad, Dallas," Janine said, smiling. She was sitting on the other end of the couch, contentedly snacking from a massive bag of crisps. "She plays this all the time."

"My turn, Conz. Stop showing off," Amelie grumbled, setting down the poker and snatching the controller away from Constance. "Who wants in?"

"I'm out," Dallas said. "I think that's enough for me tonight." She held the controller out to Brooke, who shook her head—she was busy texting Frank—and then Callie, who took it with a limp hand and shrugged.

"Sure, why not," the lavender-haired girl mumbled.

Dallas leaned back against the couch, stretching her legs out across the floor. Brooke was mindlessly running her fingers through her dirty brunette hair between texting her boyfriend, which was very welcome and also a little distracting, but she wasn't going to blame losing on Brooke's affection. Constance would have won, anyway.

She glanced down at her own phone that had been lying on the rug next to her, ignored, and picked it up to flick the screen on. The background, a picture of Chariot sticking her nose into the camera, stared back at her. No notifications. Not that she *expected* any. Why would Alice message her?

Though, they had agreed that they were technically friends...

She turned her phone so that prying eyes couldn't see, feeling Brooke's fingers working through a knot in her hair, and flipped open to her contacts.

071132687692

BARN HOTTIE

Well, since they were friends, and Dallas knew for a fact that Alice wasn't going to the show in Birmingham, there wouldn't be any harm in inviting her out with them the following night... right?

Dallas took a deep breath and flipped open the message screen, hammering something out before she second guessed herself.

Dallas 10:08

Heeeeeeeeyyyy what are you doing :3

She lowered her phone, gnawing at her lip as her eyes switched between her phone and the television. Amelie was getting thoroughly smashed by Callie, who was smirking with glee. Janine was still on the first lap and kept going off course to shovel crisps into her mouth.

Dallas glanced back down, watching the dots flicker across the bottom of the screen. Then stop. Then flicker again. Great, maybe Alice hadn't even saved her number and didn't know who she was. Play it off.

Dallas 10:09

Wrong person sorry

No wait shit that was the wrong thing to do because then Alice would get confused or upset if she actually knew it was Dallas plus how could it be the wrong person if they'd never texted before—

Dallas 10:09

just kidding

Hey Alice

Please know who she was.

Her phone vibrated.

BARN HOTTIE 10:10
You sure about that?

Dallas chuckled, leaning her head back into Brooke's nails and letting her thumbs hover over the keyboard for a moment.

Dallas 10:10
Yep

She still wasn't sure Alice even knew exactly who she was, so she figured she would clear everything up with a quick:

Dallas 10:11
how's B?

BARN HOTTIE 10:12
She's great, thanks again.

Confirmed! Alice knew who she was and things didn't even have to get awkward! Dallas smiled and crouched over her phone.

Dallas 10:12
(* ^ ω ^)
still not going this wknd?

She figured that Alice wasn't, because she had made it quite clear she didn't want to ride a schooling horse and would prefer to stay back with her mare. But it wasn't as though she had talked to the other girl since then, and Alice seemed to be like somebody who would do her own thing without letting somebody else know.

BARN HOTTIE 10:12
Unfortunately not.

Okay, well, good. That meant she was likely free to go to Last Wednesday Society with them. Dallas had thought about inviting her all week. The only other time she saw the

Alice interact socially was at the Red Stallion, and, well, she wasn't exactly being social . But she'd seemed to have a good time after she had someone to talk to. She glanced up at her friends, none of which were paying attention to her. She felt like she was doing something secretive—Amelie would probably tease her mercilessly if she knew she was texting Alice Thelwell—and so she really didn't want anybody to ask her what she was doing.

Dallas 10:13

we are going to LWS tmrw night if u wanna come!

Dallas waited, staring at the screen. A minute went by. Two. No dots. She guessed she had her answer. She had switched her screen off and was watching her friends, who were waiting to start another round, when her phone vibrated against her palm.

BARN HOTTIE 10:17

Maybe.

Maybe? What kind of answer was that? Dallas frowned, scratching at her bicep in thought.

"Yo Dallas, are you sure you don't want a go? Conz is itching for another victory."

Dallas looked up to see Amelie dangling the controller in her hand and shook her head, glancing back down at the screen and Alice's one word response. "I'm good," she said. She could see the American turn her eyes to the phone in her lap but she said nothing and instead shrugged, pulling the controller back and returning her attention to the game.

Dallas took a deep breath. She was going to get Alice to come out. Besides, maybe having Alice hang out with them would end all the weird air between the Hunt and Games

Teams. If Alice was friends with them, Hannah and Barbara would have to be nice by default, right?

Dallas 10:21
Pleeeeease? :3
I owe u drinks
2 to be exact

Dallas narrowed her eyes and threw all self-reservation out the window, thumbs hammering away.

Dallas 10:21
maybe 1 more as interest
Dallas 10:22
so 3 drinks
I guess 4 if u want 4
thats a lot tho
how about just 3
(/ ω/)

She finally stopped to let Alice have a chance to respond. Brooke was staring at her with an eyebrow raised, but turned her blue eyes back to her own phone.

BARN HOTTIE 10:23
How terribly convincing.

Dallas couldn't tell if that was sarcasm or not. She raised one dark eyebrow and responded.

Dallas 10:24
sounds like a yes

A pause.

BARN HOTTIE 10:25
We'll see.
Dallas 10:25
-_-

If Dallas didn't know better, she would have thought Alice was playing hard to get. But Alice was independent and a little shifty socially, plus had no reason to be playful as far as platonically hanging out with a girl like Dallas, so she figured the other girl just didn't want to commit to plans. She frowned and lowered her phone with no intention of trying anymore until her phone buzzed again.

BARN HOTTIE 10:25
What are you still doing up?

Okay, well if Alice was going to continue the conversation—

Dallas 10:26
texting you duh :3
its not late
wait

It wasn't, it was only half ten, but—shoot, Alice was probably one of those people who went to bed early! Of course she was. Dallas had likely woken the other girl up because she didn't bother to check what time it was. She could feel a hot flush burning into her cheeks as she typed out some quick responses.

Dallas 10:26
is it too late
ughh
Dallas 10:27
i'm so sorry
(/ ω/)

Dallas would have smacked herself in the forehead if there weren't five other people in the room who would've wondered why she was having such strange reactions to her phone.

BARN HOTTIE 10:28

lol. It's fine, Dallas.

Dallas let a long, heavy sigh slip through her nostrils. Alice was laughing. That was good.

Dallas 10:28

ok

good

:3

"You guys ready to head back?" she heard Callie ask. Dallas glanced up to see her friend looking between her and Brooke, who had both been heavily engaged in their phone conversations and ignoring everybody else. "Or did you want to stay here all night on your phones?"

Dallas pushed herself to her feet, brushing off the breeches she was still wearing and plucking up her jacket. "Yeah, sure." She looked back down at her screen. Alice still hadn't given her a concrete response.

Dallas 10:30

tmrw?

She slid into her jacket, dropping her phone on the coffee table for a moment only to see it light up and spin across the glass a moment later.

BARN HOTTIE 10:31

Fine.

Dallas couldn't stop the broad grin that spread smoothly across her face. She ignored Callie's inquiry of, "What are you grinning at?" and sent her last text before shoving her phone into her pocket and saying, "Nothing!"

Dallas 10:31
ok see you there! :3 night!

She had convinced Alice to go out with them! Though, she hadn't asked the rest of the team if it would be okay to invite Alice, but she didn't think they would care. Well, she hoped they wouldn't. They all had to get along, eventually, if they were going to spend the next few years at the same school and riding at the same barn together. It only made sense.

She didn't even realize that Alice had sent her a final text until she got home and was changing into her sleep clothes. The blue light on her phone blinked with a notification.

BARN HOTTIE 10:32
Goodnight.

Dallas grinned.

"The correspondent inference theory suggests that perception of an individual or a situation is based on the perceiver's inference, or understanding, of action and causation. Essentially, the perceiver will judge the perceived based on observation and categorize as such based on social acceptability and desirability."

Professor Badcock was droning on in her usual, "*This is super interesting, listen to how excited I am!*" voice that was her attempt at making the material interesting. It wasn't working—the general consensus, ha, Dallas had been listening a little—was that the information being put out was incredibly boring. She dragged her pen across her notebook, smoothing out the neck muscles of the rearing horse she was drawing on one half of her page. Her notes consisted of:

05 October 2018

jones and davis 1965

attribution = distinctiveness | consensus | consistency

this sucks

If most of the students do poorly on an exam (high consistency!) and everyone thinks the material is super boring (high consistency!) then the likeliest explanation for poor marks is the material (stimulus!)

Dallas groaned and let her forehead smack into her palm as she continued to shade her horse while Badcock rolled on.

"One of the main components of this theory is the idea of expectancy, of which Jones and Davis state there are two types." Professor Badcock flicked to the next slide of the lesson. "Page 267 of your text." Dallas was on 262. She made no move to change it.

CATEGORY-BASED EXPECTANCIES:

- Derived from knowledge about particular groups or sub-cultures

- Heavily influenced by stereotypes and assumptions

TARGET-BASED EXPECTANCIES:

- Derived from knowledge about a particular person

- Familiarity with the person's belief and character

Dallas glanced up only briefly, her eyes flitting through her fingers as she analyzed the slide with disinterest before scanning the classroom. For the first time, she realized Hannah wasn't there in her regular seat. She had likely already left for the show. Red eyes fell on the digital clock on the far wall.

Ten more minutes. Ten more minutes and she was free for the weekend. She could do ten more minutes.

"This theory began as an analyzation of first impressions," Professor Badcock continued, leaning against the podium and gazing over the lecture hall, at the students in the front row who were paying close attention and the students in the back who, like Dallas, were clearly somewhere else. "And sought to determine a perceiver's determination of socially acceptable behaviors versus those that were unusual. For example, we expect a certain person to behave in a specific way because we have perceived them to fall into a certain category, and when they do something outside the expectations of that category, their behavior has become unusual. However, if we take that same person and have an understanding of their identity and mannerisms, that same behavior could be completely acceptable."

Dallas's phone buzzed across her notebook, where it had been lying face down for the majority of the lecture. She set her pen down and flipped it over.

BARN HOTTIE 3:45

Time?

Maybe it was the fact that she had completely turned her brain off because it was the end of the week, she was already in weekend mode, and the lecture was particularly boring, but Dallas could not for the life of her understand what Alice was asking.

Dallas 3:45

3:45

She covered her mouth in an attempt to suppress a yawn before running her hands through her hair. Five more minutes. She wished that Professor Badcock was the type to let them out of class early, but the excitable instructor liked to go to the very last minute. Even on Fridays.

BARN HOTTIE 3:46

...

I meant tonight?

Oh.

Dallas snickered and picked her phone up, straightening her back and hiding her hands under her desk as she responded. Of course Alice had meant her invitation to Last Wednesday.

Dallas 3:46

Oh oops

after practice

BARN HOTTIE 3:47

Helpful. Thank you.

Dallas yawned again and kicked her legs out under the table in a deep stretch, raising glazed eyes to fall on the PowerPoint once again. Somebody had decided to tell a story about how they thought somebody was weird, blahblah, turned out they were just raised in a different culture, it was acceptable there, imagine that, how strange—why did people feel the need to talk? *Especially* when class was about to end?

BARN HOTTIE 3:49

Are you here?

Dallas looked back down at the phone in her hand.

Dallas 3:49

yes

no

maybe

where's here

She smirked to herself, amused by her own messages—who would entertain her if she didn't do it herself?—and set her phone down to start packing up her belongings. The class would be over in a moment and she wanted to be the first one out the door. Her Chariot awaited!

BARN HOTTIE 3:49

Nevermind, I see you're not.

Dallas blinked.

BARN HOTTIE 3:50

See you tonight.

Maybe.

"Please review the theory's studies of communicative context and subtext for the lesson on Monday," Professor Badcock was saying up front, though Dallas was sure hardly anybody heard her because everybody was already throwing their things into their bags and pushing their chairs up.

BARN HOTTIE 3:50

We'll see.

Minute possibility.

BARN HOTTIE 3:51

Very small, in fact.

Aleph-zero.

Okay, bye!

Dallas stayed in her seat even after the others around her started to get up and leave, staring at the series of text messages that Alice had sent. The other night, she had been so monosyllabic, and now she was... was she *playing* with her?

Rolling her shoulders in a shrug, Dallas tucked her phone into her pocket, slipped her bag over her shoulder, and headed off to the barn without a second thought.

The last thing Dallas had wanted to do was go out on a Friday night in dirty breeches, an old long sleeve shirt that was still damp with sweat, and the same jacket that she was *always* wearing and likely covered with Chariot slobber. But, circumstances—those being the rest of the team demanding to just go straight to Last Wednesday, because why bother wasting time to go home and change?—had determined that her weekend was already going to start in a way she didn't plan. Dallas didn't bother to argue. Her only justification would have been trying to look nice for a girl that would never have any sort of interest, and so it was probably a blessing in disguise.

The Team didn't get to the pub until almost eight and the place was still slow—the proprietor only had a couple people at the bar and the whole of the Jumping team, so a whopping five people, at one of the tables in the back. No Alice. They sidled into their usual booth with a pitcher of lager and a cider for Brooke.

"Ugh, feels good to be done with that week," Amelie muttered as she finished pouring beer into everyone's pints—she gave Dallas *way* too much head and Dallas frowned and blew on it—before saying, "Who wants a shot?"

Dallas took a breath, staring down at the phone in her lap that had been still for hours before shooting a glance to the front door. "Me," she said quickly, lifting red eyes to meet green and tracing her fingers down the sides of her iced glass.

Amelie quirked an eyebrow at Dallas but shrugged it off. "Alright. Me, Dallas, Conz, Janine—Callie, no? Brooke, I know you don't want one. Wuss."

"I prefer to call it 'knowing my limits,'" Brooke said with a shrug, bringing her Strongbow to her lips and taking a small sip as she spun her phone on the table.

"Vodka," Janine grunted, waving her hand and already chugging her beer.

Amelie snorted. "I believe I'm paying, so *I* will choose, and I can already tell you that I am not getting shots of rubbing alcohol," she said before striding away with an air of importance.

Dallas's phone vibrated against her leg. She glanced down and brushed a few copper hairs and flakes of cedar off her thigh before checking her phone.

BARN HOTTIE 8:17
Are you there already?

"What are you smirking at?" Callie grumbled from across the table.

Dallas 8:17
maybe

"Nothing," Dallas said back, burying her phone in her lap and trying to force the corners of her lips down with the reply that flashed on her screen.

BARN HOTTIE 8:18
Alright. I'm not on the way.

Why was she shaking? She flicked her screen off and dropped her phone back into her lap, raising her eyes back to the table—Callie was staring at her, but nobody else seemed to notice—before picking up her beer and taking a long sip. She swiped the foam from her upper lip with the back of her hand and tried to still her quivering skin.

There was no reason to be nervous. It was just Alice. They were just friends. Well, sort of. No. Yes. They were friends. Yes, she was one of the hottest girls Dallas had ever seen. Yes, Dallas may have been struggling to keep a crush under wraps and was failing miserably. But, at the end of the day, it was just the really hot blonde girl who rode the really nice horse and had really nice—

"Cheers, bitches," Amelie said as she dropped a handful of shots on the table and slid into the booth beside Dallas. "Enjoy the finest whiskey that this place had on well!"

Alice was going to be there any minute. Liquid courage, make her blood stop boiling and her bones stop shaking and please for the love of everything holy do *not* let her run off at the mouth with something stupid.

The whiskey burned like fire down the back of her throat and she coughed loudly, slamming the empty shot glass down on the table and throwing a closed fist against her lips. Her eyes started watering and she ducked her head to hack into her sleeve.

"What a champ." Amelie laughed and slapped Dallas on the shoulder, making her cough even more.

"I see you're already killing the poor girl."

Kuso.

Sleeve still covering her mouth, Dallas lifted her leaking eyes and red face to see Alice standing at the edge of the booth. And good lord if Dallas hadn't been focused on the overwhelming embarrassment of hacking up her lungs, she probably would have just dropped dead right there, because Alice was wearing these tight black pants and black flats and a white tank top that hugged her thin stomach and a black leather jacket that reached halfway down her waist and her long blonde hair fell over her shoulders in perfect waves—

Dallas would have taken the death. Sweet, sweet death.

She swiped at her eyes and lowered her arm.

"Fancy seeing you here," Amelie said, turning curious eyes up to their newest addition. "I thought Hannah and Barbara were at a show?"

"They are." Alice's confident smirk had faltered and she folded her arms across her chest, glancing at between Dallas and the rest of the Games Team.

"I invited her," Dallas wheezed, grabbing her beer and taking a swig to finally calm her throbbing throat and nodding at the empty seat across the table from Brooke.

Janine, who was already pouring her second beer, shrugged and said, "The more the merrier," and offered Alice a welcome grin. Dallas could have kissed her right there. Platonically. On the cheek.

Alice's smile returned—tentatively—and she sat delicately at the edge of the booth next to Brooke. The Finnish girl slid over a little bit and said, "Sorry you couldn't go this weekend, Alice."

"It happens," Alice replied. She was fidgeting with her hands in her lap and looking completely out of place, like a flighty filly that was ready to bolt at the movement of a shadow. "I'm just glad Dallas was around to notice Beatrix before it turned into a more serious situation."

Amelie swiveled to look at Dallas, who was staring down into her beer as though it was going to save her from her own humiliation. "Yeah, good thing. You never told us why you were at the barn in the middle of the night," she said, an accusing smirk twitching at the corner of her mouth.

Dallas did not want to admit in front of Alice that she had nearly failed a Hippotherapy test, so she decided to change the subject before Amelie could pry further. And what she meant to have come out was, "*Can I buy you a drink?*" but what actually came out was:

"Drink?"

In the most pathetic squeak Dallas's voice could have possibly made.

"I'll go get one," Alice said. She was smiling—no, laughing?—at Dallas.

Dallas stood up so fast that she rocked the booth with her thighs. She pressed her hands down against the edge to try to steady it and blushed. "No, I've got it! I told you I'd buy you a drink," she said quickly and was climbing over Amelie to get to the bar before the other girl could protest.

She felt some satisfaction with herself at being so sly, even if she'd had the grace of a three-legged mule, that she couldn't stop the confident smile that flitted across her lips when she set Alice's drink down in front of her to a, "Thank you, Dallas," and a smile before sliding back in next to Amelie.

Until Alice took a sip and tried to hide a strange face by bringing her hand to her mouth and Dallas squinted at her and asked, "Is it bad?"

"It's fine," Alice murmured, grabbing the lime to squeeze it into the drink, her nose twitching up a little at the corner as she added, "Just strong."

Amelie regarded Alice with a cool stare before turning to Dallas. "Well is for peasants like us. Thelwell only drinks top shelf."

Dallas was sure the glare Alice sent Amelie would have turned a normal person to stone, but Amelie was Amelie and she just grinned back as though she was the wittiest person on the planet. Dallas decided then and there that she *never* wanted to be on the receiving end of a look like *that*.

"Sorry," Dallas mumbled, looking away and bringing her beer to her lips to take a sip and glancing over at Janine and Constance, who were watching a YouTube video of last year's international competition.

"It's fine. Really," Alice asserted from across the table. She took another drink for emphasis and this time didn't make a face, so Dallas felt better. Well, a little.

The other girl seemed to relax after some time, letting herself fall into the conversation (Brooke made sure to include her any chance she could) that consisted mostly of classes and horses. Dallas didn't really know what to say to her now that she was *there*, but she supposed the point of getting Alice out was to get her on good terms with the Games Team and make sure she wasn't lonely or sad while her teammates were away at a show that she should have been at. The point wasn't for *her* to talk to Alice *exclusively*.

Though, she wished she could.

Alice got up to get her second drink. Dallas offered to get the next one, too, but Alice was resolute when she said, "No, don't worry about it, Dallas. You don't need to be buying me drinks," and dismissed herself. As soon as she stepped away from the table, Amelie took a long gulp of her beer and turned to Dallas.

"Why didn't you tell us you invited Thelwell?" she asked.

Dallas shrugged, eyebrows stitching together as she stared back at the American. "I didn't think about it. I guess I forgot." She didn't. "I mean... it's alright, right?"

"Well, yeah, I guess," Amelie said. None of the other girls said anything otherwise so Amelie added, "You just have to give a girl a heads up, you know? You can't just surprise us with," she waved a hand at Alice, who was at the bar waiting for her drink, "that."

Dallas felt herself frowning and she polished off the rest of her beer with a large swallow. "What do you mean by 'that'?"

"Nevermind," Amelie mumbled, grabbing the pitcher, empty after Dallas poured herself another half of a pint. "I'm gonna get another."

Dallas turned to watch her go, scratching at the side of her knee as she turned to regard the rest of the team. "What is she talking about?"

"They don't get along. You know that," Brooke said back, on her second bottle of Strongbow, phone in one hand where she was texting Frank.

Janine looked up from the new video that she and Constance had switched to. The screen was paused on a rider vaulting onto the back of a white pony. "Amelie really doesn't like her very much. But it's okay, Dallas, we don't mind."

Constance nodded an affirmation before unpausing the video and continuing to watch.

"I don't care," Callie said next to her, sipping her beer and staring off into the distance. "You know that."

Alice slid back into the booth next to Brooke. Dallas had almost kind of hoped she'd just take where Amelie had been sitting—which would have been stupid because she probably would have imploded—and sipped her new drink. Alice's eyes fell on Dallas, flicking over the girl's face for a moment. "How was practice?" she finally asked.

Dallas perked up. Finally, Alice was speaking solely to *her*. She ran her finger around the edge of her glass. "Oh, it was really good, we—"

"The well doth not run dry!" Amelie yelled, slamming the pitcher back down into the middle of the table and sloshing a little bit of beer over the side in the process. Alice made a face and pushed a few bar napkins at it to prevent any beer from dripping over on her, but Dallas felt a few splashes against the thighs and swiped her hands against the thin material of her breeches in surprise.

"Was that necessary?" Alice growled, icy blue eyes darting up to the American.

Amelie shrugged and plopped down next to Dallas, sliding one arm around the Japanese girl's shoulders in the process. Dallas felt her brows furrowing in confusion and she turned a gaze up in questioning, but the American's green eyes were leveling the blue that bore into her from across the table.

Eh, whatever. Amelie was just acting rowdy, like she usually did when she'd had a few drinks. Dallas picked up her beer and sipped it, shifting against the weight of the arm around her.

"You should've seen Dallas tonight," Amelie was saying, thumbing at the girl sitting awkwardly next to her with her other hand. "She and Chariot were killing it. Can't wait to see them kick ass in Glasgow."

"Well, it is a team effort—" Dallas started.

"I'm sure she'll do great," Alice said, raising her glass to her lips once more.

Amelie shrugged, her fingers twitching against Dallas's arm. "Nah, they'll do better than great. Dallas's done an awesome job with her pony and the team. Best captain we could have asked for."

Dallas flushed at the compliment and filled her mouth with another swig of beer. "I mean I think I could use some work—"

"Well, she is very level-headed and confident," Alice was saying. "Which are important qualities for a position of leadership."

A smirk tugged at Amelie's lips. "Helps that she's a total babe, too."

What?

Dallas's eyes widened and she looked at Amelie again. What was going on? "Huh?"

Alice said nothing. She glared at Amelie through narrowed eyes, color dusting her cheeks as she cleared her throat and dropped her gaze to her drink.

"Let's get you some more beer," Amelie said. She reached for the pitcher and filled Dallas's pint up, tightening her grip on the other girl's shoulder as she slid in closer and let her fingers dance along the bicep of Dallas's jacket.

Dallas, thoroughly confused and *extremely* uncomfortable with the sudden actions of her friend, just stared at the beer with slightly parted lips and a pair of huge red eyes. She brought one hand up to awkwardly push her bangs aside as she looked between Amelie and Alice—the latter looking just as perturbed.

"You know, I should, um—probably go," Alice said after a moment, pushing her glass—still half full—across the table and rising. She shoved her hands into the pockets of her leather jacket, folding her elbows into her sides. "I have a lot of studying to do."

"Wait, what?" Dallas's eyes shot up. "Seriously? You haven't even been here that long."

"Yeah. I, um—Pharmacology exam. Quite a bit of material," the other girl muttered. "See you," she added before turning on her heel and striding off before Dallas could even squirm her way out from beneath Amelie's arm and make any kind of protest.

"Aw, she was nice to talk to," Brooke said, frowning before going back to her phone.

Amelie withdrew her arm and shrugged, edging away to take a long swallow of her beer and turn her gaze away. "Anyway," she mumbled.

Dallas stared after Alice long after she'd disappeared through the front door of the pub.

Amelie. Target. Unusual.

Alice. Category. ...?

She should have listened in class.

Chapter Ten

A *LICE*

Her face was red with anger and humiliation as she threw her leather jacket onto her bed and moved to the window of her bedroom to gaze out into the darkness. By all means, she knew what Amelie's issue was. The girl *still* thought that Alice had something to do with whatever childish antics happened between her and Hannah, even though Alice had asserted numerous times that she didn't even *know* about it. But, no, apparently Alice had "said something" or "did something" (Amelie couldn't decide which) to make whatever the situation was (*because Alice had still never been privy to it!*) go to absolute hell, and couldn't be convinced otherwise.

"You're just mad about Chloe and you don't want anybody to be happy," Amelie had said the day she'd told her she was quitting the Hunt Team entirely. "I know you said something to her. You've never liked me and you've made that completely obvious."

Well, yes, she *had* been upset about Chloe, but that certainly hadn't meant she didn't wish happiness for anybody else. And, yes, she *didn't* really like Amelie all that much—the girl was crude and brass and had very little respect for others—but Chloe had been her own personal issue, one that she had been dealing with independently. Her feelings about her own break-up and dislike for Amelie were for Alice's mind only.

And neither of those things had *anything* to do with Amelie and Hannah and the tension that had flared between them in the last months of the previous semester.

It had been half a year since whatever happened between Amelie and Hannah... well, happened. None of it justified Amelie's actions or how the other girl continually found ways to get under her skin. And, yet, there they were, six months later with Amelie still doing exactly that.

"Hey there, Gaywell," Amelie had droned as she slid up next to where she was standing and smacked the empty pitcher against the bar. "So what brings you out tonight?"

Alice knew from the moment Amelie started talking to her that nothing good would come of it. She cleared her throat and looked straight ahead. "Dallas told you. She invited me."

Amelie had hummed and taken a moment to motion the proprietor for a new pitcher of lager before turning her attention back to Alice. "So what's going on with you and Dallas, then?"

"I hardly understand why Dallas inviting me out means that something is going on," Alice had replied, keeping her tone mellow and neutral. The American wanted a rise—that was always the end goal—and Alice was hard pressed to oblige.

"So you're saying that Dallas managed to pull you out on a Friday night, nights that I know you can't stand because of the crowds—hold your tongue, I know you better than you think—to hang out with a bunch of people who you've never gotten along with, by yourself, with neither of your teammates along for the ride?" Amelie leveled her with a stare, emerald eyes flickering with amusement. "And there's nothing going on?"

Alice rolled her jaw and looked away. "I hardly deign to think Dallas would ever think of me in any way you're suggesting," she said. "Though I also don't think there's anything wrong with making a friend and finding them... attractive." She had blushed when she said it and focused her gaze on where the bartender was pouring her drink. *Please hurry.*

"So you like her."

"Amelie, I hardly know her."

The redhead huffed. "You're avoiding the question."

"I said I thought she was attractive," Alice hissed through grit teeth, struggling to keep her voice low. "Is that such a horrible thing?"

"How do you know she's even... nevermind, forget that question, she lights up every bell and whistle on even the shittiest gaydar." Amelie chuckled at herself, shooting a glance over her shoulder at Dallas, who was talking to the other girls at the table, then brought her voice back to its challenging tone. "Alright, then. So you're saying you came out with no other intentions. Just to hang out with a friend. A very cute friend. Is that right?"

Alice didn't answer. She pursed her lips and stared at her fidgeting hands.

"Then I suppose I'm just here to hang out with a cute friend, too," Amelie said after a moment's pause. "If that's all it is."

Her drink had come. Finally. Alice had grabbed it and started to walk back to the table, but not before Amelie called out, "Let's see how Dallas feels."

It had all been to get under Alice's skin. Every movement, every comment, every sideways glance and mischievous smirk. And Alice was loathe to admit that it had worked. She didn't want to sit there and watch Amelie hang all over Dallas. She didn't want to spend her Friday night dealing with Amelie O'Neill. She had gone to spend time with Dallas, to hopefully get to know her better, to maybe enjoy herself the way she had the other night when Dallas sat down and talked to her. It had been eight bloody months since she last felt anything that made her stir—she just wanted to feel it *again*.

She brought her palm to her face and squeezed at her temples. She shouldn't have left. She should have just ignored Amelie and her childish comments or maybe pulled her aside and said something to her. Or, hell, she should have just let Amelie take shots at her and roll with the punches.

But she didn't, because the universe had already made it very clear it didn't want Alice to be happy. Her father, her mother, Chloe.

So why should she expect the world to suddenly shift beneath her feet?

Her mobile was blinking. She clenched her teeth and picked it up. Dallas had messaged her quite some time before.

Dallas 20:57
are you ok?
Dallas 21:13
Alice?
Dallas 21:16
if I did something i'm sorry

Alice felt her eyes glazing over as she stared down at the phone. She wanted to say something back. She wanted to message Dallas and tell her that it wasn't her fault, that she had done nothing wrong, that she was sorry she left like that and maybe they could do something together again sometime, alone-

but she did none of that, because she was weak and angry and wasn't quite sure if she even liked the way Dallas was making her feel vulnerable. Chloe had done that, once, and she had only ended up on her knees in the same dark place that she'd made her home after her parents died.

And so she dropped her phone on her desk and instead put herself to bed, crawling beneath the warm cocoon of her blankets where nothing but her own thoughts could cause her harm.

Dallas didn't send her another message, and Alice left the last few unanswered. She had wanted to reply, but maybe it was for the best that she didn't. And, the longer that went by, the more awkward she felt about trying to explain herself or offer any kind of redemption.

Hannah and Barbara had come back from the show in Birmingham with very tired horses but a slew of honors and ribbons to boot. Hannah had taken Champion in the 100cm division against 16 other horses and riders, along with 1st in Overall Equitation for the entire show, and Barbara had landed a Reserve in a modestly sized Green Horse under saddle and over fences division. The long haul had been a success for Hoofbeats, and Alice seriously regretted not packing on a schooling horse for the simple fact that she could have avoided Friday evening.

"How was your weekend?" Barbara asked when the two had finally dropped their bags in the main entrance of their flat before collapsing on the couch. She let out a heavy sigh and kicked her legs up, still clad in dirty breeches and knee-high socks littered with hay and cedar. It was raining, and both of their clothes were wet from unloading gear and horses in the inclement weather. Alice didn't have the energy to make a fuss over it, so she simply sank deeper into her father's leather armchair and let the novel she was reading drift to her lap. A bit of fiction had been a nice distraction from everything that was going on.

"Fine," Alice mumbled, hooking her thumb into the book to keep her place. She eyed her two roommates from behind her thin reading lenses. It was getting late, nearly nine, and Alice really hadn't been lying when she said she had a Pharmacology exam.

Hannah threw herself onto the floor with a dramatic sigh and wrapped her arms around one knee to stretch it to her chest. "What'd you do? Besides miss us?"

Alice looked at the tea she'd barely touched and pursed her lips. "Nothing. Studied. Spent time with Bea."

"Fascinating. You lead a life worth envy," Hannah mumbled. She switched to her other leg and turned her head on the floor to eye Alice through the legs of the coffee table. "Why are you acting like somebody shaved your mum's cat?"

Alice blinked, white-blonde eyebrows stitching together as she stared at her roommate. "Pardon?"

"Hannah, I told you to stop saying that," Barbara scolded from where she was still collapsed on the sofa. "It's super awkward and also can be taken very out of context." She tucked her hands behind her head and lifted it to look at Alice, mouth spreading in a wide yawn before saying, "She means you seem peeved."

"Just tired, I suppose," Alice said. She kicked her calves down to lower the leg rest and leaned forward on her knees, pulling her readers off and setting them on the side table next to her very full and very cold tea. "Long weekend."

Hannah hummed, eyebrows narrowing as she clambered up to sit cross-legged on the rug in front of the coffee table. "Did something happen?"

"I don't know why you would make that assumption," Alice muttered, inspecting her fingernails. They needed a trim, they were over the skin.

"*Maybe because you're acting like someone shaved your mum's cat.*"

"Hannah, nobody says that, and besides, how is that an indicator that somebody would be upset? I knew that drive was too long when you started making this stuff up," Barbara moaned.

"Look, I would be very upset if somebody shaved my mum's cat. Rochester won first prize in the York Cat Show last year in the Persian division because of his coat-"

"Please shut up, Hannah, you sound barmy." Barbara finally kicked her legs off the couch and sat up, lifting her hands over her head in a long stretch. "But she's right, Alice, you do seem upset. Last week you were dancing in your room and now you... look like someone shaved your mum's cat." She shot a glare at Hannah. "What's up?"

Alice frowned, flicking her thumb against her middle finger. She took a deep breath before finally answering. "I went out with the Games Team on Friday night," she grumbled.

"Ew, why?"

"*Hannah*."

"Pardon me. I mean, what on earth would possibly make you want to do that?"

"*Hannah*."

"Girls." Alice lifted a palm in the air before bringing it to her face and pinching the bridge of her nose. The last thing she wanted to do was listen to her roommates bicker and act like a couple of gossip girls. "Dallas invited me, and so I went."

"Dallas?" Hannah cocked her head to the side and squinted her eyes at Alice. "I didn't know you two were friends."

"Yes, we are," Alice said quickly, before adding, "Well... we *were*. I don't know." She groaned and pinched a little harder. "I thought we were starting to be friends, anyway, but then Amelie-"

"Of course it was Amelie!" Hannah moaned. "What did that bitch do this time?"

Alice lowered her hand and shrugged. "I should really get some sleep. I've got an exam in the morning-"

"If you want to be friends with Dallas," Barbara started delicately, chewing at her bottom lip, "Then what does Amelie have to do with it? Just ignore her. That's what you've always told us to do when she's being cheeky."

Alice opened her mouth to speak-

"Say it," Hannah dared from the floor.

She let her mouth fall back shut and crinkled her lip, glaring at the auburn-haired girl who was smirking back at her.

"Go on."

"Fine. It's hard." Alice tossed her hands in the air and stood, slumping her way over to their kitchen to grab a bottle of water out of the fridge.

"*She finally knows how I feel!*" Hannah yelled, fist pumping the air and letting herself fall back down against the rug.

"She gets under my skin and she knows it," Alice mumbled as she uncapped the bottle and took a swig. "She was just trying to make me jealous—you know what, I should really get to bed." She was blushing before she could stop herself.

"Jealous?"

"... jealous?"

Alice clenched her teeth together, rolling her jaw as she leaned against the marble countertop and turned the bottle in her hand. Why did she feel silly for admitting such a thing to her two best friends? They'd seen her fall from grace a million times before and would see her do it a million times again, so what was her hesitation about a simple attraction?

"You like Dallas?" Barbara asked slowly.

Alice sucked in a sharp breath through her teeth and brought blue eyes to meet the inquiring stares of her roommates. "I don't... I don't *not* like her, but I wouldn't go as far as to say that I... *like* her. I don't know her well enough. Though I find her very endearing."

"You like Dallas." Barbara was grinning. She jumped to her feet and stalked over their open kitchen, throwing herself into one of leather cushioned bar stools. "That's so sweet."

The tips of her ears were burning. "That's not what I-"

"If you're interested in Dallas," Hannah climbed to her feet and joined Barbara, brown eyes settling on her blushing roommate, "why don't you just spend some time with her and see how it goes?"

"I tried."

Barbara shook her head. "Going out with her group of friends in a setting that opens everything to outside manipulation-and by outside manipulation I mean specifically *Amelie*-is not trying, Alice. I understand it's been, like, three years since you've had to figure out dating, but even you should know that. Of course Amelie is going to mess with you if she sees you taking an interest in something. It's what she *does*." Hannah nodded an affirmation as she watched her black-haired roommate speak. "If you want to get to know Dallas, get to know Dallas. But... alone, you know?"

"So." Alice hesitated, running her index finger around the ridged top of the water bottle and crinkling the plastic in her fist. "You mean... ask her out on a date? Of sorts?"

"Well, it doesn't have to be a date," Hannah said, glancing at her friend. "You could just... get tea, or a pint, or, you know, whatever." She twirled the end of a messy French braid in her finger, unable to suppress the smile that was edging at the corner of her mouth. "Just make sure it's just the two of you."

Alice nodded, straightening her posture and leveling the two girls with a resolute stare. Her tongue darted out to wet her lips and she said, "Alright. Yes. Okay. I can do that. Thank you."

As she dismissed herself and walked off down the hall to her room, she could very clearly hear Hannah whisper-shriek, "That's so cute, Alice's got a crush!" and Barbara's, "Oh my god, Hannah!"

Dallas still hadn't messaged her back.

She had checked her mobile periodically throughout the day to see if the other girl had sent her anything. After her shower in the morning, after her Pharmacology exam, after her Nutrition class, every few steps as she walked across campus between classes. Radio silence.

Sunday, October 7, 2018
Alice 22:19
Hi, Dallas.
How was your weekend?

Alice gave her quiet mobile one more quick glance as she slid the reins over Beatrix's head. Still nothing. She likely blew any chance she had of even being friends with the girl—Dallas didn't even want to talk to her. With a sigh, she tossed the mobile onto her tack trunk and walked through the dreary, golden light of the aisles.

It had been raining non-stop for the duration and, as such, the schooling session had been canceled for the day. Though, exercise was still an option with the indoor, and Alice was itching to ride after nearly an entire week out of the saddle, so she still paid her visit to the barn and tacked the mare in her dressage saddle and bridle to get a little bit of riding in.

Alice could see the sky outside through the back stall windows, dark with clouds and sheets of relentless rain, and sighed. She had been looking forward to a lesson, and the indoor was cramped and a little small for comfortable riding, barely the size of a large dressage arena, but it would have to do. She swung into the saddle and adjusted her stirrups, bending down to stroke Beatrix's sleek neck and give her an affectionate pat. The mare had shown no signs of further colic during the remainder of the week—Alice would have known, as she scrutinized her mare accordingly—and so she felt confident that there would be no further issues and there was no harm in riding as usual.

She urged her mare forward with the dip of her seat and a squeeze of her calves, sighing into the saddle and letting a small smile flit across her lips. If there was anything to get her mind off the world outside and the confusion in her mind, it was Beatrix and the sensation of smooth power beneath her. The floating lull of her trot, the easy sway of her canter—there was nothing that compared, not even on the best of days.

Alice was halfway through her ride. Her inside hand had dropped to her thigh, seat relaxing into the saddle as her mare moved forward at a slow, upward canter in a 20 meter circle at one end of the indoor arena. There was no one else there. The only other girl, a Jumper who was only lunging her gelding at the other end of the arena earlier on in the ride, had left a little while ago. Alice was alone. She had the indoor to herself.

Beatrix felt like air beneath her. The rise and fall of her forehand carrying her forward in a smooth, rocking canter made Alice almost forget about the necessary use of her natural aids. She hardly had to correct the mare aside from a few gentle nudges of her heels. Beatrix flexed through her poll and back, large brown eyes focused, snorts rolling from her nostrils as she kept up the perfect circle that was being asked.

If Alice had to guess, she would say her mare missed being ridden, too. The mare had seemed bored and out of place without a job for the week. The short stride of the canter Alice was asking was demanding, but Beatrix delivered with the ease of a trained athlete.

She didn't even realize that there were others until the gate leading to the outdoor lane creaked on its rusty hinges, swaying open to let the entire Games team walk through. Alice brought her gaze up as she continued on in the canter, bringing Beatrix across the diagonal and asking for a smooth flying change as she switched up to the right.

Janine was holding the gate open as the riders and ponies filtered through. They all looked absolutely miserable, covered in mud and soaked from the rain, as they slipped through the middle of the arena and toward the aisle of the barn. Alice tried not to pay too much attention and instead focus on Beatrix, but she couldn't help but let her eyes fall on Dallas, who was most certainly looking her way.

She watched as the other girl turned to the rest of her team, said something, and started walking toward the center of the arena. Chariot's bridle was already off and slung over Dallas's shoulder. The equally dirty and miserable looking mare plodded after her owner with the trust and obedience of a blind best friend. The smaller girl came to a stop, Chariot along with her, and leveled a gaze at Alice, offering a weak smile when their eyes finally met.

Alice lifted Beatrix's front end, bringing her to a flowing trot. She could feel the muscular hind legs flexing beneath her, the long, blocked black tail swaying with the movement. She sat deep and brought her mare to a walk, letting the reins slide through soft fingers so Beatrix could stretch her neck out and catch a breath of air as she strode over to where Dallas stood.

"Hey!" Dallas said. Her voice was cheerful and, well, normal. She rocked back on her heels, throwing one arm around her pony's neck. Chariot lifted her head and regarded her owner with a fond expression before stretching her nose out to the larger bay mare.

"Hello, Dallas." Alice sat back and, with a squeeze of her thighs, brought Beatrix to a square halt. The mare dipped her neck and chewed at the bit.

Dallas looked like she had been through the mill. There was hardly a spot on her that wasn't covered in mud or wet sand. Her tan breeches were soaked and streaked, raindrops trailing in rivers down her black jacket. One side of her, including her helmet, was absolutely covered in mud as though she'd been dragged through the dirt and, Alice thought, maybe she had. After all, it wouldn't surprise her. The side of her face was flecked with dark smears and dots, her long brunette ponytail was drenched across her shoulder, and her cheeks were red from the cold and rain.

"You look like you had a good time," Alice said. As if to answer, Chariot let out a loud snort that sounded akin to a groan and shook her entire body.

Dallas frowned, fingers tracing underneath her pony's jugular—the only dry spot on the mare-as she stared up at the blonde. The small Japanese girl seemed even smaller from so high up and it was rather awkward, so Alice dropped her stirrups and slid from her mare's back, landing gently at Beatrix's shoulder.

"Miss Nelson makes us practice in the rain," Dallas muttered, rolling her eyes. When she noticed Alice's eyes tracing the very muddy left side of her, she clarified with, "I missed a vault. Well, okay, I missed everything, actually. Except the ground. Which is very cold. And wet. In case you were wondering."

Alice chuckled. She shifted awkwardly next to Beatrix, who leaned forward and touched muzzles with Chariot. Alice started to pull them away—she didn't really want Beatrix to squeal, she wasn't always friendly with other mares—but at the last moment she decided not to. The horse crept forward, inhaling Chariot's scent and nipping at the side of her cheek playfully. Chariot stood her ground.

After a long pause,

"I texted you-"

"I texted you-"

Both of them said the same thing at the same time. Alice looked down and dug the toe of her boot into the sand, flexing her fingers against her braided reins.

The silence grew again, awkward and uncomfortably loud, until Dallas finally said, "I... uh, right, well, I texted you Friday night after you left, but I don't know if you ever responded because I kind of lost my phone. It fell out of my pocket or something and I didn't notice for a while and I went back but I wasn't able to find it and..." she trailed off, laughing nervously as she shoved wet and dirty hands into the pockets of her jacket, shivering into it. "I wasn't able to get a new one until earlier today when the shops opened."

Alice brought her gaze back up, scanning Dallas's face. The other girl had a bunch of sand clinging to her upper lip and the outside of her mouth.

"Oh," she said at last.

So that's why Dallas had never responded.

"I just wanted to make sure you were okay," Dallas said. Her fingers were tracing a pattern against Chariot's neck, tugging unconsciously at the ends of the stringy copper mane. "I know Amelie was being a real jerk, I didn't know she would act like that. I should have stopped her, but I didn't know what to-" The other girl hesitated, her teeth rolling over her bottom lip before she made a face and swiped her mouth with her sleeve—then made another face and spat.

"Guh, sand," she muttered. "Anyway." Her red eyes found Alice's. "I'm really sorry."

Alice nodded. A gloved thumb massaged the V of a braid in the reins. "I apologize as well," she replied. "It was-" she thought for a moment, lips pursing together. "It was rude of me to leave abruptly like I did."

"No, it's okay. I understand. I get if you don' t really want to hang out with us anymore." Dallas smiled sadly, lowering her eyes. "Or me."

"That's absurd." She was blushing and she dipped her head down, hoping the bill of her helmet would hide the red of her face as she kicked the sand into a pile. "I was actually wondering if you might want to go out one night this week. For... drinks, or dinner, or... whatever." She licked her lips and looked back up, steeling herself with a deep breath of air. "You know, just us. I kind of... wouldn't mind getting to know you a little better. If that's okay." Dallas was just blinking at her with this incredulous look on her face, so Alice felt the need to continue. "I mean, if you'd like to, of course, it's just that I-"

"Yes," Dallas said quickly. She brought her sleeve to her face once more, swiping across her cheek and adding more dirt than was there originally. "I'd love to. I mean, that would be great. Yes. Okay. Good." The other girl took a shaky breath and was making sure to look anywhere but Alice. "Sorry, I just kind of thought you would hate me after-"

"Takes a bit more than that," Alice said, letting a nervous laugh pass from behind her teeth.

"Well, I, uh, have my new phone," Dallas said. She pulled it out from where she'd had it tucked in her half-chaps-

"Seriously, Dallas?" Alice's eyebrows shot up as she stared at the other girl. "You literally just lost a mobile and you take the brand new one out in the pouring rain while you're riding?"

"Well, I, uh-" Dallas chuckled nervously, bringing one hand up to scratch at her dirty neck. "I thought you might text or something, so I-"

Alice brought her hand to her face and swiped the leather of her glove against her nose, inhaling deeply and shaking her head. "Baffling," she muttered. When she finally let her hand drop, she found Dallas staring at her. The mobile—smeared with dirt already—was clutched in one hand. "Anyway, there's a great bar downtown I figured we could go to," she said. "If—er, is Wednesday okay?"

"Oh." Dallas frowned, a hard shiver passing through her body as she pressed into her wet pony's neck. "I have late practices on Wednesdays sometimes."

"Oh."

Beatrix stomped a hoof, ears flicking back and forth as she stared straight ahead, content to relax.

"And I have to go to Scotland this weekend," Dallas said. "First competition and all. I leave Friday so I should probably pack Thursday. I can... tomorrow? If you're free?"

"Tomorrow. Okay." Alice nodded. She was supposed to do gridwork the next night but she figured she could get Parker to swing it to Wednesday. All she had to do was say that she wanted to give Beatrix another day of flatwork before getting into something as strenuous as grids. Hannah and Barbara wouldn't mind, they hated the exercises their coach put them through when it came to the woman's trademark bounces with no stirrups or hands. "I can do tomorrow."

"Okay," Dallas echoed.

They stood there for another moment, both awkward and fidgety next to their very content and relaxed horses, before Dallas finally said:

"Well, I'm going to go untack and... well, shower, hopefully. Eventually. I, uh-" she lifted her mobile, wagging it a little with a half-smile. "Same number. Different phone. Okay. Bye, Alice." She turned and walked off across the arena. Chariot hung back for a moment before she realized the brunette was gone and snapped to attention, turning to find her owner and follow at a very slow, lazy walk.

Alice watched her go, waiting for her to disappear through the gate to the barn and into the aisle, before turning and burying her face into her mare's sweaty neck to shield the grin that she couldn't hold back any longer.

Chapter Eleven

D*ALLAS*
The rain was still relentless the next day, pouring down in sheets over the entirety of the campus and drenching the grounds with puddles and deep patches of mud that Dallas had to splash through in order to get to class. She was grateful that Miss Nelson had informed them that morning that they wouldn't be practicing in the miserable weather, though the alternative had been something that made Dallas groan out loud.

Dallas stared down at the message that she was about to send with a heavy sigh.

Dallas 2:35

I can't tonight. I'm so sorry

Miss Nelson had decided that they were going to have a team meeting to go through their strategy for Glasgow and, even though Dallas had tried to get her to rearrange for another night, their coach wasn't having anything to do with it. And Dallas certainly couldn't just say, "*Please, a pretty girl asked me for a drink and I'd really like to go*," because that certainly wouldn't reflect well on her role as Captain.

As Dallas sunk down into her chair, ignoring the lecture on Clinical Psychology that was droning on at the front of the classroom, falling on very deaf ears. She planted her forehead into the heel of her palm and hit send.

Her eyes felt like they were glazing over as she eyed the screen of her phone, watching as the dots of Alice's typing stuttered across the screen multiple times before a message finally came through.

Alice 2:37

Oh, okay.

She'd completely forgotten that her contacts were gone with the loss of her phone and so she'd made a point to go by Beatrix's stall to plug Alice's number back into her phone the night before. Though, this time, she figured it would make sense to put Alice in as her actual name. BARN HOTTIE was officially retired.

Dallas squeezed her eyes shut. She figured she should probably explain or Alice would likely think that Dallas didn't *want* to take her up on her offer of getting a drink. She plucked her phone back up and typed out another message:

Dallas 2:38

nelson wants us to talk about scotland.

I tried to get her to move it

;_;

another time?

Alice 2:39

Sure. Another time is fine.

Dallas frowned and turned her screen off. Alice was impossible to read through text messages—she was so formal and proper with what she wrote that she honestly couldn't get a reading on how the other girl felt. She gnawed on her lip and picked up her pen, rolling it in her hand as she stared down at the few notes she'd managed to take during the lecture. Nothing that would help her on any sort of quiz or exam. She had been too distracted, too nervous to message Alice and cancel something that she had very much been looking forward to.

Her screen lit up.

Alice 2:41

See you at the barn tonight, then?

She picked her phone back up, hiding it below the desk and resting her hands on her thighs as she thumbed out a response.

Dallas 2:42

alpha zero

Alice 2:43

...

Cute try.

Dallas rolled her eyes and chuckled.

"Miss West, if you found this class as interesting as you do your phone, you may not have done as poorly as you did on your last exam," Professor Pisces called out from the front of the lecture hall. Blushing, Dallas switched her screen off, ignoring the new message on her phone, and instead turned her attention back to the teacher with a quick apology.

Once she was sure the teacher wasn't paying attention to her any longer, she let out a small sigh of relief and let her focus stray once more. Alice didn't seem to be angry or upset, but Dallas still felt bad for having to cancel. Though, as she stared blankly at the PowerPoint that held the tiny text of a clinical study of teenagers with bipolar disorder, a sudden idea came to her.

She didn't *have* to cancel. She just had to improvise. And improvising was something that Dallas did very well.

Dallas 5:05
whatcha doing tonight?
Alice 5:06
Nothing now.
Dallas 5:07
meet me at chariots stall at 830?
:3
pls
Alice 5:10
If you insist.

Dallas was nervous as she paced in front of Chariot's stall, thumb running over the cold metal of the object in the pocket of her rain jacket. The mare was staring at her incredulously through the bars, chestnut ears flicking back and forth as she watched her anxious owner.

It was almost half eight and Alice would be there any minute. She had seen the girl riding earlier in the afternoon when she had arrived to get the barn conference room ready for the Games meeting, but she had barely managed to get out a wave before rushing off. She didn't know if Alice had stayed or gone back to her house or-

"Hello, Dallas."

Dallas froze and blinked up, crimson eyes meeting the bright blues that were staring back at her curiously. She hadn't left. She was still dressed in her breeches and the heavy navy blue coat that she had been wearing earlier during her ride, flecked with Beatrix's dark hairs and cedar bedding.

Thick, wavy blonde hair fell over her shoulder, barely contained in a messy French braid. Her hands were tucked into her pockets as she regarded Dallas coolly, glancing between the nervous looking girl and the numerous saddle pads that the other girl had draped over her tack trunk.

"Is there a... reason you wanted me to meet you here?" the girl asked at last, one white-blonde eyebrow quirking with her question.

"Yeah." Dallas stared back, reaching up to scratch at her neck and feeling a blush warming her cheeks and neck. It had seemed like a good idea earlier in the day, but now she worried it was kind of stupid. "I just... felt bad that I had to cancel and I didn't want you to think I didn't still want to be friends, so I figured if we can't go to the drinks... the drinks can come to us?" She pulled the flask, one she'd borrowed from Janine, out of her pocket and raised it with a nervous smile.

Alice chuckled. "I didn't think you didn't want to be friends," she said. She stepped over to Chariot's stall and slid a hand through the bars, letting the pony lip at her fingers. "So this is very unnecessary. But... cute. I must admit."

That was the second time that day that Alice had used the word cute in regards to something she had did. Dallas blushed harder, looking down at her paddock boots and kicking at a chunk of dirt in the aisle. When she looked back up, Alice's hand was stretched out to her and Dallas blinked between the offered appendage and the smile that Alice was wearing.

"Well?" Alice asked, taking a step forward. "Do you intend for us to drink that, or is it merely a prop?"

"Oh. Right." Dallas pressed the flask into the other girl's hand, feeling cold fingers brush against her palm before Alice pulled back, uncapped the flask, and raised it to her lips. When she dropped her arm, she was sputtering and coughing and had to bring the sleeve of her jacket—which read Leed's Hunter/Jumper Team, Dallas could now see—against her mouth.

"What did you put in that?" she asked between coughs, handing the flask back and moving to the tack trunk to plop down on the clean saddle pads that Dallas had laid out.

Dallas sat down next to her, cautiously putting enough space between them so that their thighs weren't touching, and took a swig of whatever was in the flask in solidarity.

It was so bad.

Dallas choked on the fire that burned down her throat and lowered the flask, feeling tears stinging the inside corners of her eyes as she hacked. "Dont... know..." she wheezed out, lifting one hand to shake in front of her face in what she hoped looked like an apology. "Janine," she added.

"That explains it." Alice laughed, taking the flask back from Dallas and raising it again to end up in another series of coughs. "Though," she coughed into a closed fist once more, lips curling back in distaste, "I suppose it would be rude to dismiss another's generosity."

Dallas grinned and took another sip. It seared her mouth again and her shoulders rocked forward in the effort of choking down whatever kind of vodka Janine had filled the thing with. In hindsight, maybe she should have specified a specific type of liquor or at least that it not be pure fire.

"You just want a flask of alcohol?" Janine had asked, raising an eyebrow at Dallas, who was standing at the threshold of their flat and probably looking super sketchy. "What do you need that for?"

"It's a surprise for someone!" Dallas had squeaked out, shifting uncomfortably. "I'll pay you back. I just don't have anything except Brooke's Strongbows and those things are really gross," she had said.

And so Janine had given her a flask filled with whatever disgusting Russian vodka she kept in her bar and Dallas hadn't bothered to say anything about it. After all, the girl was being nice enough just to supply Dallas with her questionable request without asking any further inquisition.

"Are you alright?" Alice asked, and for the first time Dallas realized that the other girl's hand was resting on the small of her back and sparkling blue eyes were leveling her with a look of amusement.

"Oi, yeah," Dallas said, blushing under the touch. "That stuff is just terrible."

Alice laughed, peering down the aisle at a rider from another team as they left their horses stall and stepped out of the barn. She seemed to consider something for a long moment before saying, "You know we could have just rescheduled, right?"

The strong alcohol was already making Dallas a little fuzzy. She grinned, leaning back against the wall of Chariot's stall and feeling the mare fuss with the bit of hair that stuck through the bars. "Yeah, but then I wouldn't have gotten to spend any time with you this week," she said. "And I kind of like the time I've spent with you so far."

"I... would not disagree with those sentiments," Alice said, clearing her throat into a closed fist and reaching for the flask once more. She took another swig, nose curling as she choked the vodka down. "Though I must say your idea of a substitute for what we had planned is a bit of a surprise."

"What can I say." Dallas kicked her legs out and grinned, reaching one hand over her head to poke through the bars at Chariot's nostrils, making a face when it resulted in runny snot and pulling her arm back out to swipe her fingers on her breeches. "I'm full of surprises!"

"And what other surprises can I expect?" Alice asked. She raised one eyebrow as she ran her eyes over Dallas's face.

Dallas suddenly felt nervous beneath the scrutiny, but the alcohol burning through her blood made her say, "Wouldn't you like to know?" and she hadn't meant it to sound flirty but it *did*, and so she squeezed her eyes shut and pursed her lips and mentally scolded herself for saying something so stupid.

But Alice just hummed at her side and rose, stepping to Chariot's stall door with her hands in her pockets before turning back to Dallas after a long silence. "You know that thing that you do where you jump on her?"

"Vaulting?"

"Yes, that. Teach me."

Dallas blinked between Alice's resolute stare and her pony, who was extremely curious about the two girls outside her stall and poking her nose anywhere she could. "Right... now?"

"Yes. Right now."

It was late, past nine, and they'd both drank some of Janine's putrid vodka and alcohol never mixed well with horses, but Dallas found that she couldn't back down beneath the determined pair of eyes that were gazing back at her and so instead she rose and plucked Chariot's bridle off her holder with a shrug that said, Why the hell not?

She slid Chariot's bridle on and led her willing pony from her stall, walking at Alice's side to the indoor arena. She hit the lights, listening to the gentle hum that buzzed over the arena as the massive industrial lights lit the enclosure in a warm orange glow. She could hear the rain still pounding down on the roof in a soothing rhythm.

"So... you're sure?" Dallas asked, glancing at Alice one final time, but if she expected the other girl to change her mind at the last minute she was very wrong, because Alice just nodded and grinned back.

So Dallas shrugged and led Chariot forward.

"It's best to learn from the trot first," she explained, nearly tripping over herself as she walked next to the mare—damn that vodka—and lined herself up parallel to the shoulder. She kicked her left leg up, curving it at the mare's hindquarters, and clucked. Chariot broke into a trot. "You're going to want to plant your feet and jump when the leg closest to you hits the ground," Dallas yelled in explanation before doing exactly that. She leapt into the air, digging her toes into the sand and swinging expertly onto Chariot's back. The mare burst into a canter with the expectation of racing but found herself quickly reeled back in with the snatch of the reins. Dallas stretched her legs out, feeling the warmth of her mare's bare back against her as they jigged over to Alice. "Got it?"

"I suppose we'll find out," Alice said as Dallas slid from the pony's back. She tentatively took the reins as they were being offered and led Chariot away.

Alice looked awkward, tall and lean and far too perfect next to the small pony. Dallas was grinning as she watched Alice trying to figure out where to put her hands. Finally, the girl settled with one hand gripping the mane while the other led Chariot forward. Alice clucked and Chariot jumped into a quick trot.

Alice ran next to the mare for a couple of strides before jumping—at the entirely wrong time, she clearly hadn't been paying a bit of attention—before smacking into Chariot's side. She bounced back and landed on her feet before trying again with the same result.

"Stop laughing!" she scolded, pulling the small chestnut mare up and shooting a pointed glare at Dallas. "This looks way easier than it is!"

Determined, the blonde girl halted Chariot and backed off a few steps before lunging forward. She threw her leg over the mare's hindquarters, landing gracefully on her back and straightening up. She looked tall and awkward on the short pony, her toes dangling below Chariot's knees. "Bloody hell this thing is small," she muttered, shifting her weight awkwardly and glancing back at Dallas.

"Yeah, it's easy from a halt and you're so tall it's not a big deal, so don't pat yourself on the back," Dallas said, lips spread in a wide grin. She could feel the daggers being shot back at her and raised her palms out in front of her as she stepped back in defense. "Okay, nevermind! Very hard! Very difficult! Good job! I'm impressed!"

"You know, your sarcasm is *not* welcome," Alice hissed. She kicked Chariot into a trot and sat deep on the mare's back, looking a lot more like a saltwater cowboy than the poised equestrian she was. She lifted the reins in one hand and Chariot arched her neck up, lifting her front end and bouncing a little as she bolted into a smooth canter. Dallas rarely got to see her mare from the ground and was pleased—she looked like a dancer, graceful and pretty. The girl on her back certainly did not take anything away from that aesthetic.

Dallas was still laughing when she realized that Alice had turned Chariot towards her and was charging forward-

"Hey!"

Dallas dodged out of the way just as the other girl turned at the last moment and bolted past, laughing as she pressed her hand forward and let Chariot out a little bit. The little mare took the freedom and surged forward, legs flying with the excitement of being let out.

"Give me my horse back!" Dallas called from the middle of the arena, folding her arms over her chest and watching the other girl as she zipped back and forth, occasionally feinting in.

She did it one more time, but this time Dallas was ready. She snaked her arm out, grabbing onto Alice's jacket and leaping forward as she deftly swung onto the mare's back behind the other girl. Chariot bolted a little bit to the side in surprise, but Dallas tightened her legs around Chariot's barrel and wrapped her arms tight around Alice's waist.

"What are you doing?" Alice shrieked, hands snapping back as she reined the shocked mare back. Chariot's nostrils blew loudly with irritation and she jerked forward once more.

"I'm showing you how to vault!" Dallas shouted, clucking and giving Chariot a small kick with her heel, though she seriously underestimated the response from her pony-

Chariot bolted again. Her hindquarters flew underneath her as she launched into the air, body swaying hard to the side beneath the weight of the two riders. Dallas immediately lost her balance from the odd position she was sitting in and gripped Alice's jacket hard in her fingers, yelping as she dragged the other girl down. Chariot went one way, they went the other, and in a flash the two riders were in a heap of groans and tangled limbs on the ground while the pony was galloping across the arena, riderless and confused.

"Dallas!" Alice hissed.

Dallas couldn't stop the laughter that rolled from the back of her throat as she slowly extracted herself from Alice, spitting out the little bit of dirt that she had eaten in the process of falling off. She sat up and shrugged off the swat that came from the other girl's hand. But Alice couldn't hold it in much longer, either, and soon the both of them were laughing in the cloud of dust that they'd made in the middle of the arena and Chariot was trotting over with her head down and her nostrils flaring with curiosity at what was going on.

"Excuse me, but what is going on here?"

Miss Parker voice rang, sharp and clear, through the indoor arena and Dallas looked up to see the lilac-haired woman slipping through the arena gate and stomping over. Her teal eyes were leveled on Alice as she scrambled away from Dallas and climbed to her feet, wiping dirt from her breeches and jacket as she stared back at her trainer, immediately stifling her giggles.

"I'd expect this type of behavior from someone as reckless as her," Miss Parker stated, waving a hand at Dallas, "but not from someone such as yourself. Fetch that pony and get out of here. The last thing this university needs is a lawsuit because the two of you decided to goof off after hours."

"Yes, Miss Parker," Alice said quickly, her face flushed as she brought a hand up and passed it over her braid to shake the dirt off. "I apologize."

"And come see me before our lesson tomorrow," Miss Parker growled before turning to stalk off to where Miss Willow was standing, leaning over the arena gate and watching curiously. Dallas hadn't even realized she had been standing there. How long *had* they been there, anyway? Dallas lifted her hand in a small wave at the jump coach, who returned it with a friendly smile, before snaking a hand out and gathering the reins of her pony. She watched as the two instructors strode off, Miss Parker muttering her frustration to the quiet woman at her side.

Dallas glanced back at Alice, expecting for her to be upset, but instead the other girl was letting the grin slide back across her face as she looked back over.

"Welp," Dallas said, shrugging. "Guess that's our cue." She clucked to Chariot and tugged on the reins.

"Wait, Dallas."

Dallas turned, only to step back in surprise as Alice raised a hand and passed a cold palm over the side of her face, fingers lingering at her temple in a gentle caress before dropping to her lips and swiping at the corner with a soft thumb.

The heat flared into her face immediately, burning cherry red in her cheeks and ears. "Uh, Alice?"

"Sorry," Alice murmured, though the smirk on her face said that she wasn't all that sorry at all. She dropped her hand back to her side. "Dirt." Blue eyes ran over her face for a moment before the other girl turned on a heel and started walking.

Dallas stared after her, letting crimson eyes fall on her pony's inquisitive gaze and trying to calm the implosion that had just happened inside of her at the brief touch. She let one hand come to rest on the pony's neck and took a shaky breath before following after the other girl, thoroughly confused but not at all upset.

By the time she climbed into bed after a long, hot shower, it was nearly 11 and she was exhausted. Callie and Brooke had questioned her extensively on her whereabouts, to which Dallas had only replied that she'd spent extra time at the barn to fix the line-ups for the upcoming competition. The answer seemed to appease them and they offered no further inquiry, and Dallas had slipped away beneath the shadow of her own fib.

The vodka was wearing off and instead she was just thirsty so she chugged a bottle of water before climbing into bed and curling up under her covers, snagging her new phone off her night stand. The blue light on the top was blinking with a message and she swiped across her screen with her thumb.

Alice 10:45

Thank you for teaching me how to vault.

Dallas smirked, pressing the side of her face into her pillow as she hammered out her response.

Dallas 10:58

you never learned

Alice 10:59

Then I suppose we'll just have to do it again.

She couldn't stop the broad grin that spread across her face. She would be lying if she said she wasn't confused by Alice's actions, but she would also be lying if she said she didn't like it. And, so, resigning herself to another straight crush that would never come to fruition, Dallas shut her phone off and tucked it under her pillow, drifting off to the image of her very attractive friend riding her pony—and liking it.

Chapter Twelve

A *LICE*
Though she tried not to, she often fell into thoughts of Chloe.

As she lay in her bed she squeezed her eyes shut, fingers wrapping around the edge of her pillow case as she struggled to force the memories out of her mind. But, try as she might, they were still there, plaguing her in moments of loneliness, stabbing at the backs of her eyes and flooding her vision with agonizing fragments of the past.

Chloe hadn't been her first kiss, but it had been the first that *meant* something. It had been the pinnacle of her coming out, the solidifying factor that the emotions that had dwelled within her for so long hadn't been wrong at all. Love had come in the form of a tall, French native brunette that had swept her off her feet and made her never even think to look back. Chloe was intelligent and beautiful, kind and sincere, and had the unbalanced temper of a wild alpha mare that drew Alice to her like a moth to a flame. They were inseparable and desperately in love and Alice found solace in her arms and home in her kiss.

Until Chloe left for Oxford, and Alice for Hoofbeats, and three long hours separated them.

There were still the weekends. Weekends where Alice drove to Oxford, and occasionally Chloe to Hoofbeats, though the other girl often complained about the loss of study time. And at first it was fine. Their time apart made the reunions happier, made the kisses sweeter and inevitable end of the weekend ever more painful. Every time Alice was forced to drive back to Hoofbeats, it was like she was leaving part of her heart behind and she would let herself cry for the first hour of her drive.

But, then, slowly, it seemed as though Chloe wasn't as excited about counting down the days until they'd see each other again. It was as though her life at Oxford had become more important and Alice a backseat to the new life the other girl had settled into, as though Alice was more of a burden or an interference than anything else. First there were the excuses for calling—"I have a lot of studying to do," or, "I'm going out with friends tonight"—and then there was the significant drop in texts, the nights where Chloe never even replied or the day after when Alice wouldn't hear from her until mid-afternoon.

"You suck at texting," Chloe would say, though Alice never understood because she was always prompt with her responses and nothing had changed from the first year of their relationship, where Chloe had never once complained. "And there's never anything to talk about when we talk all day."

The other girl stopped offering to drive down, cancelled weekends last minute even though Alice had already foregone her responsibilities in favor of her girlfriend, suddenly had plans that conflicted with ones they'd made months ago.

Then there was that day in mid-March. It was a Saturday and the early spring sun was bright in the sky and Hoofbeats was unseasonably warm for the time of year. A perfect day for riding, though Alice hadn't made it to the barn yet. She'd fallen asleep late after waiting up for hours for Chloe to call—the other girl had cancelled the weekend visit again and had said she'd call after visiting the library—but it never came.

Until that afternoon.

Alice had answered and Chloe was already crying, already spewing apologies without any kind of context whatsoever. At first Alice had worried that she had been hurt because Chloe had said, "I'm so sorry, babe, but something happened," and she had been ready to jump into her car and speed halfway across England to take her girlfriend into her arms and tell her everything was going to be okay, that she was there and always would be—

But then Chloe said, "I cheated on you."

And it was like her world came to a crashing halt.

She had hung up and dropped her phone, had barely made it to her bed in the stunned fog of confusion and pain and didn't even remember laying down and screaming into her pillow for what seemed like the entire day. Chloe had tried to call her, again and again, but Alice didn't answer. She couldn't. She had been feeling the constant ache of something being not quite right for weeks but she had *trusted* Chloe, had believed that the other girl loved her just as much—

She had loved Chloe.

She had *loved* Chloe.

And Chloe had sank her fingers deep into her flesh and ripped her throbbing heart from her chest to throw it on the floor and step on it with the carelessness of a stranger, had planted a seed of torment that would plague her for months afterwards. What had she done wrong? Was she not good enough? Was she not there enough? Alice had been accepted to Oxford. She could have gone, she could have followed her girlfriend, she could have and would have done everything she could to make things work. But at the end of the day she had chosen Hoofbeats, she had chosen a Veterinary sciences program that her parents were alumni of, she had chosen the riding program that she had dreamed about being part of since she was a little girl.

She didn't choose Chloe.

So Chloe didn't choose her.

And so some nights, long after the pain of betrayal had faded to a distant simmer and the love she once felt was all but a distant memory, she thought of Chloe. She thought of the firsts she had shared with somebody who eventually threw them back in her face, she thought bitterly of the comfort that she felt during those good times together when Alice thought the world was just the two of them and she had stupidly neglected the rest of her life, she thought of everything she did wrong to make things turn out the way they did.

But most of all, she thought about the heartache and the pain, the agony that followed her like the darkest shadow of night, and she knew that she never wanted to feel that way again.

"If you want company this weekend, I'll go with you," Barbara was saying from where she sat at the kitchen table drinking a freshly brewed cup of chamomile tea. Hannah had gone to the library to pick up some books for an upcoming research paper, and so the house was relatively quiet with just the two of them.

Alice shook her head, pouring her own cup of tea and sitting down across from her roommate. Her papers were spread across the table: bloodlines and lineage of the top European stallions, the pedigrees of the many colts and fillies that the Thelwell family was to offer at the upcoming auction, and the merits and earnings of former homebred Thoroughbreds. She wished that Barbara had been offering to go to Scotland with her, but that spontaneous trip had gone through the window when her bloodstock agent called and told her that she would be responsible for attending the upcoming Tipperary yearling auctions in her aunt's stead. The consignment was something that Aunt Marie would have normally attended herself, but a meeting with a stakeholder in eastern London had prohibited her from following through.

"That's perfectly alright. Thank you, though, Barbara," Alice replied, looking over the Hip numbers that were assigned to the few colts and fillies that she would be responsible for. The herd was much smaller than previous years, what with Alice in school and Aunt Marie the sole point of contact for the Thelwell Estate to include the

Veterinary business, but Alice was hopeful that they would still pull good numbers. They had two fillies sired by Galileo and out of stakes winning mares, and so those two alone would likely attract a fair number of high-end clients.

"Got anything that would be good for hunters?" Barbara asked. She was leaning forward over the table, peering at all the paperwork that Alice was perusing. "My little sister is looking for something that could take her through the long stirrup division."

Alice shook her head, bringing her tea to her lips and taking a sip. "Sorry, but no. These are all bred for racing. Maybe as a future career, but they'll likely sell for a few hundred thousand Euros this weekend." She ran her finger down the statistics for a colt by Caravaggio, who had breezed a furlong in a little over 9 seconds in his previous outing in preparation for the auction. He would get a good draw for a trainer looking for a nice turf sprinter.

"Well, nevermind," Barbara said quickly, pushing the chair out and rising. "That's a bit out of our price range, to say the least. Good luck with all that."

Alice offered her roommate a dismissive wave before continuing her studies. The mobile buzzed across one of the sire books she had been looking at earlier and she glanced over.

Dallas 19:56

aw, thats ok. Have fun!

She had told Dallas that she wouldn't be able to make it to the Games competition as planned as soon as her agent had given her the call. Though she was sure the other girl really didn't mind all that much, since what would Alice be but another bystander? She sighed and set the phone back down, resigned to her duties as a Thelwell.

The front door of their flat opened and slammed shut as Hannah stormed in, red in the face and lugging a massive bag of books. She threw everything down in the entrance hall and rounded into the kitchen, fists clenching at her sides.

Alice glanced up, plucking her glasses off her face and lowering them down onto her papers as her eyes ran over the angry girl that had suddenly appeared. "What's wrong?" she asked, watching as Hannah dove into the fridge and pulled out a Heineken, angrily popping the top off and taking a long swig.

"Amelie," Hannah grumbled, slouching down against the counter and leveling her blonde roommate with fiery brown eyes. "Imagine seeing her at the library, right? I didn't think someone like her even knew that place existed." She smacked the green bottle down on the marble counter top—an action that made Alice cringe—and continued on. "Shouldn't she be in another country right now, anyway? I swear that chav just does things to irritate me."

"I highly doubt she even knew you were going to be there," Alice said slowly, wrapping one hand around her warm mug of tea as she regarded the girl with concern. "And the girls don't leave until tomorrow and won't return until late Monday evening. I'm sure she was just getting some necessary study material for the days she'll miss." She hesitated before asking, "Did she... say something to you?"

"No," Hannah hissed, grabbing her beer and moving over to the kitchen table to flop down in the chair that Barbara had previously occupied. "She ignored me. As usual."

Alice raised an eyebrow. Whatever had happened between Amelie and Hannah, it seemed completely childish. It had been obvious the previous semester that the two had feelings for each other and their sudden falling out had come as a shock for both her and Barbara. Barbara may have known more about the situation that had taken place, but Alice had never asked nor been informed. It wasn't any of her business. Hannah would tell her if she found it appropriate.

"I doubt she meant you any discomfort," Alice replied. She brought her tea back to her lips, cooling it with a breath.

"Yeah, right. That's all she means," Hannah grumbled. She swallowed more of her beer and looked down at the papers stretched before her roommate. "What's this for?"

"Tipperary auction." Alice sighed, glancing down at the conformational pictures of her yearlings and the bloodlines of each. "I've been informed that I have to attend the auction in Ireland this weekend to liaison with prospective buyers. The burden of being a Thelwell," she mumbled.

"That should be fun, though," Hannah said. "It's beautiful there. Do you want me to come along with you?"

Alice shook her head. She appreciated that both of her roommates were offering to accompany her across the channel, but it was highly unnecessary for them to miss schooling sessions with Parker as well. They had a show the following weekend and it was crucial to get as much instruction as possible prior to. "No. But thank you, the offer is very kind."

Her mobile buzzed again. She flipped it over and swiped across the screen. Dallas had sent her a .gif of a cat sticking its tongue out. Alice chuckled.

"Dallas?" Hannah asked, glancing over from across the table.

Alice nodded, turning her screen back off without replying and bringing her attention back to her auburn-haired roommate. She and Dallas had been texting back and forth all day, the least she could do was give her sole focus to the girl in front of her at the moment. "Yes," she replied, before asking, "Do you want to... talk about Amelie? Or anything, for that matter?"

Hannah rolled her shoulders in a shrug, slouching a little bit in her chair as she wrapped her lips around her beer and nursed it in thought. "No," she said at last, pushing the chair out and rising. "Maybe another time. But... just don't mess that up," she gestured to the phone, frowning, "like I messed things up with Amelie."

Alice wanted to tell her that there was nothing to mess up, but she shrugged it off and instead watched her go, curious as to what she meant but not inquiring further. Hannah would likely tell her, in time, but Alice was also well aware that she was the last person that should be giving relationship advice. The only one she'd ever been in had fallen apart before her eyes.

"The colt looks very nice," her bloodstock agent was saying as they watched the Caravaggio yearling trotting the wrong way around the outside of the small six furlong track. His stride was short and squirmy, but at the same time his hindquarters and shoulders rippled with the muscle of a groomed athlete. He was dark grey like his sire, covered in dark dapples, with black stockings stretching up the majority of his legs.

Alice had to admit he was a very good looking colt. Hopefully he would fetch a fair price later in the day when the auction was held. As it stood, she could see a few admirers watching him from the rail. Cameras littered the hands of the observers, both reporters from the Horse & Hound and trainers scouting for their owners alike.

"And the fillies?" Alice asked, glancing over at her agent. While she was passionate about the racing industry and the young Thoroughbreds they bred, she admittedly knew very little about the economic side. That was usually Aunt Marie's forte, since she had once been married and, recently, divorced to a trainer out of Newmarket.

"They look nice on the track and have behaved themselves marvelously, but their pedigree is what will carry them far today," her agent commented. "The other yearlings should catch a fair price, but these three will bring in quite a fair sum. Especially with their sires being right up the road."

"Enough to pay off debtors, I wonder?" Alice had murmured the question to herself, though her agent answered anyway.

"I know nothing of that, Miss Thelwell."

Alice nodded and stepped back from the gap as her dappled grey yearling walked off, prancing with agitation beneath his young rider. He was pretty, but fairly small, and his brown eyes lingered on his onlookers with discomfort as his nostrils flared in a rolling snort. "Thank you, Allen," Alice said before turning and walking back to the shedrow, her hands stuffed deep into the pockets of her Leed's jacket.

Trainers, riders, and horses bustled around her, all eager to get to the track to show off in front of prospective buyers or move around the backside for conformational analysis. As she walked, she raised her eyes to glance around her beautiful surroundings.

For once, it wasn't raining in Ireland. The sky was bright blue, dotted with a few thick white clouds that drifted slowly by. The trees and grass were as green and lush as ever even in the cold, rolling in massive hills into distant mountains littered with limestone and the abandoned ruins of long since forgotten castles that remained untouched by the locals. The land was beautiful and one-of-a-kind, though Alice had seen it before and had only momentary appreciation. That moment was brought even shorter when a familiar voice grated into her ears like nails on a chalkboard.

"Ah, Alice. Good to see you," Andrew Hanbridge greeted.

Alice lifted her eyes to find the black-haired Appleton student intercepting her at a quick walk, inviting himself to link to her side as though he was welcome. She shot him a sideways glare. "Shouldn't you be in Glasgow?" she asked, frowning.

Andrew shook his head, looking straight ahead as he walked. "The Scottish competition is merely a qualifier for the upcoming international competition," he murmured. "And I hardly feel as though the Appleton team needs to subject itself to traveling to such a venue, especially when winning would be guaranteed and we have already qualified."

The words out of his mouth made Alice cringe and she looked away, watching as a few grooms walked the young horses around the shedrows to cool them out or give them a little bit of time outside of their stalls. The last thing she wanted to be doing was talking to Andrew Hanbridge, and yet for some reason he insisted on sticking by her side.

"And what are you doing here, if I may ask?"

"The same thing I assume you are doing," Alice grumbled, fingers fidgeting in her pockets. "Attending the consignment of Thelwell bred yearlings."

"I see you have HIP 262," Andrew commented, flipping open the book of sale horses and turning to her Caravaggio colt. "Do you honestly think you're going to get a fair price for such an ill bred yearling?"

"If you think he's ill bred, you clearly know nothing of European Thoroughbreds," Alice snapped, having to mentally chastise herself to keep her temper in check. "He is from one of our finest stakes winning mares by Candy Ride. He is bred for turf sprinting and nothing else. I suggest you keep your opinions to yourself, seeing as the two horses under your *father's* campaign have yet to break their maiden in their second year."

Andrew grew quiet with the retort. He buried his hands into the pockets of his jeans. "There's no need to be so hostile, Alice," he said. He cleared his throat before asking, "How is Chloe?"

Alice clenched her teeth, rolling her jaw as she lowered her head. Her stride hesitated and she deviated from her intended path and instead brought herself to a stop next to a line of tall hedges that rustled gently in the cool breeze. "I believe you have known the answer to that for some time, Andrew."

The taller male glared down at her, green eyes widening with the raise of his eyebrows as he studied her face. "Did I not warn you?"

She sighed and looked down at her feet, at the dirt that sifted around her paddock boots and stained the sides of the freshly conditioned leather. At one point in time, Andrew had been her friend. They'd both grown up only miles apart in Leeds, raised into the world of horses and bonding through the experience. He had been one of her favorite people and they would often tack one of their parents' horses and meet in the middle of their estates to ride through either town or the rolling fields that stretched the expanse of the rural areas of the province. They told each other everything—Andrew of his first love in sixth form, Alice of the inner turmoil of her own sexuality—and felt nothing but comfort in each other's presence. He filled the void of loneliness that was her life without parents.

But Andrew's first love had been Chloe.

Yet Chloe had only eyes for Alice.

And Alice didn't have the self-control to stop herself from the fairy tale that was youthful romance in the face of her best friend's feelings. The fantasy that became kissing in secret behind the oak trees lining the back of her stable, that was sneaking off in public places to steal back the time that had drifted by with the act of pretending. It wasn't long until Andrew had found them together in the hayloft of the Thelwell barn and everything had fallen apart with the bat of an eye. The girl that he had been pining for, the girl that he had *told* Alice that he was in love with, and as his best friend she had snuck around behind his back and, in his mind, stolen that girl out from under him.

She chose Chloe over Andrew.

And now Chloe had chosen somebody else over both of them, and the two former friends were left with nothing more with the ruins of what was once something akin to family. Andrew had warned her—he had friends at Oxford, friends who had seen how Chloe was changing—and yet she had ignored him and misplaced her trust anyway.

"You did," Alice sighed. She really didn't want to be having this conversation. She knew the fault that she had made well over two years ago. She was aware of the weakness that she had let take hold, the act of betrayal that she had allowed to take place. Alice never claimed to be a perfect person, but even the reflection of her own actions made her sick to her stomach. She clenched her fists and forced her eyes up to Andrew's. "We're even."

Andrew shook his head, chuckling to himself as he kicked at a rock on the ground. "I was never looking to even the score," he said, rolling his shoulders back and leveling green eyes with her own. "Though I would be amiss to say that it didn't bring me pleasure to learn the outcome of your... relationship."

"As much as I am enjoying our conversation, I think it's time for me to be off," Alice grumbled, spinning on her heel. Talking about Chloe was one of the last things that she wanted to do. Talking about Chloe with Andrew was *the* last thing she wanted to do. "Good luck with the auction, Andrew."

"I think luck will be on my side," Andrew called after her. She could hear the grin in his voice. "There's a very nice Caravaggio colt that I have on my agenda."

DALLAS 06:47
www.imga.eu/2018/gs101318
if u want to watch
we ride at 2

Back in her lodging Alice flipped open the MacBook she'd brought with her and put in the address that Dallas had provided. It was after 15:00, but she hoped they were still riding—after all, the competitions seemed to take quite some time. She had a couple hours before the auction took place and she was determined to catch some of it.

She wasn't disappointed.

The video player buffered into the middle of a game. There were six teams, all at varying parts of the same race, and she recognized Brooke racing through the center of a lane with something clutched in her hand. The Hoofbeats team was wearing matching jerseys, long sleeved navy blue athletic shirts with rings of gold around the sleeves and their names in bold lettering on the backs. Alice didn't even know they wore uniforms.

"*St. Andrews is in the lead here for the bottle exchange but Hoofbeats is close behind. Brooke Thornwood with the hand-off to Dallas West,*" the announcer droned.

And Dallas was off like a rocket, the white band around her helmet a flash of light, the gold WEST bright on her back. The chestnut mare was hurtling towards a blue barrel close to the start line and her rider was leaning far to the side, the bottle clutched in her right hand raised high-

She slammed it down on the barrel with the wide arc of an arm, losing no speed. Her legs were wailing against the pony's side, one arm pumping furiously through a whipping chestnut mane, head low and focused.

"St. Andrews has missed the barrel and Hoofbeats has taken over, Grenoble not far behind-"

Chariot swung by the second barrel, closest to the far end of the arena, and Dallas snatched the final bottle from the top. Her limbs were flailing wildly as she pushed her mare forward, asking for as much speed as the pony had to offer. As soon as they flew across the white line that designated the finish, she could see the girl rising in the stirrups and grinning with excitement before the camera panned away.

"One more race here before the end of the first day but Hoofbeats is commanding a dominating lead here with 41 points."

Alice sat back in her desk chair, folding her arms over her chest as she watched the remainder of the competition. Dallas didn't ride in the last race. It was jousting, which Alice vaguely remembered Dallas saying was something that she wasn't that great at, but the team won nonetheless with Amelie crashing home and slamming the final target down at full speed ahead of the other teams by a large margin, throwing the massive stick onto the ground without a second thought and rising in the stirrups to try to calm Star. She could see Dallas, half hanging off her pony as she cheered and high-fived her teammates.

She sighed and stared at the screen of her MacBook, fingers drumming a rhythm against the wooden desk as she watched some of the highlights and glanced over the program for the sale. All of her horses were scheduled to enter the ring that night. Which, wait—

If her horses were going to be sold that evening, that left the entire next day. She might have missed the first full day of competition, but that didn't necessarily mean she had to miss the second...

It wouldn't be hard to rearrange flight times. All she had to do was reroute to Glasgow, which would likely get her there around noon and then all she had to do was call for a driver to get her to the equestrian center by the time the games competition started. All that was required was a little bit of finagling time on her part and she'd be able to actually go—

But she decided she wouldn't do that, because as she stared through the window of her small room for the weekend, at the towering hedges that lined the narrow, unpaved road that led to the bustling stable full of yearlings, she thought of Chloe. She thought of heartbreak, she thought of pain, and she thought about which choice was more likely to lead her there.

And so she closed the page of prospective flights, shut her MacBook, and chose to stay.

Chapter Thirteen

D*ALLAS*

The second day of competition had gone just as smoothly as the first and they had won by a landslide, the closest team near them being St. Andrews by over twenty points. The whole team had done so well that Miss Nelson had even granted them Tuesday and Wednesday off practice for a little bit of much needed rest and relaxation. Even Amelie had given Dallas a pat on the back and a job well done for how well the line-up worked out over the weekend, but Dallas couldn't take all the credit. Amelie had helped with that one, too.

Dallas was still reeling from the excitement as she slumped in the tiny space she'd been alBrooked in the van, letting the droning monotony of the drive tug at her weary eyes. Her earbuds blared SPECTRUM as she stared through the window at the rolling green hills that spanned along the motorway, unchanging for miles. Beside her, she could barely hear Callie and Amelie having some kind of heated debate that was including wild gesticulations and a whole lot of sarcasm. Constance, next to them, quietly played a game on her Switch.

Brooke and Janine had long since fallen asleep next to her, with Brooke's hands limp in her lap and her head resting comfortably on the Russian girl's broad shoulder. Dallas had tried to sleep, but every time she was close to slipping off, some bump in the road jostled her awake. Plus, her legs were already cramping, both from the exhaustion of the weekend and the narrow portion of the seat she was crammed into.

Dallas brought her eyes to the stuffed pony that she held in her lap. She'd seen it at one of the vendor stands. It was cute and bay, with a stripe and a forelock, mane, and tail of black yarn made from hand-spun Scottish wool. It had immediately made her think of Beatrix, obviously, and so she'd bought it for Alice. The other girl had gotten stuck in Ireland and wasn't able to make the competition and visit Glasgow like she wanted, so the least Dallas could do was bring her a memento. If Alice couldn't go to Scotland, Dallas would bring a piece of Scotland to her.

She flipped on the screen of her phone and stared down at the messages. She and Alice had hardly talked all weekend because they had both been so busy. Not that she *expected* it, of course, but every time she got a text from the other girl she felt a rush of excitement.

Sunday, October 14, 2018
Alice 7:59
I saw you won. Congratulations!
Dallas 8:07
thanks ^_^ hows the sale?
Alice 8:37
Colt sold for €550,000. Fillies for €605,000
and €450,000.

Dallas hadn't responded because she'd passed where she'd been laying on her stomach on her way-too-hard bed in her hotel room. She had sent Alice a text that morning when she woke up early as all get out to load the ponies on the van and begin the long journey back to Hoofbeats:

Monday, October 15, 2018
Dallas 5:15
good morning! hope u got back ok

But the entire day had yielded no response. Though, she had messaged the other girl super early—hindsight was 20/20—and Alice was *probably* busy with classes and all, so she shouldn't have really been looking forward to a conversation...

The stuffed horse in her hands suddenly seemed like a really stupid idea. With a heavy sigh, she planted it between herself and the cold van window and leaned her head against it, squeezing her tired eyes shut.

She hadn't even realized that she'd drifted off until her phone vibrated in her hand.

Alice 1:56
When do you get back?

Dallas blinked the sleep out of her eyes and stared at the message for a moment before replying.

Dallas 1:57
a lil over an hour
Alice 1:59
Okay. See you at the barn?

She felt herself grinning. Okay, so maybe the pony hadn't been the worst idea ever. Dallas sat up and caught it before it dropped between the seat and the door, gently swiping the little bit of drool off its back and settling it into her lap. She smiled down at her small rendition of Beatrix.

She couldn't wait to see her friend and tell her all about the competition, to hear about the yearling sale in Ireland, even though Alice had said it would be boring and there wouldn't be much to hear about.

With a deep breath, she glanced at the front of the van, where Miss Nelson looked zonked out of her mind driving, and stared at the expanse of road ahead. They'd been on the road for seven hours already.

What was one more?

Dallas wanted to fall asleep.

And she could have. Right there. On Chariot. Her pony wouldn't care—it wasn't like Dallas hadn't done it before. Many times, in fact.

She had finally finished unpacking and putting her gear back in place and was ready to pass out. After getting her mare settled back into her stall, she had climbed onto the mare's back and wrapped her arms around her neck, fluffy with the incoming winter coat, and buried her face in the stiff hair of her mane. Chariot stood quietly, occasionally stretching her neck to grab a mouthful of hay from her feeder before munching contentedly, ignoring the antics of her owner.

Dallas breathed deep the scent of her horse. Hay and cedar, some leftover Cowboy Magic from the competition to make her coat sleek and shiny. It was nice. She smelled like coming home after a long day away.

"That looks safe," came a familiar voice from outside the stall.

Dallas pressed her hands against Chariot's shoulders and pushed up, swinging her legs down to sit bareback on the quiet mare. She sighed with the effort. Her whole body felt stiff and sore and she really just didn't want to move.

Alice was leaning over the stall door, arms folded against the polished wood. Her wavy blonde hair was pulled back into a loose ponytail, a little damp around the temples from the effort of riding. Her blue eyes were bright with the smile that her lips failed to show.

"What would you know about safety?" Dallas asked, squinting her eyes at the other girl. "I seem to remember you stealing someone's horse and then trying to run them over with it."

Alice smirked and unlatched the door, slipping into the stall and stepping over to the pair. She reached out to Chariot, who regarded her with a glance and a small snort before returning her focus to the hay. "You look positively knackered," she said, running her hands down the mare's soft neck and giving her a gentle pat beneath the mane. "You. Not Chariot. She looks like she could run in the Mongol Derby."

"Well, that's rude," Dallas pouted. She felt Alice's fingers graze against her own as the girl brought her hands down to Chariot's shoulders and pulled back quickly, a hot blush searing her cheeks. She swung a leg over her pony's back and slid back down to her feet, dusting the hair and dirt off the insides of her thighs.

"I managed to catch some of it on the live feed," Alice murmured. She stepped back from Chariot and shoved her hands into the pockets of her jacket. "You looked good." Her tongue darted out and wet her lips before she added, "The team looked good. I apologize for not being able to attend in person."

There was a piece of hay in her ponytail and Dallas resisted the urge to reach out and pluck it away, instead busying her hands in Chariot's mane, her fingers tangling with the hair as she affectionately flopped the muscle back and forth. Chariot ignored her. "That's okay," she replied. "I brought you something."

Dallas stepped outside the stall into the aisle, waiting for Alice to follow before shutting the door and latching it. She threw on a clip—Chariot was smart enough to open her own door and would do so occasionally—before reaching for the pony that was sitting on her wooden tack trunk. She shoved it unceremoniously into Alice's arms and stepped back, clearing her throat behind a closed fist.

"It looks like Beatrix," Alice said, regarding the little stuffed pony in her hands. "I—thank you, Dallas. I... didn't bring you anything, though." She looked up and frowned.

"Sure you did." Dallas flashed a grin. "You came—"

"Ah, Miss West. Just who I was looking for."

Dallas blinked away from Alice to find Miss Willow striding quickly toward her. The woman was wearing a pair of navy blue breeches—though Dallas had never seen her ride—and a thick gray coat that engulfed her thin body. Her straight blue hair was tied into a low ponytail that swayed at her back.

"Oh, I'm sorry, girls." She offered a small smile as she came to a stop, glancing between Alice, who was hugging the stuffed pony tight to her chest, and Dallas, who looked like she had been caught doing something she shouldn't have been. "I'm not interrupting anything, am I?"

"No, Miss Willow," Alice said quickly, stepping back. "I'll take my leave. Dallas... thank you. Again."

Dallas frowned. She had hardly gotten to spend any time with Alice at all. She dipped her head to Alice, briefly meeting blue eyes before the other girl turned and strode off.

Once the blonde was out of earshot, Miss Willow leveled her bright red eyes on Dallas. "I meant to speak with you last week, but I didn't realize you left for the competition on Friday. I wanted to speak to you about a position on the Jump team. Mary recently accepted a transfer to a school in the United States in the coming semester and will be taking Sebastian with her. Hoofbeats will no longer have a rider or horse in the Pony Jumper division."

The Pony Jumper division? Dallas narrowed her eyes and shot a glance at Chariot, who had wandered over to the stall door and was draping her neck over it—as much as she could, being so short, anyway—and huffing at the instructor. Miss Willow reached an arm out and gently stroked the mare's face.

"You want to use Chariot for jumpers?" Dallas asked. It wasn't the first time somebody had approached her about leasing the mare to jump. After all, that's what she had done before Dallas had acquired her. It was her job until the girl who owned her grew to be even taller than Alice and couldn't ride her anymore, which was the only reason she'd come under Dallas's ownership in the first place.

Miss Willow shook her head, lowering her hand and turning back to Dallas. "Not... just Chariot. I was actually interested in the both of you."

"Me?" Dallas's eyebrows stitched together in surprise and she couldn't help but let her mouth drop open a little bit. "I'm not a jumper. I mean, I've done it before, but it's been a long time and..."

"Your position could use some work, yes," Miss Willow countered before Dallas could finish. "But your ability to effectively ride is not even a question. Pony Jumpers is a competitive division and takes somebody with a lot of grit and tenacity. Not to mention a mount with the speed and agility to challenge the others. I see a lot of potential in the two of you."

Dallas felt like she had just been smacked in the head by a wooden plank. She reached up and rubbed at her temple, shoving greasy bangs out of her eyes and taking a deep breath. Miss Willow wanted her... for jumping? The very idea was still something she wasn't sure she believed. If it wasn't coming from someone that was her elder, she would have thought it was a prank.

"I've already spoken with Miss Nelson," Miss Willow added. She shuffled her feet, moving a few pieces of hay into a pile on the stone floor. "I understand that you are here on a scholarship for the Games team and of course that would be a primary commitment. We would only incorporate you in one practice a week and only expect you to make the shows that didn't interfere with your Games competitions."

Dallas stayed silent, so the jump instructor continued.

"There's a show this weekend, if you'd like to just try it and see if you like it. Of course I don't expect an answer straight away. I know this is quite a bit to ask, but I truly think you could go far. I would love to have you on the team. So... just think about it, okay? You can get back to me with your decision."

Dallas nodded, linking her fingers together and tugging at her knuckles. It wasn't as though she hadn't thought about jumping before. When she was a kid, she used to set up her own jump courses in their family's apartment out of couch cushions and pillows. She'd race around on her hands and knees, pretending she was an Olympic show jumper, ripping holes in the knees of her pants along the way and constantly getting scolded by Okaasan.

Not to mention, Octavia Chariot had been a jumper. She knew that she never wanted to do it professionally—she had other plans—but she'd never even had a horse to really try outside from goofing off and it had looked like a lot of fun...

Miss Willow had turned on her heel and started to walk off.

"Wait," Dallas said, stepping forward. Her teeth nibbled at her very chapped bottom lip as she brought her red eyes to meet the instructor's. She was letting her impulse take over, but she could consider those consequences later. "I can give you my decision now."

"You joined the *jump team*?" Brooke asked, staring at Dallas—who was stretched out on the floor of their common area still in the dirty jeans and jumper she'd traveled in—with a look of pure confusion. She'd lifted her glasses off her face and was staring at the other girl with wide blue eyes. "What about Games?"

"Oh, she's abandoned us," Callie deadpanned from where she sat next to Brooke on their very hard plaid couch that had likely been made by people who had never felt comfort in their lives. "What will we ever do without her?"

"I didn't *join*," Dallas said, sitting up and stretching her arms above her head with a wide yawn. "I just said I'd go to the show this weekend and try it out. I'd still be focused a hundred percent on the Games team!"

"Well." Brooke shrugged, flopping back against the couch's equally hard pillows and glancing between the puzzle that she and Callie were midway through (a stock image of wild horses galloping across a field) and Dallas. "If you think you can balance both of those and Miss Nelson and Miss Willow are willing to work with you, I think that's great. I used to jump. It's a lot of fun."

Callie just yawned and folded her legs underneath her. "If that's what you want to do, you know I don't care." She reached into her bag of dried seaweed and plucked one out, shaking her head at Dallas's outstretched hand and burying the bag in her lap. "No."

"I made you ramen last week," Dallas grumbled. "Come on."

She stood and made a lunge for the snack but Callie jerked it away with another resounding, "No!"

And Dallas fell right on top of the coffee table, sending puzzle pieces flying across the floor, under the couch, under the television stand, and into the mini-kitchen that their living area opened into. Probably the hallway, too, but Dallas didn't check.

"Dallas!" Brooke shrieked. She threw herself to the floor and immediately began to shovel puzzle pieces into a pile. "We've been working on that for a week!"

"Oops."

"You're so graceful," Callie said, unable to hide the snicker that worked its way past her lips. "You'll make a very good jumper. Every single pole will be on the ground."

"Aw, come on, I'm sorry," Dallas mumbled. She backed away—but not before snatching a stick of seaweed when Callie let her guard down—and started digging under the couch for puzzle pieces. "Should have just given me one and it wouldn't have happened."

"Well that's a manipulative way of looking at things," Callie said. "Besides, I can't help you're so food aggressive."

"I am not food agg—"

Brooke shot up onto her knees, her short strawberry blonde hair a mess across her forehead, and huffed. "I am way too tired to listen to you guys bicker!" she moaned. "But, Dallas, I think you and Chariot would be good at it. Besides, it's really cool that Miss Willow even offered you a position on the team. It's very hard to get onto. Alice's been trying to get on it since she came to Hoofbeats."

Dallas pulled herself out from under the corner, one fist clutching two puzzle pieces and a whole lot of dust bunnies, and leveled narrowed eyes on Brooke. "Alice wants to be on the Jump team?"

"Yeah," Brooke said. "Well, she did anyway. Last year. Her mom won top honors for the team when she went to school here." She shrugged. "I don't know anything else about it."

"Don't look at me," Callie murmured, raising a palm in defeat. "I don't know and don't care."

Dallas blinked, dropping the handful of dust and cardboard on the table before rising. "I didn't know that," she muttered, reaching up to pass a hand through her dirty hair. Alice had wanted to be on the Jump team. She'd never mentioned that. She always seemed so focused and dedicated to Hunters that Dallas couldn't imagine her wanting to do something else.

"Hey, space cadet, are you gonna help us clean the mess you made or what?" Callie snapped.

File that away for later under Things To Ask Alice About. But that was for the future. With a sigh, she shoved those thoughts away and focused on the present—which was crawling on her hands and knees picking up the puzzle pieces she'd thrown everywhere.

Dallas was struggling to keep her eyes open as she stared at the bright screen of her phone. It felt good to be back in her own bed, which was significantly softer and more comfortable than the one in Scotland, and she burrowed under her heavy blankets, kicking her bare feet against the cold sheets. They hadn't turned on the heat for the dormitory just yet and the bitter air outside meant that she had to sleep in sweatpants and a long sleeve instead of her usual t-shirt and shorts. She pulled her favorite fleece blanket (the one with the horse who looked just like

Chariot) up to her chin and took in the text message that flashed on her screen.

Alice 8:47

Willow asked you to ride in Pony Jumpers? That's great, Dallas.

She had texted Alice to tell her about her conversation with Miss Willow when the other girl messaged her to ask about it. After thanking her—again—for Mini Beatrix.

Dallas 8:48

but I'm not a jumper

and I didn't say yes yet

i'm going to try it in the show this weekend

Alice 8:50

The show in Bedford?

She was pretty sure that's what Miss Willow had said. In all fairness, her mind had been blown just by the proposal of joining the jump team, so the words that left the woman's mouth after that had sounded like a voice calling to her while she was drowning.

Dallas 8:50

yes

I think?

Alice 8:51

I'm going to that show.

Well, that would make sense. Hunters and Jumpers often rode at the same events, they were just critiqued differently. Dallas stifled a yawn and nuzzled the side of her face into her pillow.

Dallas 8:51

*^_^*

Her phone vibrated in her hand and she felt it, but her eyes had drifted shut and she didn't have the energy to turn her screen back on and respond. The weekend and the thoughts running through her head weighed as heavy as the blankets that she was comfortably buried under, and Dallas couldn't stave it off any longer. She fell asleep.

"Kick, kick, kick. Kick! Outside leg! Eyes up, look at the jump!" Miss Willow was hollering across the arena. Dallas and Chariot had just leapt over a low vertical and were expected to roll back immediately into another that was placed right at its side. She pulled Chariot to the right, arcing out in a small circle, before dipping her torso heavily to the left. Chariot switched trajectory with the skill of a cutting horse, pausing only briefly mid-stride to regain her composure before bounding forward. She left the ground too far away from the jump but still managed to clear it, though Dallas popped up in the irons, completely left behind by the movement.

"You have to stay with her," Miss Willow called. Look for the line—good—now breathe. Count your strides in rhythm. One, two, one, two. One, two—jump!"

Chariot's ears flew forward with her body as she hit the first vertical and charged to the oxer. She let one hoof drop and nicked the wooden pole, which rocked uneasily in its cup, but stayed. Dallas stayed with her that time, bending over her neck and shoving her hands forward in the only crest release she knew how to do.

"Bring her back," Miss Willow called. "Girls," she said to the other four riders, who were waiting in the center of the arena, "Go cool your horses. Great job today."

Dallas was breathing heavily as she walked Chariot over to Miss Willow. It was bitterly cold, close to zero degrees, but she was sweating beneath her heavy red coat nonetheless. Only her hands were numb. She would definitely have to get gloves for this. Chariot's nostrils were rolling in heavy pants from the effort of jumping.

Dallas could see the Games team in their own arena. Amelie had stopped to watch and stood in the irons on Star's back, throwing her a thumbs up before turning and walking away. Dallas smiled.

She had been surprised that the Games team rallied with support. Especially Amelie. "At least it's not the Hunt team," the American had said, patting Dallas on the back. "So you're definitely still cool in my books."

"Not bad," Miss Willow said, reaching out to pat Chariot's sweaty neck and ruffle her mane. "She is a wonderful little jumper. The two of you shouldn't have a problem this weekend. I want to see a couple things from you. First, heels down."

Dallas glanced down at her feet. She wasn't used to having the stirrups jacked up so short and had to admit it wasn't at all comfortable. She was used to letting her legs go wherever they wanted. Now they were expected to be securely locked at the girth and her heels had to be pressed down at all times.

"If she were to quit a fence, you would go flying. If you can't get them down, at least keep them parallel with your toe."

Dallas nodded. On instinct, she pressed her weight into her heel and pulled her toes up.

"Next, stay back a little when you get into two-point. You don't need to get so far forward. Just bend at the hips." To demonstrate, Miss Willow pretended she was in a riding position and moved forward. "You're also releasing too much. Your hands barely have to move. Just let them slide forward with the movement of her neck."

"Okay." Dallas shifted in her saddle and scratched at Chariot's withers—at the little white spot she adored—with her cold fingers.

"Finally, I need you to *always* be looking at your next jump. Right now you're caught up in exactly what's happening as it's happening. You need to be ahead at all times, always planning your next move. What corners you're going to cut, what angle you might need to take a fence at. It can be easy to fall into the moment, and I understand why you're doing it right now, but keep that in mind." She gave one final pat to Chariot's neck before pressing one hand to Dallas's knee with a small squeeze, bringing her eyes up to meet Dallas's. "And don't worry about a thing. No one in that division is going to know what hit them this weekend. Good job today."

She turned and walked off. Dallas felt herself smiling as she slouched back in the saddle. She wasn't used to keeping her posture so *rigid* and it felt weird. She nudged her heavily breathing pony into a walk, letting the reins (stiff leather ones that she'd found in her tack trunk, because apparently cotton wouldn't fly) drop against Chariot's neck.

When she finally looked up from her pony, her eyes fell on Alice. The other girl was perched on Beatrix in the middle of the Hunter arena next to her own, where Hannah was going leisurely around a course on Cello. Long blonde hair fell over the front of her shoulder, face pale, nose cherry red from the cold. Beatrix's neck was arched low, lips brushing against her chest with the tight hold on the reins, mouth rolling over her bit and white slobber dripping everywhere.

At first she thought the girl was mad—her expression was stiffly neutral—but then a wide grin spread across Alice's face. She threw her arm out straight and pressed the heel of her hand down, tilting her fingers to the sky, before pointing at her lower leg and mouthing, "Heels."

In response, Dallas kicked her legs free of the stirrup, slumped back low in the saddle, and folded her arms across her chest. She pointed her toes straight at the ground.

Chariot bolted in surprise at the sudden change in position of her rider, flying out to the side with a loud snort, and Dallas had to lurch back upright and grab at the reins to keep the mare from leaping forward and herself from falling off. But in the moment before goofing off and looking foolish, she had seen Alice laugh—and that was worth it.

Chapter Fourteen

A *LICE*

She laid in bed and squeezed the small horse against her chest, staring down at her phone and the few text messages she had shared with Dallas the night before they were set to leave for Bedford. The other girl hadn't replied in a while—she said she was going to go make dinner, a few meals to take with her, and a shower—and Alice was using the time to think about herself and what she wanted.

Well, she knew what she wanted. She wanted Dallas. Her heart and body were screaming for the other girl, struggling in vain against the brain that said, "*That's stupid, it's just asking for hurt.*" It had been a long time since she met anybody that made her feel the way Dallas did—since Chloe, really—and just beating down the feelings that the other girl stirred only made them flare up with a vengeance, brighter and stronger than before. And then, just when she thought that maybe she had control of herself, that maybe she could regulate her emotions, Dallas went and did something impossibly cute and the cask shattered. Again.

She was starting to think that maybe she didn't *want* to hold them back anymore. Maybe the way she felt was a good thing, because when she looked at Dallas she didn't think about heartbreak or Chloe or *anything*, for that matter, because her brain flat-lined with the rest of her.

Alice ran her fingers through the yarn mane, gnawing her bottom lip and letting her eyes glaze in thought.

She had noticed Dallas the very first week she'd come to Hoofbeats. It was impossible *not* to, really, because the other girl was so upbeat and radiant that she drew people to her like a magnet. She was positive and kind and rode that spunky little mare like a rowdy cowboy from an old American western movie. Not to mention she was *desperately* cute.

And so the first time Alice's eyes had fallen on Dallas, she knew she was doomed.

It had been easy to not have feelings for anybody for a long time. First there was heartbreak, when she didn't even want to eat or drink, much less go to class or interact socially with other people outside of mandated situations. Then there was the sadness of solitude, the desperate urge for something, anything to ease the loneliness that gnawed at the inside of her mind like an insatiable parasite. She had shut herself off, hiding in her studies and in Beatrix and behind the closed door of her room and let herself drown in it, let herself be pulled under by wave after wave after excruciating wave-

and then there was the recovery. Where she threw herself into her routine: wake up early, take a shower, eat breakfast, go to class, study between class, go to more classes, go to the stable, ride Beatrix, spend time with Beatrix, go home, study, bed, rinse, repeat, rinse, repeat, rinse, repeat.

Then Dallas.

And she was going out with her friends. She was staying at the barn late to break rules and ride a horse after drinking, past hours and without a helmet. She was telling herself that she shouldn't go to Scotland, that she *couldn't* go to Scotland just to attend a competition just because it happened to have a girl that she very much wanted to watch ride and spend time with. Because that would be absolutely absurd.

And then that same girl came home with a smile on her face and a gift that Alice clutched tight in her arms and wished that it was her instead, because Dallas had this way of making her heart stop and start again with a single smile, made her nerves flare with heat with a single look, made her brain fog in a cloud of desire-

Maybe it was time. Maybe she was ready.

A text message lit up the screen of her phone.

Dallas 21:33

i'm clean and fed so u can stop worrying! :3

not that you were

maybe you were

anyway

Dallas 21:34

hi

A smile crept across her face. The rest of those feelings smashed through that wall she'd built and she didn't even know if she wanted to put it back up again, because she had the feeling that this was going to get

so

much

worse.

And maybe it was worth it.

Dallas was passed out in the passenger seat, her head resting on the pillow she'd smashed against the window and was hugging the life out of. In the backseat, Hannah and Barbara were slumped against each other. Barbara was asleep and had been since about five minutes into the drive, but Hannah had woken up recently and was browsing something on her phone.

"You doing okay, Alice?" the auburn-haired girl asked, lowering her phone for a moment and turning her head to look at their driver. Barbara grunted with the movement and readjusted herself on Hannah's shoulder.

Alice glanced in the rear-view. "I'm fine, thanks."

She had chosen to drive. The van would have been packed to the brim between the Hunter/Jumper teams and Alice decided she would rather be behind the wheel for the four hour trip than piled uncomfortably into a small place with a bunch of other girls. She'd invited Dallas to ride with them for company, because the girl knew nobody on the Jump team and she had the extra seat. Plus, they were friends. Right? Friends.

Hannah and Barbara had insisted the other girl take the passenger seat. Alice knew why, but Dallas just thought they were being nice. She'd taken it without a fuss. Alice didn't mind.

She could hear the music still blaring from the earbuds that had long since fallen out of Dallas's ears. They lay draped across the pillow, tousled into knots with the bumps in the road and the Japanese girl's constant squirming. Her brunette hair was splayed everywhere and there was a wet spot under her mouth where she was drooling, open-mouthed, against the dark fabric. Her hands were buried deep in the sleeves of a baggy hoodie.

Alice rested one hand on her gear shift and readjusted in her seat, rolling her shoulders in a small stretch. There wasn't much longer left in their drive, though it had been dark for quite a while and she couldn't wait to climb into bed. Between classes earlier in the day, packing her own gear, packing Beatrix's gear, plus loading all the horses and getting them settled in the van... she was exhausted. Plus they still had to get the horses unloaded and into their temporary stables for the weekend along with water, hay, and their supper.

Sleep would be a welcome respite, especially with the early morning that awaited them.

Dallas took a sharp intake of breath at her side and pushed herself up, lips smacking as she glanced down at the puddle of drool on her pillow before lowering it to her lap. She swiped her mouth with her sleeve and arched her back in a stretch, reaching forward and planting her hands onto the dashboard as she yawned loudly.

She turned to Alice. "Where are we at?" she mumbled.

"Half an hour outside Bedford," Alice replied. She glanced over, watching as the other girl rubbed her temple and smoothed her wild hair. Red eyes blinked sleepily into her own and she smiled in a way that made Alice's stomach turn. She brought her eyes back to the motorway and the dark of night. "So, almost there."

Dallas hummed. She swiveled in her seat, her arm brushing against Alice's elbow as she peered back at Hannah and Barbara. Hannah's phone had fallen back down against the seat with her eyes were shut, breath coming slow and peaceful. "Sorry," she chuckled, straightening back up and rubbing the back of her neck. "I guess we're bad company."

"Not at all." Alice slowed with the van of horses in front of them, following the other vehicle off a slip road and into a more rural setting. Green hills and trees loomed on all sides, towering shadows against the dark sky. "I don't mind." She let the corner of her vision travel to Dallas's lap, where the tips of her fingers fidgeted in her lap beneath her sleeves. "Are you doing okay?"

"Mhmm." Dallas looked over and gave that half-smile again. Alice felt a pang in her gut and took a sharp breath, pulling her hand away from the gearshift and instead placing it on the steering wheel.

"Are you nervous?" Alice asked after a few moments. Dallas had turned to look through the window at the passing scenery, none of which was very discernible at night. Her feet were kicked forward far under the dash and she was slumped into the seat, looking almost childish with the seatbelt nearly digging into her neck.

"Nah." Dallas straightened back up and started messing with the radio, pressing buttons at random in exploration.

"Knock it off," Alice grumbled, swatting her hand away. Dallas brought it back up. A challenge. Alice swatted it down again. "Stop that. You're going to make it 40 degrees in here."

"Like this?"

Dallas started pressing the temperature gauge to crank it up.

"Damnit, Dallas." She pushed the girl's hand away and turned everything back to the usual setting. "I really don't want to sweat the rest of the way there, stop it."

Dallas's hand crept forward once again and Alice grabbed it on impulse. Clutching the soft fingers between her own, she lowered her hand to the gearshift and rested her wrist on top, clasping Dallas's hand in her own. She could feel the muscles twitch for a moment before her hand relaxed, though she made no move to pull it away.

So neither did she.

She could sense crimson eyes on the side of her face. Her heart slammed hard against the front of her chest, her foot stuttered on the accelerator, and she felt a hot blush spreading to the tips of her ears. She swallowed. Hard.

Dallas's fingertips danced against her palm. The edge of her sleeve brushed against the soft part of Alice's wrist.

Alice set her jaw hard, focused on the back of the van ahead that read *CAUTION, HORSES* and below that *HOOFBEATS EQUESTRIAN TEAM.* Dallas's hand closed around her own and squeezed.

"Um, Alice?"

Alice took a deep breath and let her gaze drift momentarily to Dallas. The girl was staring back at her, wide eyed, her face a bright cherry red and her teeth clamped down on her bottom lip.

"You can... let go," the other girl squeaked. "I won't mess with it again."

"Oh." Tendons and ligaments tightened in her hand as Dallas slowly squirmed free. "Right." She clenched her fist tight with embarrassment and pulled her arm away, gripping the steering wheel with both hands until her knuckles were white against the dark leather. She could feel how clammy her palms were, how her skin itched with the boiling of her blood, how the throbbing muscle in her chest threatened to burst from the confines of her ribcage.

And Alice sweat the rest of the way there.

Alice realized two problems very quickly.

One, she was going to have to spend the entire weekend with the same girl that she was trying very hard not to crush on.

Two, *she was going to have to sleep in the same bed as the same girl that she was trying very hard not to crush on.*

Alice stared into the lodging that she was sharing with Dallas, Hannah, and Barbara. At the two double beds that were feet apart on one side of the room. One of which she was most definitely going to have to share with Dallas.

She knew that, because Hannah had turned and given her a wink as soon as they opened the door to the room.

"Alright, we're going to go find the vending machines!" Hannah exclaimed, grabbing Barbara's sleeve and yanking her from the room as soon as they'd dropped their luggage.

"We are?" Barbara squeaked, glancing furiously between Hannah and Alice. She seemed to understand very quickly, because she nodded her head resolutely and said, "Yeah, we are!" and stormed from the room along with the other girl.

"Don't know what they'd want so late," Dallas mumbled. She threw her bag on the ground and started rummaging through it before jerking her hoodie off over her head. Alice tried not to stare and swallowed hard as she began searching for her own sleep clothing. "I'm ready for bed, they're out of their mind."

"Same," Alice said quickly. She pulled out a t-shirt and shorts and raised her eyes to Dallas, who was already fumbling her way out of her long-sleeve shirt. She could see the abs rippling beneath smooth skin, the muscles shivering along her sides below the black sports bra that hugged her chest, and felt her face grow hot and flush. "Uh—I'm going to change... in the loo," she said quickly and rushed into the small washroom, slamming the door shut with probably way too much force. She let her body collapse against the sink to take a deep breath. She didn't know if she could do this. She already found the other girl insanely attractive and had already accidentally held her hand and had to look at that perfect body *again* and now she had to *sleep in the same bed* and try to be *completely normal.*

By the time she was sure her face wasn't so red, she slipped cautiously from the washroom. Dallas was already laying in bed on the side she deemed would be her own. Hannah and Barbara still weren't back. She pictured the other two girls off in a stairwell somewhere, sitting down while they wasted time and goofed off amongst themselves, probably laughing at how much Alice was panicking.

Dallas was sitting up against the pillow, staring down at her phone as though in some deep state of concentration. She looked up and stared at Alice for a moment before saying, "Of course you're the kind of girl who folds your dirty clothes."

Alice looked down at the stack of laundry in her hand and shrugged. "How else would I pack efficiently?"

Dallas shrugged. "I always just cram it in there. What's the big deal? Just gonna go in the laundry anyway."

"And of course you're the type of girl that does *that*," Alice shot back, setting her folded clothes down on her closed luggage bag. She hesitated for a moment as her cool blue eyes fell on the other side of the bed, where the blankets were still pulled up beneath the pillow.

How was she supposed to sleep next to an impossibly hot girl and *not* have inappropriate thoughts? She let her eyes trail to Dallas, at the confused expression that was etched across the other girl's face, at the smooth neck and collarbones peeking out from beneath the neck of her shirt. At the teeth that rolled over her bottom lip as she gazed back at Alice.

She forgot she was staring.

Dallas's dark eyebrows scrunched together. "Are you okay?"

"Uh, yes. Yes." She cleared her throat and rolled her shoulders, slowly climbing into the bed next to Dallas. It was small—way smaller than her own bed—and she was acutely aware of the proximity of Dallas's warm body, of the bare legs that whispered against her own.

Where in the bloody hell were Hannah and Barbara?

"Um, where are Hannah and Barbara?" Dallas asked.

As if on cue, they heard the swipe of the keycard on the door and the other two girls stepped into the room, whispering between themselves before striding into view.

Hannah was wearing a devious grin. "Found the vending machines," she said, though she held nothing in her hands.

"Yup," Barbara confirmed. She held nothing in her hands, either.

"I'm surprised you two were able to keep your clothes on," Hannah added.

Dallas sat up next to Alice. The covers slid to her waist and Alice let her breath catch in her throat as she stared at the other girl's side and the blatantly obvious fact that she wasn't wearing a bra beneath a white t-shirt.

This was lesbian torture.

Alice shot at glare at Hannah, one that she hoped very clearly said, "*If you say anything more, I will kill you and carve your skin off your body to use as a throw rug at the entrance of the Thelwell Manor so that everybody who enters and leaves will trample on your once very smug remains*," though she was fairly certain Hannah didn't get the message because she just smirked and walked into the washroom.

If Alice thought it had been bad then, the lights being off were worse. She could feel the gentle rise and fall of Dallas's chest next to her as she settled down on her side, her face buried into the same lumpy pillow that she'd drooled all over in the car. She was facing the middle of the bed, one hand shoved contentedly between the two pillows, and Alice stared at the fingers that were inches from her nose, at the peaceful face with the eyelids pressed delicately closed. At the soft brunette hair splayed over the pillow and the thin white shirt that covered one of the nicest bodies she had ever seen.

All she had to do was sit up, to plant one palm on the other side of Dallas's head. To bend down and take those lips in her own. Dallas would kiss her back and Alice would grind her body down against the other girl's athletic frame, roll her hips against those impossibly smooth thighs, nip and kiss down the pulse point of her neck until Dallas was squirming and begging-

Her heart was slamming against her chest, throbbing into her skull and pounding against her ears. She rolled over onto her back and took a deep breath, squeezed her eyes shut, and tried very hard not to think about it.

But she did make a mental note to add batteries to her shopping list for that week.

She and Beatrix were in the 120cm Division, which consisted of one under saddle class and three over fence classes—one based purely on equitation. The next two over fences classes would take place on Sunday, so she only had one remaining for the day as she had already completed the under saddle class. She'd taken first, which she had humbly stated was a difficult class and therefore couldn't be sure of the victory, but inside she knew Beatrix was one of the best looking movers around and her equitation was unrivaled on the flat.

Hannah had already finished, taking Reserve Champion in the 100cm Division, and Barbara had taken Champion in her Green Horse Over Fences classes, which Alice was especially proud of as it was the pair's first award of that caliber. She'd been sure to tell her such.

Perched on her tall bay mare, Alice watched one of the riders on the line-up ahead of her cantering quietly around the arena. The horse had hardly enough impulsion to make it over fences of that height and his rider was much too forward. He was straining to get over the jumps, and it finally paid over a three tier oxer. His hoof nicked the top rail and it fell. Alice felt bad—the rider looked absolutely devastated.

Alice was next on deck, right after the rider on the tall flea-bitten gray gelding waiting nearby. She swiveled in her saddle, finding the group of other riders gathered near the other arena.

The Pony Jumper division hadn't started yet. First they needed to finish up the 130cm Jumper classes before the course was rearranged and the the riders had a chance to walk through and discuss strategy with their trainers.

She could see Dallas standing with Chariot, looking entirely out of place. The other girl had dug old show clothes out of her closet—a pair of white breeches and a navy hunt coat that was very out of season (though Alice supposed it didn't matter for the Jumpers), a white dress shirt that collared tight around her neck, and a stock tie that Alice had to help her with earlier in the morning. She was wearing the same jockey-style helmet she wore in her Games competitions.

The other girl's hand was running down Chariot's neck in slow movements, the other clutching the hard leather reins that Alice had told her that she absolutely *needed* to condition because their current status was *unacceptable*. She was wearing a pair of Hannah's older gloves—the other girl had hands around the same size and happened to carry an extra pair—because Alice had insisted that she not blister her hands against reins that rough.

Alice had personally taken it upon herself to braid Chariot's mane. Dallas had told her that it wasn't necessary, but Alice had very slowly stated:

"I beg to differ, Dallas, because you can tell you hacked this pony's mane off with a dull pair of scissors and you will not represent Hoofbeats looking like this."

to which Dallas had merely grumbled and kicked cedar in the aisle while Alice got to work, twisting her fingers monotonously through the pony's thick mane.

And then she'd braided *Dallas's* hair, because she wasn't about to let the other girl walk out there in a messy bun and call it show fashion. The girl hadn't protested. In fact, she had sat quite still while Alice ran her fingers through the long, soft brunette hair, feeling it fall through her fingers like liquid, before carefully bringing it back into a french braid and tying it off with Dallas's stretched out hair tie ("This one's about to break in half," Alice had said, but Dallas had countered with, "It's my favorite," and that was that) before sending her on her way.

Miss Willow had thanked the Hunt team profusely when she came by and saw the appearance of her newest pupil. Alice humbly accepted the gesture as she watched Dallas and Chariot walk off with pride that she figured was akin to a proud parent.

All in all, the pair didn't look to bad. Out of place, yes, but not bad. Chariot desperately needed a clip—she was starting to look like one of those ponies that stood in the mountains of Iceland and stared into photographer's lenses—and a few other aesthetic corrections. If Dallas chose to stay on the Jump team, Alice would help. If she didn't,

Alice would still help, because the pony looked like it had walked out of someone's backyard and into Dallas's rowdy hands and she was *not* about to let them go to an International competition looking like that.

"Miss Thelwell," the ringmaster called. "On deck."

Alice squeezed her calves against Beatrix and the large mare perked up and stepped forward. The rider before her was coming over the last line, looking elegant and, all in all, like a challenging competitor, before finishing with the traditional circle closest to the arena gate. As the ringmaster let the other pair out, Alice nodded to a very quiet, "Good luck," from the previous rider and urged Beatrix in at a flowing trot.

"Now in the arena is number 184, Alice Thelwell riding Beatrix."

She could feel eyes on her from the stands, from around the edges of the arena, from the judge's booth. But it didn't bother her. She let herself get lost in her mare, in the bold stride that flowed beneath her, in the swivel of large bay ears as Beatrix responded. She sat deep and Beatrix transitioned easily to a smooth canter.

The fences were large and imposing, but neither Alice or Beatrix were phased. Alice counted in her head, felt the length of the strides beneath her and altered her aids in minor adjustments as needed. Which was hardly an issue, because Beatrix was a learned professional, an athlete at the top of her game, and so each jump came and went with the ease of the last. When she had finished—arcing her body over her mare's rippling back and neck over the final oxer—her onlookers had erupted into applause. She let herself drift back into the saddle and brought the mare back down, offering a small nod to the judges before leaving the arena at a slow trot.

She would have to be present for the results, but there were still a handful of riders left to complete the course and, so, instead, she walked Beatrix directly over to the jumping arena, where Dallas was standing in front of the printed jump layout and moving her fingers in the pattern of the course. Her lips mouthed each number.

"Are you nervous?" she asked, not for the first or last time that weekend. Dallas turned and looked up, giving Chariot a soft tug on the reins before the mare could bend down and snatch a mouthfull of grass.

"Oh, hey." A small smile flickered across her lips. "You looked really good!"

She had been watching? "Thank you," Alice said, forcing down the hint of a smile and letting her face fall neutral as she glanced between the printed course and the arena, where the jump crew was setting everything up.

Dallas hummed and turned back to the course. She stretched an arm out and ran her fingers between the jumble of lines and numbers. "This is hard," she groaned, frowning. "There's so much to memorize."

"That's why you walk the course," Alice said. Beatrix shifted underneath her and Alice let her take a step forward to get more comfortable. "Miss Willow will take you around and make sure you've got everything down. It's only twelve fences, Dallas."

"Eh, I don't know," Dallas mumbled. "I have the memory of a lobotomized goldfish."

Alice chuckled. "I'm sure it's not that bad."

Dallas turned her gaze up with a raised eyebrow that said, "*Yes, it is that bad.*"

"Miss West, are you ready?" Miss Willow was walking over when the announcer called out for the course walk. "Wangari can hold Chariot for you."

Dallas passed off her pony to her not-yet-teammate and stepped off with a small nod to Alice and a, "Good luck!" just as the announcer called for a final under saddle portion and line-up of Alice's division.

Alice lingered for a moment, watching the short girl stride off with a confident step but a nervous glint in her eyes. Her gloves fingers were rapping against her coat as she walked carefully, awkward in the tall black boots that she clearly hadn't broken in all the way.

Yes, Dallas looked very much out of place, but also so gorgeous that Alice had to force the blush out of her cheeks as she turned and walked Beatrix back to her own responsibilities.

The Pony Jumper Division was massive. Alice had plenty of time to cool Beatrix, untack, and quickly brush her off before putting her back into her temporary box with a flake of hay. She slipped the mare a few pieces of carrot before tossing her helmet onto a hook and rushing across the show grounds to catch Dallas's class. Hannah and Barbara, who had been hanging out chatting on a few overturned 20 gallon buckets with what Alice *knew* was a bottle of something that was very against show rules (she chose to ignore it, she was in a hurry) came along with her.

It seemed *everyone* was curious to watch the new pony and rider pair, because the whole Jump team—Alice knew they had finished earlier in the day—was there to watch. She slid in with them, nodding to Wangari as she took her place on the fence and raised one boot to rest on the rail.

The ponies were fast and agile, zipping around the arena and flying over fences at a pace that was unfathomable for a larger horse. They cut turns, jumped verticals and oxers at unlikely angles, dashed over long distances in a burst of quick strides. Some of them pulled rails in their rush to beat the best time. A bright red digital clock, counting milliseconds into seconds into minutes, added another four seconds for each.

Dallas still didn't look that perturbed. She sat atop Chariot, quietly watching the other riders with an expression mixed with curiosity and admiration. The small chestnut mare seemed calm, but Alice knew that she would fly into action as soon as she was asked.

"Geez, this seems reckless," Barbara murmured at Alice's side. She was watching a small gray pony launching itself over a massive oxer after coming in extremely short to the fence. The poorly timed ride paid its due diligence and a few of the rails came crashing down.

Hannah shot a glance at Barbara. "We're talking about Dallas here. Reckless fits. Have you *seen* the way she hangs off that pony? I'm surprised she still has all her limbs."

"Girls," Alice scolded. She folded her arms across the top of the fence and watched.

Finally, it was Dallas's turn. Alice could see the gears turning in the girl's head. Dallas's face was more serious than

Alice had ever seen it, lips pursed in thought as her crimson eyes scanned the jumps that spanned the arena. At the gate, Miss Willow called out, "Good luck, Dallas."

"Now in the arena is number 208, Dallas West riding Swift Chariot."

The announcer hacked her name to all hell and Alice rolled her eyes and grumbled under her breath.

Dallas trotted Chariot to the middle of the arena where she brought the mare to a skidding halt—Chariot rose up on her two rear legs, reading the anxiety of her rider—and dropped one hand and the bill of her helmet in a quick salute, just as Miss Willow had taught her. A whistle blew, and the pair were off.

Dallas looked so different. She was sitting deep in the saddle, not throwing herself all around like she usually was, with her hands pulled back nearly into her lap as she guided Chariot to the first fence. The mare's front legs danced in front of her as she set back on her hindquarters, teeth flashing around the bit as she raised her head and strained for speed that Dallas wasn't letting her have.

The crossed between the cones that started the timer, and Dallas gave Chariot a little bit of rein.

The mare flew forward.

They caught the first vertical a bit long but Dallas stayed with her pony all the way and her hooves cleared the rails with space in between. Five strides, another jump, this one at a better distance, and the two landed and swung to the left.

Dallas's legs were swaying a little underneath her—she hadn't quite gotten accustomed to having to keep her body in the same place—and Alice watched as she thought about it and corrected herself. She pushed her heels down and threw her toes forward, rocking back in the saddle and bringing her mare up under her a little bit more as they took one final stride and flew over a wide wall. A small circle back across the arena, a triple bar. Chariot was confident, excited, and Dallas was looking good. She was swiveling her head, looking for her next obstacle, the mare beneath her hopping and ready at her fingertips-

Dallas eased her back a little bit, planting her seat deep in the saddle and scanning.

She was still looking, even as Chariot rounded the corner and was guided around an oxer at the end of the arena. One that Alice was *pretty* sure was the next jump.

She could see the confusion, the flash of pained desperation as Dallas just picked a jump and went for it.

Alice didn't have to hear the whistle to know. She stepped back from the fence, sighing heavily. Beside her, Hannah and Barbara groaned in shared empathy.

Dallas had forgotten her course and gone off. She'd been disqualified.

Chapter Fifteen

D*ALLAS*
She forgot the course.

Her heart was thrumming against her chest as she stood in the irons and glanced around the arena, feeling her own confusion feeding to Chariot as she desperately searched for the next jump. She had been so focused on the moment, on speed and accuracy and the power of the pony at her fingertips, that the rest of the course had slipped out of her mind and she had no idea where she was going.

She guided Chariot around an oxer at the far end of the arena—kuso, was that the next jump?—but she had no time to dwell on it because if it was, she would be disqualified for passing over her own line, anyway, and so she picked a vertical across the diagonal and just went for it.

As soon as Chariot's feet left the ground, a whistle shrilled from the gazebo that overlooked the arena. Dallas and Chariot landed, easily clearing the fence, but it didn't matter. Nothing that she did had mattered, because she had been disqualified for going off course.

Dallas clenched her jaw and turned to look at the judges, who weren't even looking at her but down at something they were writing on. She stood, pulling the reins up to her chest and dropping her startled pony to a trot—Chariot wanted to keep going—before heading to the gate that was already open for her. She could see Miss Willow standing near the rest of the Jump team, watching. She didn't look upset or mad, but she definitely didn't look happy either. If Dallas had to guess, her expression was... disappointment.

And Alice was there. She hadn't even noticed that Alice had come back to watch. She was standing with Hannah and Barbara and was wearing a rather sad smile, hands shoved into the navy blue Hoofbeats Equestrian Team jacket she'd thrown on over her stark white show blouse.

She could feel the color flooding her face as she sat down on the saddle and brought Chariot to a walk, kicking her feet out of the stirrups and wishing that she could disappear, or, better yet, just take off galloping with her little chestnut mare and not look back.

"It's okay, Dallas," Miss Willow said carefully as she strode forward and closed a hand around Chariot's nose. She reached out with her other hand and placed it on Dallas's lower leg and the stiff leather boots. "It was your first time and these courses can be confusing. You have another two courses tomorrow, we'll make sure it doesn't happen again."

Dallas frowned and looked down, idly scratching at Chariot's neck for a moment before sliding down off the mare. She could feel the blisters hot on the back of her heels from the boots and was suddenly hyperaware of exactly how uncomfortable she felt. She missed her team, her coach, the freedom of charging across the arena and not worrying about a thing except a single task at hand. Games was one at a time, step-by-step, and she could always count on her teammates to have her back if she made a mistake. This was all her. And she had failed.

"Go take care of her and try not to worry about it," Miss Willow added. She gave Chariot one last stroke on the face. "It's not a big deal. I promise."

"Alright," she choked out, nodding sadly and sliding the reins over Chariot's head. She took the stirrups and tossed them across the saddle, not even bothering to run them up, before slackening the girth. The mare was still blowing a little bit and turned to press her flaring nostrils against Dallas's leg, her breath warm and wet in the brisk air.

Dallas could see Alice turn and say something to Hannah and Barbara just as she was turning to lead Chariot back to the temporary stables across the show grounds. She didn't know if she wanted to face the other girl just yet—she was humiliated and so angry with herself—but she said nothing when the blonde caught up and matched stride on the other side of Chariot's shoulder. It wasn't Alice's fault that she was an idiot.

"You looked great," Alice said. Her braid was still perfect—how was it perfect after wearing a helmet all day?—and her show attire looked like it had been freshly laundered. The white collar that wrapped around her neck gave her usually pale skin a little bit of color. Her nose and cheeks were red from the cold.

Dallas glanced up momentarily before bringing her gaze back down. The other girl was looking at her in a way that made her feel vulnerable. "Thanks, I guess," she mumbled.

Alice reached a hand out and set it on Chariot's withers as she walked, fingers threading around the last braid and squeezing. "I mean it," she said. "You don't have to worry about forgetting your course. It happens to everybody. I've forgotten plenty of courses in my time."

"Really?"

Alice shrugged and pulled her hand away, shoving it back into her pocket. "Of course."

Dallas sighed and reached up to unbuckle her helmet as she brought Chariot up in front of the stall. Beatrix poked her head over the adjacent stall door, contentedly munching on some hay as she looked at the three new additions. Alice stepped over and took the mare's head between her hands, gently stroking the soft muzzle.

Dallas watched the blonde as she picked up Chariot's halter and replaced it with the bridle, affectionately scratching the mare's forehead before tying her off to a piece of twine she'd hooked around one of the wooden posts. Alice had tried to make her feel better and she *knew* that, but it didn't stop her from feeling stupid. Her pony had tried so hard and was doing so perfectly and all she did was let her down. She unbuckled the girth and dragged the saddle off, tossing her helmet to the ground with her other hand, and stared at Chariot's sweaty back with frustration.

All that for nothing.

"Are you alright, Dallas?"

Dallas focused on the mare in front of her and swiped the palm of her gloves against her eyes. She ducked down and started pulling off Chariot's splint and bell boots, throwing them to the side with the rest of the gear she'd unceremoniously dropped to the ground. Brown sweat had trickled down into Chariot's white stockings and she ran a thumb thoughtfully against the damp hair. She was well aware of Alice dropping Beatrix's head and rounding her pony, of the tall boots that had stopped next to her.

"Dallas."

"I'm fine," she grumbled, rising and planting her palms against Chariot's back. Her mare let out a rumbling snort and stomped a hoof.

Dallas felt warm arms closing around her and pulling her in tight. Her breath hitched in her throat, her muscles stiffening on impulse against the sudden contact. She let her arms hang uselessly at her sides, one hand still clutching one of Chariot's small rubber bell boots, and slowly let herself relax into the strong arms that enclosed her. Her head fell against Alice's shoulder and she breathed deep the scent of helmet sweat and horse that was clinging to the other girl. She squeezed her eyes shut and crinkled her nose in rigid determination not to cry. It wasn't as though she was sad. She was just so *frustrated.*

"Don't be so hard on yourself," she felt Alice say into her hair. "You looked lovely out there. There's no reason you don't belong. Your riding made that very clear today. It was impressive. And, don't forget, there's always tomorrow. If not tomorrow, the next day."

Dallas's heart was echoing a desperate rhythm in her chest and she hoped that Alice couldn't feel it. She let the boot slip from her limp fingers and hit the ground as she wrapped her arms around the other girl's waist, pressing into the warmth and the comfort that enveloped her, and let out a long sigh.

"Thank you," she murmured, and let herself enjoy the contact while it lasted.

After a few moments, Alice let her arms drop and stepped backwards, clearing her throat into a closed fist. Her face was a little more flushed than before as she met Dallas's eyes before turning back to her own horse. "Don't forget to put her neck nylon on to protect those braids," she said. "I'd prefer not to have to do them again tomorrow."

Dallas nodded, even though the other girl wasn't even looking at her and probably didn't see, before bringing her attention back to Chariot. But her movements were interrupted and she didn't really know what to do next. Sweaty pony. Right. Brush. She reached into her grooming kit and pulled out a stiff brush and slowly began to drag it over Chariot's damp hair, putting her focus completely into the monotonous action instead of the tall, gorgeous girl that was standing only feet away. The tall, gorgeous girl who had just hugged her, whose warm breath had ghosted over her ear, whose fingers were just gripped into her shoulder blades.

The tall, gorgeous girl that was going to put her into cardiac arrest before the weekend was over.

Dallas had let herself get dragged out.

Not that it had been *hard* for Hannah and Barbara to convince her. She really felt like she deserved a beer after the events of the day, and so she'd agreed after initial hesitation. Alice had at first joined her in a refusal, but she relented once Dallas said that she would go.

And so, freshly showered but lazy in jeans and her Mounted Games jacket, Dallas found herself in a pub in downtown Bedford at the bar with Alice and the two other Hunt team girls at her side. She sighed with relief as her lager was placed in front of her and brought it to her lips with a long, slow sip. Alice pulled over her own gin and tonic, fingers running around the edge of the glass.

Dallas was starting to realize that all English pubs kind of looked the same. Small, dark, and filled with the resounding call of football games and chatter of groups of friends. This particular bar—which Hannah and Barbara explained they went to every time they were at the Bedford show—was decorated with stuffed, fluffy white mountain goats and colorful ducks that were mounted between electric torches on wooden walls. Dallas eyed the goat closest to her, who was staring back with black glass eyes. It had three horns, one of which was clearly a later addition to the top of its head.

She figured that was the reason the pub was called *The Three Horned Goat*. She grunted and turned her attention back to her beer and the tired girl at her side.

"Can I ask you a question?" she asked after a moment. She ran a hand through her clean and still somewhat damp brown hair and tousled it over her shoulder, leveling crimson eyes on the side of Alice's face.

"Depends," Alice responded. She lifted her drink to her lips and took a sip, carefully holding the small straw out of the way. "Question for a question?"

Dallas watched as she lowered the glass back to the wooden bar before ripping the straw out completely and tossing it onto the side of the napkin with a huff. "Okay. Deal," she agreed.

"Go ahead, then."

Alice was peering at her with bright blue eyes, shimmering against the pale light above the bar, and she had to take in a sharp breath before remembering her initial question. She could hear Hannah and Barbara chatting animatedly on the other side of the blonde, both looking at something on Hannah's phone. "Is it true that you were trying to get on the Jump team?" she finally asked.

Alice brought her drink back to her mouth and hesitated before sipping. "I—yes, I was trying to get a spot on the team. Last year," she replied. She looked down at the bar, wavy blonde hair framing her face in gold.

"What happened?" Dallas sipped her beer, sliding her fingers down the cold and sweating glass, as she took in the change in attitude. She turned in her barstool, feeling her knee brush up against the other girl's thigh, and awkwardly adjusted her leg.

"Nope." Alice shook her head, momentary look of sadness quickly switching to a playful smirk. "My turn. Why Hoofbeats?"

Dallas chuckled and brought her hand to the back of her head, gently scratching at her scalp. "Uh, it's going to sound really stupid, but it's always been my dream to go to Hoofbeats. It's where Octavia Chariot went to school."

Alice hummed, a wistful smile coasting across her lips. "So you chose a university based on where your childhood idol went?" She chuckled and drank her gin and tonic, the ice clattering against the sides of the glass. "What a marvelous reason to choose a place of schooling."

"Hey, it's as good a reason as any!" Dallas said defensively, swallowing some beer and lowering the pint onto the bar with a much louder than intended bang. The bartender shot her a look and she glanced away sheepishly. "I don't see an issue with it. Besides, I kind of figured this would be a judgment free zone," she grumbled.

"I never said that," Alice replied. She looked amused at Dallas's reaction. "I'll judge you all I want. Who says I haven't already?" She smirked. "And as for what happened, yes, I was actively competing for a spot on the Jump team. My mother rode in Jumpers when she went to Hoofbeats, and so it was *my* dream," she placed heavy emphasis on the statement, "to follow in her footsteps. Unfortunately, Beatrix was injured late last spring. She tore a suspensory. Jumpers would have been too demanding and placed too much stress on her, so I chose to stay on the Hunt team." She looked down into her drink, turning the glass in her hand. "Bea was the last horse my mother bred. I would have had to get another horse."

"Oh." Dallas looked down at her own half-finished lager. She kind of already knew the answer to her next question, but she asked it anyway. "Is your mom—"

"Yes," Alice interrupted, shifting her seat on the barstool—her thigh pressed up against Dallas's knee again, but Alice didn't move and so Dallas didn't, either—and swallowing the last of her drink in one quick gulp. "She passed away when I was young. My father, too. I was raised by my Aunt." Glistening blue eyes turned to meet crimson and she offered a reassuring smile that said, *Don't worry, I'm perfectly okay*, but Dallas still felt remorse tugging at her heart. "And you're terrible at this game. I get two questions." She waved the bartender for another drink and settled back.

Dallas pouted and rolled her eyes.

Alice waited for her new drink before asking, "Why Mounted Games?"

Dallas's eyebrows scrunched together. "I don't know." She shrugged. "It's fun. Do I need any more of a reason than that?"

The other girl's eyes scanned her face for a moment. "I suppose not."

"Alright, you've got one more. Then it's my turn."

"Right."

Alice looked away quickly, wrapping both hands around her new drink. She tossed the straw out again before holding it to her mouth and taking a *very* large gulp. Dallas took the opportunity to drink some of her own beer while she waited and—hold on, was Alice *blushing*?

"I—I was wondering," she started when she lowered the glass, her hands fidgeting around the edge, "If you maybe wanted to—"

Alice froze. Her eyes locked on something across the bar and a shadow passed over her face. Her nervous smile faltered. "I... um. I actually...," she stuttered, then finished with very enunciated, "*Fuck*." Dallas swiveled in her stool, following the other girl's eyes but seeing nothing but a bunch of other people gathered around a table.

"What's wrong?" she asked, returning her attention to Alice.

"My ex," Alice hissed. She shrank down into her jacket and looked away, face shielded beneath a wall of blonde, and stared pointedly at her drink.

"Your... what?" Dallas turned to look over her shoulder again.

"*My ex-girlfriend,*" Alice growled, snagging the sleeve of Dallas's jacket and tugging. "Stop staring, would you?"

Flames burst into Dallas's cheeks. She brought wide eyes to Alice's face, which was drained of all color as she locked her eyes straight ahead. She could feel her ears burning and she opened her mouth to speak, but all that came out was a very squeaky, "Huh?" A moment passed, in which Alice's thumbs were pressing into her temples, before Dallas managed to say, "Ex... girlfriend?"

Bright blue eyes peeked from around a palm as Alice leveled a very neutral stare at Dallas. "Seriously? You didn't know and you choose *now* to have a revelation about my sexuality? I figured Amelie would've told you. How much more obvious can I be without being that chav, anyway? What did you think I was—you know what, nevermind, Dallas, can we just get out of here?"

"Why? Is she mean?"

Alice squeezed her eyes shut. "How would you feel if your ex-girlfriend showed up in a completely unexpected place?"

"Wow," Dallas mumbled, grabbing her beer for something to hold on to because she had to do *something* with her hands. "You think I'm—wow—bold assumption—way to..." she trailed off, blushing furiously. Her hand was sweating more than her pint class. "I've never had a girlfriend." She clenched her jaw before throwing a brief glance over her shoulder at the group. There was one girl looking over at them, tall with long, wavy brunette hair, and Dallas assumed that was who Alice was referring to. She turned back to the blonde and said, "Why should we have to leave? Besides, Hannah and Barbara—" she pointed to the two girls who had gotten up a while before and were mingling with a few members of the Jump team, "—rode with us." She sat up straight and puffed out her chest, leveling Alice with what she hoped was a resolute grin. "Besides, I'll make sure she doesn't mess with you!"

"Will you?" Alice hissed. "Because she's looking over here."

Dallas grabbed her pint and threw it back to polish it off, dribbling a little down her chin and swiping it away with her sleeve, before tugging her barstool closer to Alice. She slid an arm around the other girl's waist with practiced ease—no, really, she had practiced being smooth with her stuffed animals—and leaned in.

"Dallas—what are you—"

"Just follow my lead." The bartender placed another full beer in front of her and she looked over and nodded a thanks, even though she hadn't asked.

She reached up, trying to keep her hand from shaking, and traced her fingers over the other girl's jaw, her neck, threading into thick blonde hair. She pushed it back. Alice shuddered underneath her as she brought her face next to her ear and whispered, "Pretend you're with me," before dropping back a little.

Dallas heard Alice suck in a sharp breath of air. She brought her eyes up to meet Dallas's and whispered a very weak, "Okay."

She felt Alice's warm hand—tentative and slow—coming to rest on her thigh and tried to force down the sudden explosion in her gut as the other girl's thumb rolled in slow circles against her jeans. Dallas moved in closer, her arm pressing against Alice's, and snagged her beer with her other hand to bring it to her lips and take a sip. As she did so, she glanced behind her. The girl she figured was Alice's ex-girlfriend was watching them. She turned back to Alice and asked, her voice low, "Does she ride or something? What's she doing here?"

"Her best friend rides for Oxford," Alice mumbled. Her warm breath ghosted against the side of Dallas's face. "She probably came to watch."

"Watch her friend, or you?" Dallas grumbled. She lowered her beer back to the bar, her other hand still combing through Alice's hair. It was soft and tickled the skin of her palms. Dallas slid her fingers against the back of Alice's neck, her breath shuddering under the look the other girl was giving her. She could feel the grip on her thigh tightening.

"I—I don't know," Alice choked out. Her cheeks were bright pink, topaz eyes flickering between Dallas and the group behind them. "I blocked her number last month."

Dallas hummed. She let her other hand drop to Alice's and squeezed. Was this act for Alice, or for her? She wasn't sure. Her lower abdomen was lurching in a way that made her wish that this was real, that this wasn't a show for whoever this other girl was, that Alice was touching her because she wanted to—

A long, heavy sigh slipped through Alice's partially open lips. She brought her eyes to meet Dallas's, her gaze drifting from crimson to settle on chapped pink lips, and Dallas felt the heavy drone of desire pounding in her skull as her own trailed down, found Alice's. They looked so soft and for a long moment she wondered what they would taste like before Alice whispered, "It worked. She left."

But her hand didn't move. It lingered, warm and complacent, on Dallas's thigh. Her thumb was still tracing slow patterns on the inside and Dallas felt like her blood was boiling. Her heart was thrumming hard in her chest as she let the hand on Alice's neck slowly trail down her arm before dropping entirely.

"I... um..." Dallas started.

Suddenly Alice stood, her hand falling away from where it rested on Dallas's leg, and she cleared her throat. Her face was a bright, burning red as she grabbed her drink, tossed back the rest, and quickly said, "I have to use the washroom," before bolting off.

Dallas stared after her, her breath still shuddering and rasping in her throat, the place where Alice's hand had been on her thigh now cold and empty where the warm touch once was. With a heavy, shaking sigh, she turned back to the bar, lifted her beer, and chugged.

Dallas was glad it was their last night in Bedford, because if the first had been hard, this one was downright painful. She was grateful for Hannah and Barbara sharing their room, because if they hadn't... well, her insides would have likely painted the walls and housekeeping would have been *very* upset over the mess.

"Was it my imagination, or did I see Chloe?" Hannah had asked when they got back to their lodging. "Tell me she came with Hayley just to see you. That right cunt, I swear—"

"She didn't bother you, did she?" If Hannah had held the anger, Barbara held the remorse. She had placed her hand on Alice's shoulder and looked at her with eyebrows knit in concern. "And are you okay?"

"No, and... yes," Alice had said. For a brief moment, her blue eyes had flickered over to Dallas, who was freshly changed into a pair of baggy sweatpants and a t-shirt and was trying to mind her own business as she texted Brooke about the day. It was late and she really wanted to go to bed, but the other three insisted on talking, so instead she had curled up cross-legged against her pillow and placated herself. Really, she was trying to calm her own body down. She was still burning from earlier and the skin on her thigh twitched with the phantom reminder of Alice's touch and the way Alice's thumb circled like she knew exactly what she was doing to Dallas's insides.

She was so zoned out she didn't even notice when the others started flicking the lights out and Alice said, "Dallas, are you not ready for bed? We have to get up early tomorrow."

"Yes," Dallas said, her voice somewhere between a breath and a squeak, and shoved her phone under her pillow as she climbed under the covers. She lay on her back, thinking that might be the safest place to be, and coiled her arms on her chest as she stared up at the dark ceiling.

She didn't know how long she stayed like that. Long after Hannah and Barbara's breath had trickled into the rhythm of sleep, long after she knew that she *too* should have been asleep, but her brain was still alive with thoughts of Alice and the radiating warmth of the girl's body so close to her own.

"Hey, Dallas?"

The whisper was low, hesitant. Dallas felt the tips of Alice's fingers ghost against her shoulder and turned her head to see blue eyes staring back at her. Moonlight streaming through the window lit the side of her face and the pale gold of her hair, wild against the pillow.

Dallas said nothing as she blinked back. Her heart, which she had *finally* managed to talk down from the cliff it was hanging off, had immediately started to flare into action again. It was loud in her head and she wouldn't be surprised if Alice could hear it, too.

The other girl leaned up on a propped elbow, her eyes flickering over Dallas's face. Dallas felt her vision fog, her skin burn with the anticipation of whatever was happening as Alice leaned slowly in, her breath warm on her cheek, her temple, rustling her hair.

Alice leaned in, her lips tickling against the shell of Dallas's ear. Dallas couldn't stop the very sharp intake of breath at the sudden sensation and froze completely, clenching her fists against her chest.

"Thank you," Alice whispered, her voice a soothing breath that sent warmth flooding through Dallas's entire body, coursing through her blood at the speed of sound. It was like somebody running through a house and turning on every single light as they went, screaming, *Wake the hell up, something is happening!*

She felt warm, soft lips pressing against her cheek and her breath hitched. She choked down a whimper that fought to get loose behind her teeth and turned her head up, red eyes wide as she found the small smile that had slid across Alice's face as she retreated.

Alice settled back onto her side of the bed and rolled away from her. Dallas squeezed her eyes shut hard, forcing her lungs to take in air as she struggled to quiet her raging nerves. She rolled her jaw, nails digging half-moons into her palm, and tried to distract herself from what just happened.

But she couldn't stop thinking about it, and she most *certainly* couldn't sleep. She knew she needed to get rest—she had to be up early the next day and had courses to memorize—but the lights were still on in her mind, and so she resigned herself to exhaustion and the sweet, sweet suffering that came with the beautiful girl who was only inches away.

She didn't forget her courses.

She didn't win, either, but that didn't matter. Miss Willow had instructed her to go slower, to take her time, to focus on where she was going next. Plus, they had pulled a rail in one course—Dallas's fault, she had rushed Chariot to the fence—and so that had drastically knocked their time down in the second round. But, she *did* come in third and fifth, respectively, which Dallas thought was quite good since she was facing over a dozen other riders in her division and it was her first time.

Dallas was especially proud of Chariot. She had hugged her mare tight and told her how much she loved her and what a good pony she was as she pulled the braids out of her mane ("I am fixing that mop when we get back to Hoofbeats," Alice had grumbled from where she stood getting Beatrix ready to travel) and prepared her for the van. She tugged Chariot's plaid sheet over her body and fastened the buckles, gently running her hands over the long, soft hair and digging peppermints out of her pocket every other moment to shove into the waiting pony's mouth.

She had just loaded the mare up, still giggling to herself at Chariot stepping with exaggeration in her thick shipping boots, when Miss Willow finished a conversation with Miss Parker and strode over with a huge grin.

"I'm proud of you, Dallas," the instructor said, placing an affectionate hand on Dallas's shoulder. "You did extremely well. Once we get you used to memorizing courses, all you have to do is add a little bit of speed and you'll be wiping the floors with everybody else. Well... that is, if you decide you want to stay on the Jump team."

Dallas had blinked back at her with wide red eyes, unable to stop the smile that tugged at her lips. She knew the decision would be coming on whether or not to take on the added responsibility of an extra team, but she was also ready. While she preferred the rush of Games, she had to admit that jumping was fun and Chariot was good at it. In fact, Chariot *loved* it. And if Alice had made a decision on discipline based on her mare, why shouldn't Dallas do the same?

"I would like to," she said after a moment, fidgeting with the empty peppermint wrappers in her pocket and shooting a glance at Alice, who was talking to Hannah and Barbara at the other end of the van. Alice looked up and met her gaze with a timid smile before turning away.

Okay, so it wasn't all based on Chariot. The Jump team traveled with the Hunt team. And so, if Dallas rode for them, she would be able to spend more time with Alice and, well, now she knew she had a *chance...*

It was stupid, but Dallas never claimed to always think with the smart part of her brain, and so the addition of Alice to that slightly tilted scale made one end drop like she'd thrown a two ton weight on it.

"Really?" Miss Willow was grinning, one dimple dipping into the side of her freckled cheek. "That's great, Dallas—" when had the instructor started calling her Dallas? "—I'm really excited to have you. I'll talk to Miss Nelson when we get back and make arrangements. Wow, I feel like a divorced parent in a custody battle. Don't worry, we'll make sure you aren't overwhelmed."

And so she had joined the Jump team. Officially. Which meant she had a lot to think about. Games. Jumping. School.

Alice.

But that could all wait, because she didn't sleep for a single minute the night before, and so as soon as she climbed into the passenger seat of Alice's car, she had curled up against the window and passed out.

Chapter Sixteen

A *LICE*
"Pretend you're with me," Dallas had whispered into her ear. Shivers ran down her spine like she'd been dunked into freezing water. She had to squeeze her eyes shut at the sensation of the other girl's arms around her and the soft words that tickled her skin. She took a deep breath and met Dallas's bright red eyes with a wavering stare.

"Okay," she'd managed to say, trying not to focus on the fingers threading through her hair and the shockwaves that Dallas's touch was sending through her body. She slowly reached out and placed a hand on Dallas's thigh, her thumb dragging across the material of her jeans on impulse.

Dallas took a sip of her beer, glancing over her shoulder before returning her gaze to Alice. She was pressed in so close that she was sure Dallas could feel the heat radiating off her burning skin. "Does she ride or something? What's she doing here?"

Dallas had fallen into her role as Alice's pseudo-girlfriend with ease, and Alice let herself admire the sudden confidence and protectiveness that had encompassed the other girl in mere moments. It was... really attractive, if Alice had to put a label to it.

Okay, she would anyway. It was really attractive.

Alice eyed Chloe over Dallas's shoulder. Hayley was lingering at her ex-girlfriend's side, occasionally glancing over as she spoke with the tall brunette. *Please don't come over here*, Alice thought, and turned back to Dallas. Had she moved in? Her face was so close that she could have just tilted her chin a little—

"Her best friend rides for Oxford," she said, keeping her voice low. "She probably came to watch."

A shadow passed over Dallas's bright eyes and she tightened her grip on Alice's neck, sending a pang through her lower abdomen and making her choke on a breath. She unconsciously squeezed the other girl's thigh a little tighter, feeling the muscle squirm beneath her. "Watch her friend, or you?" Dallas asked, and for a moment Alice thought she could pick up a hint of jealousy in her voice.

"I—I don't know," Alice somehow managed to say through the sensation of fingers tugging at her hair. She guessed that she had about thirty seconds until she lost her mind. She shot a look back over at Chloe, who wasn't looking any longer, and said, "I blocked her number last month," because she definitely didn't want Dallas to think she was still hung up on her ex.

Dallas's warm hand fell from her beer to cover her own and squeezed gently. Alice flicked her thumb against the inside of Dallas's thigh and took a shuddering breath. She watched as Hayley seized Chloe's arm and, with a final glance back at Alice and Dallas, led the other girl from the pub. She let out a long sigh of relief, blue eyes flickering back to red before drifting to the soft lips that were only inches from her own. Dallas's breath was ghosting over her face in warm waves. Her eyelids felt heavy with lust—all she had to do was close that gap in one quick move. The thought made a warm desire pulse through her body.

"It worked. She left," she finally managed to choke out, although she almost didn't even want to tell Dallas because then everything would have to end. She *wanted* Dallas's fingers in her hair, she *wanted* Dallas's arm around her waist. So she kept her hand where it was, feeling the warmth of the other girl's thigh beneath her. Dallas was staring at her with a look in her eyes that she had never seen before. Her chest throbbed.

"I... um...," Dallas started, her fingers dragging across Alice's neck, her arm.

It was too much. Her thirty seconds had long since been up and the ache between her legs was so powerful that she didn't trust herself to sit there another moment. She stood quickly, nearly knocking over her barstool in the process, and blurted out, "I have to use the washroom," before rushing off.

And thank everything that ever existed that it was empty because she ripped open the door and slammed it shut behind her, letting her back hit the wall hard as she sucked in air that she desperately needed. She felt like she was on fire, like her heart had dropped into the pit of her stomach. She brought her hand up to her face and pinched the bridge of her nose, hard, and let out a loud groan that she'd been holding in the back of her throat.

She could still feel the soft fingers on her neck, in her hair. Dallas's breath against her cheeks and lips. Those crimson eyes staring back at her with a look that said that maybe she wanted her just as bad as she wanted Dallas.

Alice had stayed there for long enough that she knew it would draw questions, but she couldn't go back out to Dallas just yet. Not with her face burning so red, not with her breath hitching in her throat as she struggled to compose herself. This was ridiculous. She was Alice Thelwell, poised and confident and always in control. Even when it came to Chloe, she had been able regulate herself. But with Dallas she was some teenage girl that withered beneath the touch of an attractive girl who she *very* much wanted to pin against a wall or just curl up against in blissful peace to let the world fall away—

She was in trouble.

She was in a *lot* of trouble.

But, God, if it didn't feel *so* good.

Alice had been trying to ask Dallas out on a date—a *real* date, not getting tipsy on Janine's Russian hooch and terrorizing Dallas's pony—when the whole Chloe thing had happened. She'd felt like she was finally brave enough to call it that, brave enough to solidify her attraction, subject herself to that vulnerability, and put those words into the air between them. To let Dallas know exactly what her intentions were.

Sure, Dallas was leagues beyond her. She was friendly and outgoing and well-liked, all things that Alice wasn't, and she was sure the other girl would be more interested in somebody who wasn't emotionally crippled by the weight of an elite status. That's what Chloe had once said, anyway. Those exact words.

"You have no idea how to show your feelings," Chloe had told her one night during a particularly heated argument when Alice had told her she was upset about a cancelled visit the previous weekend. "How am I even supposed to know how you feel about something if you can't properly convey anything? You are literally emotionally crippled. It's not anyone else's fault that you learned to repress your emotions."

She wanted to explain that she *had* to—she'd lost her father and her mother and if she let her emotions take control she wouldn't have made it through a single day of her life—but she'd just thrown in the towel because she hated confrontation and didn't want to deal with it anymore. Besides, Chloe was probably right.

Alice rapped the tip of her pen against her open Equine Nutrition book, sighing down at the wall of words that had blurred together with her thoughts. She'd been trying to study for a majority of the night, and thus far it had been completely ineffective. It was a good thing she had already reviewed this particular chapter twice, because she could not seem to get her head into it.

The only time she'd had respite from her own mind was when she rode Beatrix earlier in the evening. It had been cold, bitterly so, and so Miss Parker had let the Hunt team hack in the indoor arena. She'd barely even seen Dallas, who'd had her usual outdoor Games practice and only waved in passing as she and Chariot pranced by the doors to the indoor with the rest of the team.

Alice had left long before Dallas had even finished.

The blue message indicator was blinking at the top of her mobile where she'd set it down on her notebook. Alice dropped her pen into the spine of the book and opened it up—she didn't even try to suppress a smile, she was alone in her room—to find her latest message from Dallas.

Dallas 20:22

are u going to Janine's party this wknd?

She blinked down at her mobile. This was the first thing she'd heard about any sort of party, and to be quite frank, house parties were certainly not her scene. She preferred her surroundings more docile and controlled.

Alice 20:23

I haven't been invited to any party.

Dallas 20:23

yes u have :3

| Dallas 8:19

| can I invite the hunt team pleeeeeeease

| Jazz Hands 8:21

| they eat two vodka gummies at the door.

| and don't start anything with Amelie.

| if they're not in costume they're taking another shot of the worst vodka I have and getting kicked out.

| only conditions.

| Dallas 8:21

| deal!

see

Alice propped her forehead against the heel of her hand and stared at the messages. She wasn't sure about going to the type of party that she knew this one would be, but if Hannah and Barbara were allowed to come—and, well, Dallas—

Alice 20:26
Well, it seems you've already committed me.
Dallas 20:26
YyYYEYEYESSSSSSss

Alice chuckled and set the mobile back down, packing up her text and notebook and returning them to her satchel for the next day before turning off the pale glow of her desk lamp and climbing into her bed. It was early, sure, but she knew she wasn't going to accomplish anything further.

Not that she really did in the first place.

She stuffed her Beatrix plush between her arm and torso and lay on her back, clutching her mobile between her hands.

Dallas 20:31
whatcha doing
Alice 20:31
I'm in bed.
Dallas 20:31
it's 830
are u 19 or 85?

Yeah, well, she woke up at 5:30. And she knew for a fact that Dallas didn't wake up until after 10 (she'd even missed her morning class, which Alice had scolded her for) because the other girl didn't respond to her good morning text until then.

Alice 20:33
Easy to say when you skip class and sleep in.
Dallas 20:33
THAT WAS ONE TIME
this week

one time this week
so far

Alice gnawed at her bottom lip, running her fingers through the little Beatrix's soft yarn mane and mulling her options before deciding to go for it. If she didn't get a good response, she could always play it off.

Alice 20:35
Come keep me awake.

Dots darted across the screen and then disappeared. And then again. She was starting to feel really dumb for saying that and was trying to force away the heat in her face when a new message flashed—

Dallas 20:36
and how would u like me to do that?

Her tongue darted out and wet her lips and she squirmed beneath the sheets, unable to keep herself from blushing furiously as she responded. She felt her lower abdomen surge and she slid her fingers beneath the waistband of her shorts, tapping out a text with her thumb.

Alice 20:37
I'm sure you'll think of something.

More dots flashing across the screen. Stop. Start. Stop. Start.

Dallas 20:39
i'll make ur bed rock

Oh, this was going exactly where she wanted it.

Dallas 20:40
FROM
JUMPING
ON

IT

She rolled her eyes and pulled her hand back out of her shorts.

Alice 20:41

Wow, Dallas.

Dallas 20:41

what? I'm a master bed jumper

Alice squeezed her eyes shut and shook her head against the pillow, switching the screen of her mobile off and dropping it on the edge of her bed. With a heavy sigh, she pushed her hand back into her shorts to feel exactly what thoughts of Dallas—repressed, ignorant, useless Dallas—had done to her, and she took care of it anyway.

She had been riding Beatrix much longer than she meant to, but her heart was pounding and her anxiety was through the roof. She barely focused on the rhythm of her posting as she guided the large mare in a 20-meter circle, hands resting quietly against her thighs as she tried to sink into the smooth flow of the trot.

Dallas was still practicing. Alice occasionally raised her eyes from her own task at hand to watch the team, galloping back and forth and recklessly jumping on and off their ponies as they ran the same races time and time again. They had one more competition in November, Dallas had told her, before the international meet which was to take place at the end of the year. The host country was yet to be announced—it all depended on which teams remained after qualifiers in the divisions around the world.

She watched as Dallas and Amelie bolted side by side, carefully weaving through poles as they held a string taut between them. They worked pretty well together, despite their clashing personalities, and the two ponies were a flash of bay and chestnut as they broke apart at the finish and went galloping in different directions. Dallas was standing up straight in the irons and gesturing with one hand and a wide grin on her face.

Cute. Alice smirked and brought her attention back to her own mare, who was huffing with the effort of the lengthy work. Alice sat deep in the saddle and let the reins slip between her hands to feed Beatrix her freedom. The mare responded by dropping down to a walk and dipping her nose to the ground with a quick shake of her head. She snorted and stepped over to the rail on instinct.

The Games team was gathered in the middle of their arena speaking with Miss Nelson and Alice knew that practice was about to be dismissed. It was long past dark and the arena's floodlights had sparked to life hours before, though the team had continued practice. It was astounding, really. None of the other teams ever went that late or that hard-the Games team went rain or shine, snow or sleet—and Alice couldn't understand for the life of her why. Dallas never seemed bothered, though, and always greeted Alice with the same smile whether she was soaked to the bone, freezing cold, or dripping sweat.

Alice stopped Beatrix in the middle of the arena and swung off, her boots thumping gently into the sand, and slowly ran the stirrups up. Anything to take longer, anything to give her another moment to take some deep breaths and reassure herself that there was no harm in asking. Dallas would either say yes, or she wouldn't. Still, she couldn't soothe the way her skin was shivering—it wasn't from the cold—and the fog that had consumed her mind all day. Ever since she had finally worked up the courage to message Dallas. The courage to commit to the question she wanted to ask.

Alice 14:44

Hey, do you think we could talk after your practice?

Dallas 14:45

sure, everything ok?

Alice 14:45

Yes. I'd just like to talk to you.

Dallas 14:46

ok...

sure?

She slipped the reins over Beatrix's head, stopping to undo the noseband, throatlatch, and affectionately scratch her mare behind her large ears, and headed for the gate. She shoved her hands into her pockets, trusting the mare to walk quietly behind her, as she undid the latch and pulled the mare into the middle lane. Beatrix's shoes echoed and scraped on the cobblestone as she stepped forward and turned with her owner.

Dallas was already headed toward her. Her black cotton reins were still hung over Chariot's neck, stirrups tossed carelessly across the saddle. Dallas's helmet was unbuckled and the strap dangled at her neck. The right side of her body was sprayed with wet sand—the arenas were filled with puddles from rain the night before—and the bottom half of her breeches were soaked.

"Should I be worried?" Dallas asked as she grew near, chuckling nervously and shoving her hands deep into the pockets of her thick red jacket. Her long brunette ponytail hung, tangled and limp, in a straight line down her back. Her bangs were scattered across her forehead and her temple, sweaty and messy.

Alice took a deep breath.

"Of course not," she said quickly. She clenched her jaw and looked down at her boots, shuffling them against the edge of a stone as she tried to gather her bearings. "Would you... like to walk back together?"

"Uh, sure," Dallas replied, brown eyebrows knitting together. Alice could feel the crimson eyes searching her face and knew that the other girl was staring at the way she was blushing.

They started walking together. Chariot obediently following her owner, Beatrix obedient with the lead of the reins that were shoved into Alice's pocket. She switched to the wrong side so she could walk next to Dallas, her breath catching as their sleeves rubbed together. Neither girl moved away.

A long silence had passed before Dallas said, "What was it you wanted to talk about? You're kind of worrying me." A pause. "I didn't... do anything, did I?" She turned her head, red eyes peeking at the side of Alice's face as they walked.

"Of course not," Alice repeated. Okay, this was it. No, she'd never done this before—Chloe had asked her out—and yes, she was internally panicking. But she'd rehearsed this—she was Alice Thelwell, dammit—and she could *do* this.

"I—uh—you see—well—"

She rehearsed this.

Dallas raised one eyebrow. Chariot snorted and the other girl cringed and swiped the snot she'd sprayed all over her sleeve onto her wet breeches.

"You owe me a question," Alice breathed at last. Yes, this was right. She swallowed hard.

"Oh." If it was possible for Dallas to look more confused, she did. Her step faltered, but she carried on to the bright white lights of the stable that wasn't far in the distance. The rest of the Games team had already disappeared. "Do I? I don't remember asking you anything. Was I supposed to?"

"No," Alice said. She shivered into her jacket and bit her lip, forcing her gaze straight ahead because she knew if she looked at Dallas she would lose her train of thought again and she wasn't about to look like a bumbling idiot doing this. Dallas wouldn't want to go out with somebody who couldn't express themselves. She, herself, was a walking bundle of human emotion. And she certainly wouldn't want to go out with somebody who couldn't ask a single question without tripping on words. "You... owe me a question. To ask you. From last weekend."

"Ohhh." Dallas nodded, looking down at the stone as she walked. "Right, right. Okay, go ahead. Ask whatever."

They were near the stable entrance, and Alice didn't want to go in just yet, so she came to a stop. Beatrix dipped her head at her side, sniffing at the ground. Dallas took an extra step but, realizing that Alice wasn't moving anymore, turned and faced her. Chariot walked over to the grass along the side of the lane and lowered her head to start snapping greedily at the little bit of green grass that was left with the colder weather. Dallas let her.

"I—" She paused, licking her lips nervously before tugging her eyes up to meet Dallas's. God, she was cute. She forced her mind to focus once more and took a deep breath before saying, "I was wondering if you would like to—"

"Yo, Dallas!"

Alice groaned. Out loud.

Amelie was rushing out of the stable toward them with her trademark grin, pulling her untacked and still sweaty pony along with her. "You gotta get in here, Connie's made the coolest automatic treat dispenser. Cookie's already figured it out and it is *funny* as—"

Alice cleared her throat and leveled blue eyes on the rowdy American. "Pardon me, but do you mind?"

"Mind what, Thelwell?" Amelie grumbled, pulling up next to them. Star made a lunge for the grass beside Chariot but she snatched him back with a jerk of the rope. Dallas had turned, confused—the emotion she'd clearly chosen to represent for the evening—to face her teammate.

Alice grit her teeth. "Would you consider taking a walk? A long one? Perhaps across the country and back? We're having a conversation."

"And I'm sure that's *very* important," Amelie said, disregarding Alice with a roll of her eyes before turning back to Dallas. "Anyway—"

Alice brought a gloved hand up to her face and pinched the bridge of her nose, sucking in air through her nostrils before letting her arm drop. She forced her expression back to neutral as she regarded Amelie and said, her voice far more clear and confident than she expected, "If you would be so kind, I am kind of trying to ask Dallas out on a date right now. So, yes, it is important."

Whatever Amelie was going to say disappeared with any resolve that the other girl held onto. Alice could feel two pairs of eyes on her, both flickering with shock.

"Huh?" Dallas squeaked out.

"Oh," Amelie mumbled. Her red eyebrows stitched together and then relaxed as she took a step back, tugging Star to get his attention. She raised her hand and thumbed down the lane in the opposite direction and muttered a quick but decisive, "Right, okay... I'm going to go... take that walk."

Star's shoes rang out into the bitter night as the American hurried away.

Dallas was still staring at her, red eyes wide with surprise. Her cheeks had been pink from the cold, but now they were a bright red fire. What Alice would have given to warm her hands on them.

"So..." Alice took a deep breath, suddenly nervous again, and forced her eyes to meet Dallas's. "Would you... like to go out? With me? On a... date?"

Dallas's lips were slack and her tongue darted out of her mouth to wet them. A chill breeze picked up the end of her ponytail and sent her hair scattering across her shoulder. There was a long quiet between them—one that was probably much shorter than it felt—before Dallas finally spoke.

"Please," she breathed.

Alice wanted to say something, but whatever it was died in her throat at that single word.

"I mean... yes. Yes. I would love that. I mean, like that. I mean... a date would be... cool. With you." Dallas brought her hand up and scratched at the back of her neck, the corner of her mouth tugging into a grimace at her own words. "Yes?" she squeaked, followed by a more confident, "Yes," and a firm nod.

"You... will? Okay." Alice let out a long breath and shifted on legs that she didn't even realize had completely frozen with the rest of her. Beatrix brought her muzzle down to her lower leg and gave it a small nudge. "Great." Her heart was throbbing in her ears and she felt the urge to run away and scream into something until her body stopped having a total critical meltdown.

"When?" she heard Dallas ask, but the question didn't really register because her brain was disintegrating inside her skull, and so she replied with:

"Huh?"

Dallas chuckled and looked down at her feet, burying her hands back into her jacket. "When... did you want to go on the, uh... the, uh-"

"Date," Alice said quickly. Though she had to admit, she had been panicking so much over asking Dallas that simple question that she hadn't bothered to work out the logistics. It was already Friday, and so it was too late to say then, and then they had Janine's party, and she had an exam Monday morning so Sunday wouldn't be all that great—"

"I'm free Wednesday," Dallas said. "And I promise this time. I was supposed to have a Jump lesson but Miss Willow is visiting family this week, so..."

Weird. Miss Parker was visiting family that week, too. "Wednesday. Yes," Alice confirmed. "I... will arrange everything else."

"Okay," Dallas replied.

Another silence spread between them. It was awkward, and Alice had no idea what to say, but she knew she needed to say *something*, so she said, "Well..."

Just as Dallas said, "Alright..."

Alice chuckled nervously.

"Right. Well, I'm going to go untack. Are you coming?" Dallas asked.

Alice glanced at her horse, who was staring off at the wood line, at the shadows of the trees that stretched like monoliths over the stable grounds. She shook her head and turned back to Dallas. "I'm going to stay back for a minute."

Dallas cracked a smile and nudged the toe of her paddock boot into the side of Alice's foot. "Okay, weirdo," she joked. "I'll see you, then." She turned on her heel and started walking off to the stable, turning back only to call Chariot ("Come on, lazy pony!") who was still grazing next to the lane. She perked up at her owner's voice and broke into a trot after her.

Alice let out a very, very, very long sigh and wrapped her arms around her quiet mare's neck. Beatrix leaned into her a little bit, nipping playfully at the bottom of her jacket and earning a swat of Alice's hand, before grunting and looking back at the stable, where Dallas and Chariot were disappearing into the bright light of the aisle.

Alice buried her face into her mare's black mane, took a deep breath, and screamed—internally, of course—until she felt like she could function again.

Which turned out to be a *significant* amount of time.

Don't miss out!

Visit the website below and you can sign up to receive emails whenever Hannah Conrad publishes a new book. There's no charge and no obligation.

https://books2read.com/r/B-A-PDRK-SMJKC

BOOKS 2 READ

Connecting independent readers to independent writers.

Did you love *Mounted Games*? Then you should read *The Perfect Distance*[1] by Hannah Conrad!

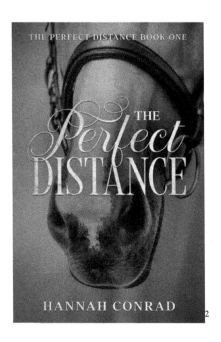

Sometimes you need to find the perfect distance.

For Lucy, it's always been easy. You count the strides, make sure your horse is lined up correctly, ask, and then complete the jump. But college is full of new kinds of distances. When Lucy joins the university's equestrian team and has to navigate not only courses but interacting with senior girl Elise, she learns that measuring distances may apply to more than just riding horses.

---

1. https://books2read.com/u/mVg5gZ

2. https://books2read.com/u/mVg5gZ

The Perfect Distance is a series set in the Akiyama Quest Universe and can be enjoyed with no previous books from this universe being read.

Also by Hannah Conrad

Elemental Fate
Watersong

Fantasy Unleashed
Fantasy Unleashed

Fantasy Unleashed: Akiyama Quest
The Journal of Irene Summerset

Fantasy Unleashed: Apprentice of the Night Empress
The Orphan

Fantasy Unleashed: Riders of Alvilda
Welcome to Alvilda

Fantasy Unleashed: Standalone Adventures
Falling Feather
Dragon Knight

Fantasy Unleashed: The Perfect Distance
The Perfect Distance
Legacy
Letting Go

Mounted Games
Mounted Games

Sherlock Holmes Fantasia
The Mystery of the Red Rose

The Magic We Make
The Magic We Make

Standalone
The Ravens

The Legend of Lady Robin Hood
A Study in Souling
Always, Anna
Hallows Happenings

About the Author

Hannah Conrad has been been passionately writing and reading her entire life. Early on, she became enthralled by fantasy novels as well as by horses. She desires to write the kind of books she would want to read. Hannah specializes in portal fantasy and fantasy books involving horses. Her main series take place in the Akiyama Quest verse.

About the Publisher

Dimension Seal Studios is a new, multimedia studio that aims to bring new and engaging stories into the world of entertainment. The studio was founded in 2019 by Hannah Conrad and Walker McMullin.

With an emphasis on film, television, and literature, Dimension Seal Studios creates fresh and entertaining stories in a variety of genres. Our stories encompass a wide variety of genres and we have something for everyone. Check out Dimension Seal Studios' works and meet your new favorite characters!

Milton Keynes UK
Ingram Content Group UK Ltd.
UKHW021825041023
429927UK00014B/408